Icarus

JOHN E. ANDES

iUniverse, Inc.
Bloomington

ICARUS

iUniverse books may be ordered through booksellers or by contacting:

iUniverse
1663 Liberty Drive
Bloomington, IN 47403
www.iuniverse.com
1-800-Authors (1-800-288-4677)

ISBN: 978-1-4697-8128-0 (sc)
ISBN: 978-1-4697-8129-7 (ebk)

Printed in the United States of America

iUniverse rev. date: 03/05/2012

Dedicated to my sons

You stand by me and I stand tall
I have your love, I have it all.

Prologue

*L*aps. I hate the damned laps. Running in circles is too much like life. It's the *Circle Game* Judy Collins warned us about thirty-five years ago. And we are the painted ponies. Running is something totally different. I really do like to run. Over hill, over dale even on the dusty trail. I do like to run. My preference is to run in the dark. Anytime after sun down and before the first piercing rays of God's one eye. I have even awakened at three-thirty AM just to run. It's amazing the number of drunks who are trying to pull into their respective carports, exit their cars and find a key that matches their doors. These same assholes were just on the road. It certainly makes you want to work the swing shift.

Back to my bitching about laps. I have to run them before and after. I have to lift more weight more often. My muscles and joints have to ache everyday for two months, so that when the time comes I can be faster, stronger and have more stamina than the others do. The others are thirty years younger than I am. They have not had the opportunity to ingest great quantities of rich, fatty foods, alcohol of all types and forms, and drugs, both prescribed and street level. Their bones are strong. Their muscles have not yet begun to evolve to flab. They are the mighty warriors; the hunters. I am not a gatherer. I am an elder seeking one more day on the hunt, one more day in the sun. And, this is it. This is the time to go back and recapture the physical exuberance that is youth. Exuberance that is expressed in physical combat, in a stadium, on a freshly mowed battlefield, in front of a few hundred peers, theirs and mine, who are also the parents of theirs. This is my time.

About three months ago, I asked the Athletic Director of Saint Sebastian if I could practice with the football team and play in the Spring Jamboree against Saint Peter. After he picked himself off floor, he protested adamantly. It was dangerous. It was a precedent he wished not to establish. It was a violation of the state high school athletics association's rules. The school positively prohibits parents from competing with their children in a sanctioned sport. I was too old. I could be seriously injured. The kids would make fun of me.

I listened stoically. I said nothing until the flush left his face and the volume of his voice became conversational. I was willing to sign a waiver releasing the school from any liability or harm. It would be a precedent, only if he wanted it to be. He could and should treat this event as a one-time only event. It would never happen again. The state high school athletics association need not know since the practice was a school function and the association did not sanction the Jamboree. I would be under a doctor's care and would willingly submit myself to the school/team doctor for weekly monitoring. The kids would love it. At long last, they would be able to beat up a dad, if only in a metaphorical sense. I would even make a substantial contribution to the school's athletic budget, a new whatever-was-needed. Reluctantly, he allowed that we should talk to the Headmaster.

In his soul, he was intrigued by the request. He needed the Headmaster to relieve him of the decision responsibility. As he started to reiterate his objections, a small smile appeared. He knew that I knew that he knew that I had gone over all these points before and rehearsed my rebuttals and answers. Coach Lewis was weakening ever so slightly. A bulk of an athlete. Two hundred and forty-five pounds of male beast arguing with a smaller parent, an older parent, a parent who would be a major contributor to the coach's world. He almost wanted to lose the argument. Could it be that I represented a secret wish of his? Undoubtedly, my wishes were the wishes of every ex-high school jock, of every ex-college player and of every Walter Mitty. Did I represent a dream saver? Salvation of the last drop of testosterone? Maybe to Coach Lewis. Hopefully to the other parents. The mansioned gentry of Country Club Hills. These were the few, the proud, the incredibly wealthy of Lansdale. They of the rich wall tapestries, real oak floors, the floor-to-ceiling widows, two lanais, swimming pool, and walk-in fireplaces. House size: minimum forty-five hundred square feet. Autos: one big sedan, a Sport Utility Vehicle, a Wrangler for Eric, and a Camry for Ashley. Despite all these trappings of money and status, most of the families, parents and children, were disarmingly warm and friendly. They opened their hearts and doors to all whose children attended the right school. Saint Sebastian was the door to their domain. Education is everything. These people know it. They are doctors, lawyers, bankers, and business owners. While many of them had inherited a ton, their grandparents and parents stressed the absolute critical nature of a better education. More than a good education. Many of them had been educated in New England. So, if out-of-towners have the right educational pedigrees and they send their progeny to the right school (Saint Sebastian), the entire family is acceptable and accepted.

But I have gotten ahead of myself. Or am I behind myself. In a continuum, I just don't know where I am.

White Sixty-three Power Rush

*W*hite . . . sixty-three . . . power push. White . . . sixty-three . . . power push. Mid-zone coverage. Sideline to ball. Do not bump. Give six-to-eight yard cushion. Stalk receiver no more than ten yards deep. Safety takes over. Watch for speed . . . cut block attempt. Keep one eye on motion man. Shift glance to QB. Three down linemen. Two shifted to the power side. Two linebackers blitzing from the weak side. Others roll into positions on the blitz. Here they come. Unbalanced line. Power away. Wideout mid-spread. Motion away. Watch QB. God they're big. Hope not fast. QB spins. Pitches to motion man. Wideout bumps me. He is skinny and tentative. A dangerous combination for him. I smack him on his ass real hard and push to cut off any cut back. There is none.

The invitation, tucked behind the driver's seat visor, reads:

Christmas with the Kileys
Join us to celebrate the season of giving and love
Tuesday, December 22nd, 2012
Six to Nine PM
Prince Court
Gifts and contributions for CitiMinistries lovingly
accepted
RSVP

The quintessential holiday, charity, socially preeminent event. The Kileys, Billy Ray and Jeannie, have thrown this Christmas-giving-being-seen event for the last ten years. Each year just the best, most visible, most reliable, of the movers and shakers are invited. *Creme de la creme.* Three hundred families. Those who don't RSVP or just skip the event do not make the cut next year unless they apologize and ask to be included. Two gaffs and the big black ball is dropped. I'm still not sure why I am here. Maybe the Kileys feel this dear friend is a party favor. He sure as hell doesn't fit the mold. But, I do know the rules. I've always been there for both Billy Ray and Jeannie. And from time to time they have shielded me from the slings and arrows of outrageous fortune.

Arriving at the gatehouse, I present my numbered invitation. The young boy at the guardhouse recognizes me. It's Tommy. Curly black hair. Lots of it. Brown eyes, about the size of quarters. A smile that would light up a football stadium. These looks in combination with his physique moisten every cheerleader's lips during the fall.

"Hey, Mister McCaa. Nice to see you again. How's Two doing?"

Tommy Serrano is a big-time running back. Six feet even, two-hundred-ten pounds, four-point-five speed, very physical and the smarts to know what to do and when to do it. Almost three thousand yards last year as a junior. Twenty-one touchdowns. Unanimous All State and third team All American. Led the Cats to the state championship game only to lose to Osalooki and the "Looni Lookis." Tommy is back, his line is back, and the quarterback can pass to a set of younger, faster receivers. This is the *Year of the Cat.* After this, who knows? A big school where he can test his pro potential.

"Tommy, it's nice to see you, too. You're looking a little bigger since I saw you in October. You must be living in the weight room. Don't forget the laps and the stairs."

"I won't. We could use Two at DB, but I guess he is happy at Sebastian. And he gets to go both ways. Can I see your invitation? Sorry, but I have to check. Yep, I should have known. Number seventeen. Always at the top. Right after the really big guys. Go through. One of the boys will park your car. See you later. How's 'The Terror'?"

"Terry is great. He lives in Minnesota. Happily married with two daughters."

Everybody remembers Terry "The Terror," my first son. They remember the night he got the nickname. The night he picked up a defensive lineman from Eastside Christian, carried his screaming body to the sideline, and tossed him like garbage onto the team's bench. It seems that the D-lineman had poked Terry in the eye twice. Once may have been an accident. Twice was intentional. Terry was ejected and barred from the next two games until the incident was reviewed and the truth unearthed. It seems that video evidence confirmed the eye poking and the D-lineman was barred from high school sports for life. This was a little action he learned from his godfather, Billy Ray. Terry earned his bones that night. Opposing teams feared him thereafter, which was the remainder of the season and his senior year. He even carried his nastiness over to the basketball court. Though not the tallest, he was a hulk in the middle. When opposing centers tried to back him down, he would drive his knee into the back of their knee and they would slump. Failing this he would scrape his shoe down the back of the center's calf. Shredding the hairs caused the center to stop and think of the pain. This gambit was very effective at disrupting plays. He was never found guilty. He bulked up and played tackle for a very good D-III school. His reputation enrolled before he did.

I float through the stone pillars that hold the two-story gate. Two is my son, James Buchanan McCaa, Junior. I am Jimmy B. He is Jimmy B, Two or just Two to his close friends. And Tommy is a close friend. Two is the only kid Tommy ever faced who could stalk him and bring him down like a wolf does a deer. Two does not have exceptional speed. Just fierce determination and the uncanny knack to sense what's going to happen, where, and when. The bond between the boys has been solid since the Lansdale Area Youth Football League. Two will be inside somewhere. I haven't seen in him in six days, but who's counting.

This party is not only for elite adults; it is for elite high school juniors and seniors, and not necessarily the children of those invited. Every October, the Kileys request, from guidance counselors at the all the county high schools, public and private, the bios of students who might be deemed worthy to serve at this gala event. Worthiness is based upon academia, as well as the student's overall contribution to the school in athletics, clubs, societies, etc. The applicants are then screened by the Kileys, primarily Jeannie.

From this herd of hungry, are selected twenty boys and twenty girls to work the party. Boys park cars and other physical jobs. Girls serve food, clean up, get drinks, and basically manage the house. This is the division of labor that will continue for the rest of their lives. For their labors, they receive service hours (mandatory for graduation at the private schools), recognition in the social pages of the local fish wrap, and, most important, the introduction to Lansdale society, both the bright and the dark sides. All this said, this special birthday part functions as a debut for both sexes. For this reason, preference is given to seniors. But, if a junior is invited to serve, he or she is marked for future greatness. And parents revel in this unseen but very special laurel wreath.

The culling process for the kids is often heart breaking, and has, on numerous occasions, drawn the pleadings and wrath from the parents of the unworthy. There was even one instance in which the parents of a rejected declined their own invitation. They were banished to social Siberia forthwith.

Oh, there's another thing. I can't explain why, but the holiday spirits, emotional and liquid, seem to encourage sexual exploration and explosion. I suspect there is more behind the scene hanky-panky at Christmas than at all the weddings in May, June, and July combined. During the summer couplings, bridesmaids and best men, long lost cousins and even strangers are caught up in the moment. It's been that way since fire and through all the ages of Europe. Christmas, in twentieth century Western society, is just a lot more of the same.

My car creeps along behind the ten or so wending their ways o'er the quarter-mile drive way. Double S like in Germany. Just a hell of a lot slower. The pines and the oaks shield the house and property from prying eyes, as if the fifteen-foot flagstone wall wasn't enough. Add to this the black six-pack and you have a keep. Two Rots, two Shepherds, and two Dobermans. A fighting force that can best any opponent. A black, five hundred and fifty pound monolith with twenty-four legs. This cloud of ferocity has three-point-two speed and a collective appetite equal to the training table for a professional football team. But they don't bother the horses or family and friends. Sort of an MCI thing. They have treed a few interlopers and even pinned down two would be robbers who were wasted on crack. The guys were happy to go to jail. I have been blessed. They like, tolerate, or just pity me. Not sure which. In any case they show their idea of affection to me by wagging their tails and barking. I have petted them and retained all my digits and limbs. Their combined growl is frighteningly feral and their stare is terrifying, but they are just big babies around the Kileys.

You can't see the stables from the driveway. If the wind is right, you can take a deep breath and know stables are somewhere nearby. Four horses. Like the family, two stallions and two mares. The groom lives in the tack house. In total, the horses cost more than most of the houses in the county. But with land, money, time, and a wife and daughter who could ride six hours a day, what's a hapless husband and father to do? Build the best stable and fill it with good horses. Every so often the four humans spend a few days on the trail, their own, riding into the eight hundred acres and pitching tents for a family camp-out.

The auto unraced course is outlined by bagged candles. Why doesn't the paper burn? Flaming stars at the shoulders of the Yellow Brick Road. Except it's not yellow, brick, or a road. The moon is full. Seems to be that way every Christmas. Maybe it's part of the script. The dancing orange candlelight and the constant blue from the fluorescent orb in the black sky casts an eerie aura reminiscent of many tab-induced visions. Add to this the shadows and shapes of the trees moving in the wind and I begin to sense an old paranoia. Most of the chosen frozen are oblivious to the visual experience of the holding line. Like theme parks, the emotions experienced in line before the ride are integral to the whole experience.

The small stones on the path to Oz dance a multi-colored Flamenco as they mirror the changing light composition and the shadows. They crunch sensually beneath the tires. Unlike most Floridians, I keep the car windows down all winter long. Fresh air is such a rare commodity in the land of over-construction and grandfathered utility air pollution. Mine is the smallest, least significant vehicle in the caravan. I guess, when you have lots of money you can afford a really, really big penis. Implants be damned,

I like my Mazda. At the serpentine terminus, there are six young men, three for each car, two for the doors and one to drive the vehicle to the beginning of the horse field, behind a big stand of trees, behind the guest bungalow cum gymnasium cum pool house. Out of sight from the house. Ain't money grand?

The boys are dressed in the uniform *du noir,* gray slacks, white shirt, red tie and blue blazer. Black shoes and matching belt. That is it. No deviations. No sweaters. No school patches on the blazers or ties. No running shoes.

I've reached the end of the line. It's my turn to off load, approach the castle, and be announced. Rabe Miller, Tryson Windley, and Albert Torres are my team. Unfortunately, I am alone and Tryson has naught to do. As Albert opens my door, the boys greet me with a cacophony of recognition.

"Hello, Mister McCaa."

"Hey, it's Jimmy B."

"Good evening, sir".

They can get away with infernal familiarity because their very presence is proof they have been accepted. But, their pubescent confusion is manifested in the different salutations. Soon personal salutations, to even the dourest of the adult land, will be common place outside of the work place, but only outside.

"Two is inside. He drew KP, the lucky stiff. The fox is in the hen house. A little dish washing, a little pot scrubbing, and lots of time to check out the talent." Rabe sounds genuinely jealous.

Tryson chimes in. "All that food and drink. Besides, it's warm in there."

He is a real Floridian. When the thermometer hits sixty, it's time for the woollies and a heavy coat.

Albert is simply non-communicative. Shyness is his way. I suspect he is embarrassed. His family. It's a shame. Hide all that talent and intelligence under a bushel basket of social stigma. A few more years and he'll be gone to become himself. Hopefully, far away where he feels comfortable that no one knows the whole sordid story of alcohol abuse, embezzlement, and murder suicide. A burden no child should carry. He is already a man in many ways.

Parking costs fifty dollars. This goes to CitiMinistries. Somewhere over six grand in foldable green. *No Tipping* says the sign. This would violate the rite of passage and the earned service hours. However, the boys clear a couple of hundred each. Under the table starts early. It can become a way of life.

Up the long flagstone double S path (there are patterns and motifs everywhere) to the two story double oak doors with the perfect patina. More bagged candles. Just smaller. As I approach the entrance, one-half of the double-door swings open and Eben, the major domo, the sentinel, smiles as he recognizes the latest guest.

He extends his hand to take the invitation and then accepts my hand in friendship. This latter is an uncommon gesture for Eben. His position as the diplomat for the household does not foster familiarity. But his strength and depth of character allow for an exception to every rule, particularly where love is concerned.

"Welcome to Christmas, twenty-twelve, at the Kileys, Mister McCaa. Sir, it is truly nice to see you again. I guess now the party can begin in earnest."

"Thank you, Eben. It's always nice to see you. How is Dorothea holding up with all the extra help in her kitchen?"

We both chuckle. His eyes twinkle with glee.

"Well, she'll manage. Always does. They're such nice young men and women. I noticed yours doing dish and pot washing duty. No mistaken' the father-son resemblance there. And, he's so close to all the young ladies. Wonder where he got that?"

"Now, Eben, someday someone is going to believe all those rumors you've been spreading about me."

"Please come in. Mister and Missus Kiley have been asking about you. May I introduce Kellan Connors Kiley and Christina Kathryn Kiley, your hosts for this evening?"

KC and CK are festively, if not comfortably, gussied-up for the holidays. He with a tux and heavily starched, wing collared shirt. She with a long dress, Kiley tartan with Irish linen ruffles at the arms and bodice. These are not their normal uniforms. He would prefer coveralls from the boat yard and she loves jodhpurs and a pullover. Nonetheless, they look handsome and lovely. They are trim and stand tall, each with a deep heartfelt smile, yet an almost mischievous look in their eyes, obvious traits from the parents. I get a hug from both. I am the Dutch uncle. Listened to and respected when parents are ignored. Two years apart. College is over for both of them. Life at home is sweet, perhaps a bit stultifying, but the nest from which the young birds choose not to fly. Parents don't want to toss them to the wolves quite yet. That time comes all too soon. And, there is a certain finality to it.

"Hey, Jimmy B. is here. Now its time to *paaahtay*." KC even sounds like his old man when he speaks loudly.

CK whispers, "Pay no attention to the youngster. The loudmouth lout. Someday he may even grow up to be human. Welcome. You're looking devilishly scrumptious for an older man."

She has acquired the coquettish traits of her mother. Both Kiley women love to tease and occasionally flirt. But in the safety of friendship and in good taste and good fun. I have warned Jeannie. If anything were to happen to Billy Ray, she is not to consider me as a replacement. This always gets a chuckle and wink from her.

Through the foyer, a scant twenty feet long by fifteen wide, by twelve high. Curtained windows on both sides. Benches and built-in hooks for outdoor boots, jackets, and hats. The highly polished brass, pewter, and the slate floor sparkle in the light of ten three-foot candles on four-foot, hand-hewed oak stands and the light from the entrance hall. The scents of pine and potpourri mingle to tingle the olfactory sense. The noise from the assembled throng is muffled by the size of the house and configuration of the rooms. Suddenly there is a huge shadow cast across the slate. Billy Ray the Jolly Flesh Colored Giant. All this and a smile wide.

William Raymond Kiley. Six feet four and one-half inches. Anywhere from two hundred and thirty-five to two hundred seventy-five depending on his work and work-out schedule. Like Jackie Gleason, he has multiple wardrobes for body size. He is trim for this party. Thirty-four inches in waist and forty-eight in the chest. The remnants of a cherubic face. A full head of white hair. Gray-blue eyes and a nose that has been broken more than once. Definitely a countenance that Hollywood would call rugged. Trunk and arms of a linebacker. Gait of a tight end. Hands that can still palm a basketball, despite the fact that the little finger on both hands is gnarled by numerous injuries, some administered, some self-inflicted. His limp was acquired in Vietnam. The helicopter in which he was being ferried to a firefight was hit from the ground.

Sitting on his pot saved his ass and life. The pilot next to him exploded in a flash of flesh, bones, and blood throughout the cabin. The chopper spun lazily then furiously right before it hit the ground. Eight went up. Five were rescued. The back never healed properly, ergo the limp.

Years later Billy Ray and I were out on the Gulf, sort of fishing, sunning, bullshitting, and napping. It was my birthday and we always did something totally wasteful with each other on our respective natal celebrations. One year it was wild pig stalking, one time parasailing, once a drive to Atlanta for dinner. Wives know boys must be boys. On the forty-five footer called *You Bought a What,* we were just hanging' and chilling' and he asked me to go to the ice chest for another round of beers. There was a filthy sock on top of the ice. As I was about to toss the sock, Billy Ray advised me that it was my gift.

Inside was a bracelet made of brass. The bracelet was inscribed in some oriental symbols. He told me it was a gift to him from a chieftain of a tribe of *Mounties* in Nam. Mounties are the fierce mountain people who hated just about everybody, took from everyone, and loved only their tribe. They were not afraid to die or kill. All of this is very reminiscent of Highland stories. Nam was theirs long before there was Ho or Madam Nu. And, within a few centuries, it will be theirs again. The bracelet was given to Billy Ray as a token of honor. He had set up a fire base in a valley. Forward protection for the troops that would follow. Many tribes found shelter, or, at least a base of protected operations, from which they could go out and kill the bad guys, all the bad guys. One tribe was grateful. The bracelet was a form of acknowledgement, not only of his deed but also his attachment to the tribe. He was accepted as a fierce and loyal clan leader. The brass came from shell casings expended in defense and offense of whatever.

Bill told me two truisms learned in the jungle. First: "If no one is shooting at you, it's a great day." Second: "When you awake and right before you go to sleep, click your teeth. Because if you can hear your teeth click, you are alive."

These are basic, and once understood, easy rules to live by.

He was giving his gift to me. For what I had been through, who I was to him, and what I could do. He knew I would kill for my clan (Gaelic for children) and my freedom. These two ideals are fundamental for men. It's what distinguishes the real men from those who simply go through life with their hands out and produce chaos. I was, am, and will be forever honored.

Billy Ray Kiley was the first Saint Sebastian graduate to play really big-time football. He has always been big. He was faster when younger. Weren't we all? He was drafted and played three years for the Bears before his knees became his unwanted ticket out. This did not stop *tio sucre* from seeking his killing talents. Apparently, football players, and particularly linebackers, make excellent *mercs*. That's what they are even though they are on our side. The chopper incident was his wanted ticket out. He came home. Entered law school. Then prematurely exited stage left answering his dad's call to come home and fix the family business. Plus, Pop and Maggie were in declining health.

Kiley Boat Yards (KBY) had been under investigation for outfitting boats in such a manner as to avoid inspection of the cargo by certain authorities. The Irish Republican Army gun running business was never proven, but the boat yard was more prosperous than other yards twice its size. Oh, well, just really tight management.

Kiley Boat Yards. Service and repair only. No sales that require inventory and take up profitable space. KBY works on all manner, shapes and sizes, for anybody with the money and the desire for the best. Not cheap. This tradition dies hard. They're working credo is that: *There are three forces governing our work; the finished quality, time of work, and money to pay for work. The customer can control two and only two of the factors. KBY controls the remaining one.* After nearly five decades, the credo has helped create a very profitable business, which employs one hundred seventy-five to two hundred people depending on the season. Billy Ray and his business brood want for nothing. His full-timers are well paid with a stack of benefits, health and dental, 401(k), three weeks paid vacation, and nice year-end bonuses. No one leaves unless they die.

KBY is as computerized as possible, thanks to KC. Very efficient systems, estimates and production schedules. The third generation is nearing take over. In a few years Billy Ray can consult, sail, and fish whenever he wants.

Billy Ray took over for Pop when the yard was doing about a reported million a year. Small and profitable. He went to work, hand-in-hand with the men, for as long as the men could last. Billy was more than just respected. One, he was the boss's boy. Two, he could and would do whatever it took to complete a superior quality job on time and on estimate. The men loved his get down and dirty attitude. And three, his fierce devotion to the company was manifested by his periodic outbursts of temper. The men had seen the film clip of linebacker Billy Ray tossing the wideout from the out-of-bounds-line to the bench, eight yards, because he was in Billy's path to the running back. Broke the wideout's shoulder, jaw and wrist. Enough said by the clip to fill volumes.

Soon he secured capital to expand the facilities and prayed for a terrible hurricane season. The storm gods are Celtic. Three *Level Fours* came through Florida during the season and the boat salvage and repair business was bigger than ever. Insurance companies, which have a tendency to be *r-e-a-l-s-l-o-w* payers were caught between the rich yacht owners and a very imposing boat-yard owner. Fifty-percent of the money was due after insurance inspection and estimate or no work would begin. The balance was due upon inspection and delivery. The sailors didn't want to miss the winter season and the fishermen could not afford to be out of water too long. They opted for time. And the insurance companies opted for quality, because this saves them money in the long run. So, the best work was done within a short time frame and KBY became exceedingly profitable. But, not without work. Hard work.

Billy Ray and all his people worked doubles seven days a week. There was even a graveyard shift to do the not very precise set-up work for the next two shifts. Part timers and temps filled needs. The pay was better than they had ever dreamed. They knew this work had a life span, but hoped that they would be able to hire on full time if they proved themselves worthy during the massive crunch. That's how the work force grew to its present size.

Today there is nearly too much business. Old customers. New foreign money, able to pay for the best repair and refitting. Sons and nephews of men who wish to move things undetected. They know loyalty and silence can be purchased. There is talk of further expansion. KBY owns the shoreline on both sides. Expansion is always risky. Billy Ray knows this. KC knows this. It will be accomplished, or not, under KC's aegis. That's Billy Ray's promise.

Jeannie Connors Kiley. The queen. Black hair and delft blue eyes. A trim figure, even at the ripe old age of forty-six (yeah, right). She's wrapped in something dark blue and gossamer, floor length with lacy shoulder straps. Abundant cleavage made possible by the latest in under garment technology and the right amount of femininity.

Jeannie managed a line of marine supply outlets for her family. She grew up a smart and tough businessperson. Learned to decode truth. How to cut a deal. She was beautiful—is beautiful—and will be beautiful when she turns seventy, in twenty-four years or less. Underneath the smile and twinkle. Underneath the very expensively tailored but casual looking clothes, is the female animal, a real woman. She would kill to protect her children and anyone who fucks with her husband. Her devotion exceeds the norm. Consider a wounded tigress protecting two cubs in a cave and you have vague understanding of her ferocity. But, make no mistake about it, she is not a jungle stalker. She is the queen of the realm.

Jeannie met Billy Ray when he was trying to buy supplies for KBY during the year of the hurricanes and good fortune. She negotiated a lot more than a good price for a huge order purchased on one hundred-twenty-day credit terms. She held a large piece of Billy Ray's heart as collateral. It was his to give and he did so willingly. He made trips for special, made-to-order items and to renegotiate the terms. All of this could have been done by telephone. But, they both felt that face-to-face was critical. The day trips spun into overnights, which evolved into four-day weekends, which evolved into forever.

After the marriage, she applied her expertise of the parts and supply business to KBY. She wanted to stand by her man and take a minutia-filled time consuming activity off his shoulders so that he could concentrate on the work in the yard. Beneath the noble exterior motives, was the truth. She was better at this job than he was and they both knew it. They divided and they conquered. In a few years, the rug rats. By the time the darlings could be left alone and she could go back to work, she deemed it not necessary. This was her decision. The family fortune was planted and growing. So, she devoted her energies to *giving back*. Became an unbelievably great, believable community leader. Fund raising for CitiMinistries has been the cornerstone of her efforts. She has also helped the not-for-profit hospital. Established shelters for the homeless snowbirds flocking south to escape the freezing winter streets up north. Between the money contributed and time devoted, even at minimum wage, she has been worth well over twelve million to the community. Her fan club of politicians, clergy, business leaders, and educators will do what she asks, when she asks it, because she never asks without doing first. And she doesn't ask much or often. Silent strength is real power.

Here they stand at the entrance to the citadel. The god and goddess. Behind them all the joy and gayety continues. Jeannie moves to embrace me. Just a tad personal. Body contact above and below the waist is always nice, but not with a husband so near. Sometimes her flirtations can be right up to the edge. CK has learned from the queen. Maybe this is in female DNA. A smile, a giggle, a wiggle and a touch. Men are helpless. The flood of testosterone is overwhelming and manifests itself inappropriately. We separate. I have lipstick high on my cheek.

I jump up onto Billy Ray's chest like a child to a parent. We've been doing this for years. The size difference makes it physically possible and our concept of theater makes it emotionally desirable. I squeal like a leprechaun. He chuckles. He puts me down and kisses me on the forehead. This is a form of male bonding they don't acknowledge in oh-so-polite circles. It's visceral. I would kill for him and he would maim for me, because he still likes to administer pain. I would do whatever he asked and he would only ask what he could not do for himself. Love like this is eternal and universal. It's brotherly and fatherly.

"Well, Jimmy B, what brings you to the sticks in the dead of winter?"

Jeannie's huge grin belies her sarcasm. She is talking with a clenched jaw so no one nearby can really tell what she is saying. It all looks just too nice for words.

"I guess the holiday season is upon us. Here is the Christmas elf, Santa's oldest helper."

I whisper to Billy, "Would it be appropriate to say fuck you to your wife?"

"How is my godson?"

"Terry is great. Lives in Minnesota with two daughters. He is a consultant in the health care industry. So far he hasn't thrown anybody from an office or beneath a bus. I guess he has mellowed."

"You know Jimmy anger and intelligence are correlated. People who are highly intelligent like Terry and me, can become very angry at the fools with whom we work."

"I guess my lack of intelligence is reflected in my *laissez faire* approach to life and idiots."

"Au contraire, *mon petite ami*, your mellowness is a residue from the '60s."

His false basso profundo causes people behind him to pause and stare. By then, Jeannie and I are giggling.

Jeannie, now the lady of the manor, continues the dig with a very phony Southern Belle accent, "Where did Two get those good looks? And that gracious charm? He certainly has a way with the scullery maids. They are falling all over their feet to help him, even if this means ruining their manicures in hot soapy water. God, you McCaa's have such power over us helpless females. I hope you stay away from CK tonight. I'm not sure she's strong enough to withstand your charm."

Wink, wink.

Billy interrupts, "Come in, oh favored son, enjoy the eve, sample the tarts, the baked variety, asshole, and drink your fill from my supply of Celtic whiskeys. Seriously, it's great to see you. Hope all is well. How goes the legal battle?"

"Yes, Jimmy, welcome. Why do we spar each time we meet? You didn't touch my daughter did you?"

"Now, Jeannie. I would never sully the princess. And, besides, she is not my type. She is single and over seventeen. The deep-seated reason you spar is that you lust after me and this is your way of rejecting your own primal urges. As for me, I have always teased women. You know, *Georgie Porgie* and all that. I am here because I love you both more than you could ever know. And, I like most of the crowd you assemble. It's a different flavor each year. I wouldn't miss the sycophantic, over-indulging *High and Mighty*, who tries to score points in your home. Billy, the legal battle rages. Flames licking at my feet. I will win, just not unscarred. Now where is Two?"

I kiss Jeannie again, this time on the lips, with just a slosh of passion. I can tease, too. Billy is looking inward to the milling throng awaiting his return. Heading for the kitchen, after my stop at one of the three bars for an Balvenie and two cubes, I notice the servers. Their uniform is unmistakable. Kiley tartan long skirt with a black patent leather six-inch wide belt and gold buckle. White silk blouse. Only the top one of the two collar buttons may be left opened. White hose and black leather shoes with gold buckles.

In the hair, regardless of style, is a tartan bow held with a gold buckle. The shoes, hose and blouse they buy; the rest is provided. They look snappy, a word most associated with green beans and an activity level required by your mother.

Full Bore Thirty-four

ull bore . . . thirty-four. Full bore . . . thirty-four. Three down linemen. Four linebackers. Three of them blitz. Always weak side heavy. Corners give ten yards. Keep receiver inside. Safeties protect mid-depth, but a little wider than normal. Lone non-blitzer drops to center of field. Net is six rushers and five coverage. Speed is critical. Any slow down creates major holes and gaps. Unbalanced my side. Wide out on other. I have tight end. Play off shoulder three yards. Give him the lane I want. Toward center field. Motion toward weak side. Extra pressure for safety on that side. At snap QB steps back out of the way of the pulling guard. Guard runs into blitzer. Both bump running back. He goes deep. Tight end tries to seal me off. I run behind him toward linebacker depth. He tries to turn. Tackle busy with our end. I get caught in tangle of bodies and legs. Go down grabbing arms. Blitzers force runner out of bounds three yards deep. My side is kicked and hand stepped on. These guys are rough.

One of Gino's guys called and told me that Gino wanted to see me. I heard and I obeyed. When Gino spoke, people I knew listened. Gino had been a friend of a friend for a couple of years. He is connected. He also was about as high as I would see. On the surface, Gino sells building materials for a wholesaler on Long Island. The construction trade is lucrative. He makes a few telephone calls and personal visits each week and earns about four hundred grand a year. But, he lives in a three-story brownstone on the East Side of Manhattan. The house and his three cars are worth about five and three-quarter million. I'm not sure of his family affiliation and will never ask, because it does not exist. And, I like life.

He works out of a small office in Midtown. No secretary. Just three telephones, each with four lines. He knows each one of them is tapped. They are for his legit business, or, in extreme emergencies, elaborately coded conversations. Never up the tree. Only down or sideways. Any meetings with Gino are held during a sidewalk stroll. I went to the office about nine AM. Gino was on the phone. His voice flip-flopped from threatening near scream, to slimy singsong, to hefty jocularity. He waved me to come in, sit, and be quiet.

"Listen, here's the deal. I need the pipes and fittings delivered to the job site by noon tomorrow. Not Friday. Tomorrow. Thursday. Got it? Get it done. You know you'll be paid in cash on delivery. Is there a problem? That's not my problem. That's your problem. You fix it. You're a big boy. Remember, there are lots more where this came from. OK? Thank you for your help in this matter."

"Putz. Where da' fuck does that little kike get off telling me he can't deliver and wants more time. I tell him what I want. He does what I ask. Or, he'll never do business with us again. I don't give a fuck who his uncle is."

"Let's get some coffee."

We leave. Lock the door. I'm not sure why. There are more cops and feds watching this place than a bank. Only a junkie would be dumb enough to steal anything. And this assumes there is anything to steal, which there is not. The elevator is one of the very old varieties with the metal grate door on the cab. You can see the inside of the shaft as you go up and down. From the thirty-sixth floor to the lobby is a surrealistic three-minute, shuddering and fluttering, musty, dusty ride. Outside, on the sidewalk we find the coffee-and-sweet-roll guy. His cart is two blocks away. Gino never walks to the cart the same way twice in a row. I suspect this makes it tougher to keep the voice gun on him.

Two large. Double cream and one sugar. One prune and one apricot Danish. We walk toward the benches by the river. Sit beneath trees to shield the listeners.

"I would like you to do me a favor. I need an unknown to help with a delivery. I would like you to deliver a package for me. Yes, you do have a choice. But I figured you might like the money for no risk. I need to know now."

"Gino, I would be honored to help you. You knew that before you asked. And yes, I could use the money. The 'Cuda wants his nut and I ain't got it."

"How much you owe 'cuda?"

"Twelve."

"The delivery pays twenty. You pay 'Cuda. But the delivery must happen tonight. You must be very invisible and do exactly what I say. Do not even think of peeking into the package. And, if you are nabbed, it's your ass. Silence will extend your life regardless of where you wind up. Talk will end it. OK?"

"OK. I can do that. But what about my family, if I get stopped? Will you take care of them? What's next?"

"If you are unlucky enough to be spotted and stopped, we will pay for your attorney. If you have to do time, we will take care of your family better than you have been doing. And, if you keep silent, they will live. If not, then not. Go to the dry cleaners at ninety-sixth and Madison, ya' know, Jerrob. Be there at six sharp and ask for Marvin. Tell him you are with me. He will give you a case, just like this one. Make sure the new one is sealed. Just like this one. Take the case to 3414 Bedford Boulevard in Brooklyn. You'll find a storefront, ABC Hardware. Enter and ask for Willy X. He is a very tall, thin blonde. He is a swisher. Give him the case. Give the case only to him. He will give you an envelope. Take the envelope to Ellen's bar at Seventy-Third and Third. Ask for the maitre de, Alphonso. Introduce yourself as a friend of mine. He will drop a menu. Put the envelope in the menu and hand it to him. You're done. Have a drink or dinner. Or, just leave. One last thing. Take all forms of transportation. Take the subway. A few busses. Take short cab rides. Got all that?"

"Yes, Gino. But, when . . ."

"The money will be paid tomorrow. Come to my office at seven in the morning."

Unemployment led me to the 'Cuda, a loan shark of great evil. His smile is an eerie reminder of his evil loose with the money and very precise with the payback. His approach to collection is like his name. He would bite a finger off to prove a point. He wants his money every Friday by five. I could make the vig by hustling backgammon and poker. That would keep him happy. But, I would never be out of debt without a big score. This was my chance. I was in heaven. A few errands. A nap. Buy tokens in advance. Eat early. Dress inconspicuously. The key is to blend in. I know someone will be tailing me. I can't let them know I know. Lose them as soon as possible on my journey.

The case at the dry cleaners is exactly like the one I walked in with . . . one of the knock-offs from the street vendors, cheesy Tourister. No problem at the pick-up. I look like a thousand other *schlubs*. Subway downtown. Change from local to express at Forty-Second Street. Switch to Brooklyn line at Wall Street. At the Bridge exit in Brooklyn, get off and on the Bedford Boulevard Bus. Bed-Sty is a frightening, bombed out, black neighborhood. Truly a war zone. Renowned for its flames and fights. Death and destruction. What the hell is a short white guy doing here at night? One hundred block. Two hundred block. The bus ride goes on forever. Deeper into the *Heart of Darkness*. About a year later I exit the bus at far end of the Thirty-Four hundred block. Hardware store across the street. I am scared. Lost and alone is not a healthy combination. Lost alone and carrying contraband of great value could be deadly. The sweat is beginning to run down my spinal concave.

"I'm here to see Willy X."

"I'm Willy X."

"No offense but Willy X is tall, thin, and white. You're zero for three on those counts."

Laughter all around.

"I am he?"

"Yes, you be." More laughter.

"I have a package for you. From Gino. Here. Now do you have something for me?"

"Let me examine the case first."

He disappears into the back room. Now I'm in deep shit. If he disappears with the case, I'll disappear with special shoes. He appears with an envelope.

"This is for you. And, if you like, my friend will drive you anywhere you wish."

The envelope is not fat. Not packed with cash. There are a few folded sheets in the envelope . . . certificates?

"If he would take me to the Wall Street subway station, I would appreciate it. And he can go any route he wishes."

The ride takes an hour and a half. A bus for the entire time would have taken much less time. But no one could follow us over the circuitous route he took. Three bus routes and I am at Ellen's. It's one of the many trendy, Upper East Side, over-priced, eateries. The maitre de and I make the switch. He never bats an eyelash. I head for home via the streets. Walking a very round about route.

Seven AM on the dot I'm walking through Gino's door. He holds up his hand for me to stop. Nothing said, we exit and move to the elevator. He hands me an envelope and signals for me not to talk. Shakes my hand, a rarity, and whispers in my ear:

"You'll like Lansdale, Florida a lot. It's a great town to hide in. Call Billy Ray Kiley. His dad and I are old friends. Good luck."

I do what I'm told. Particularly when the teller is in a position to enforce the request. Gino said go and I never looked back. The envelope contained a note to return to Jerrob's dry cleaners. Marvin had a case for me. I opened it when I got home. Twenty large. A fair wage for a job well done. I have wondered many times what was in the case that could be worth a total of twenty grand for its delivery. Bearer bonds? Diamonds? Plates for hundreds? It was small and very valuable. Some questions are better left unasked. So, here I am in Lansdale.

*   *   *

The entrance hall is brightly lit by the forty-eight candle chandelier. Imported from Ireland, the dining hall lighting of the castle Duncannon now graces this entrance every holiday season. The Kileys remove the brass candelabra electric lighting and temporarily install this magnificent oak fire-burning unit every December seventh. Only to take it down on January fifth and reinstall the brass one. It's what they want to do.

Into the kitchen, through the in door, not the out door. This causes me to contemplate. The out and in doors are not what they appear when one is on the other side, and just which is the other side? I'm I getting tied in philosophical R.D. Lang knots.

There he is. Two and his harem. Up to his elbows in greasy, hot, soapy water. A filthy apron protecting his shirt and pants, sans jacket and tie. An aproned blonde to his right is handing him freshly scraped plates and platters. An aproned brunette to his left, accepting the washed plates and platters, is rinsing them and stacking them for two other brunettes to towel dry. A fifth young thing is moving the scraped, washed, rinsed, and dried serving and eating ware to two large trays. The fresh platters are loaded with food, and, along with the plates, are taken back out to the party to be emptied and soiled respectively, only to return to the kitchen and the previously detailed cycle. Henry Ford would have envied this process, and Two's older brother would like to reengineer it. All the food is prepared according to Dorothea's recipes. Two is the bub at the hub.

His face is strong, almost chiseled, but not sharp angular. He has the look that wets lips. Many people claim to see the resemblance between us. It is strong, so they say. Frankly, I've never seen it. One of his baby pictures is a Xerox of a shot of my father. There is my dad, in 1904, wearing a baby frock that looks like a dress. He is holding a ball. Well, Two's face and dad's face are the same. So there must be some resemblance between, dad's son and my son. Two has not picked up the pounds of excess which seem to appear and stay after thirty-five. These little pounds which plop up around the waist and under the jaw bone. Maybe, if he works at staying in shape, he can delay the pound-on process for many years.

But, it is his eyes. Hazel with minute flecks of red. Not blood. Just red flecks. They add a sparkle, a devilish glint to his countenance. This he got from me and I know it. This is what drives the little girls wild. One peek into the peepers and a chemical imbalance occurs in the female body. It has been this way for at least three generations (I never saw my grandfather's eyes). It is a blessing and a curse. But it is a fire starter.

And, he is "jacked." Having spent hours and hours in various weight rooms during the past three years, his physique is something to behold. Very trim, yet rippled and bulged where it shows. He has his six-pack. Once known as a washboard. The change in designation is a reference to the visible muscles from the sternum to the navel and not an amount of beer.

Occasionally, one of the girls will say something or glance into Two's eyes; otherwise the young lions and lionesses are there to work, not socialize. Except, and this is a big except, they seem to be in some level of nirvana. I think I saw a touch. Oh-so accidentally the scraper touched Two's hand. My whistle crashes the hum of the kitchen like a bomb. This whistle has called both my boys, hailed taxis, and caused dogs to return to my side for nearly two generations. My dad whistled and I responded. I whistle and my sons respond. Two looks up from his putrid pond, smiles and flashes me thumbs up. He's in hog heaven. I motion as if I am driving a car, point to him. He looks right and left, and back to me with a sly grin and shakes his head. He does not need a ride home from me. Home is where he lives with his mother. Not my home. It is obvious, even to an *alta caca* that Two has multiple ride options, if not multiple orgasms, after the party. Truly, youth is wasted on the young.

I am confronted by Dorothea. This is her realm. Her people. Her responsibility is to train these young men and women in the importance of preparing, serving, and cleaning. Neither seen nor heard. They are the medium through which culinary enjoyment is experienced by guests. Therefore, the kitchen is run like a small company. Dispensing food in a quiet, dignified atmosphere. No shenanigans. Orderly.

"Who told you you could come in here and disturb my kitchen? You are always makin' noise and causin' a commotion. These young people are learning to be adults and you're behaving like a child. What kind of example is that?"

Two's smile widens. His old man has been busted.

Properly upbraided, I grin sheepishly.

"Dorothea, I'm sorry for disturbing your kitchen. I just wanted to see Two and make sure he was all right."

As she takes me by the arm and leads me to the out door, she says, for the benefit of her brood, "You shouldn't be here at all. Of course Jimmy Two is all right. In fact, he is a far sight better in the behavement area than his daddy."

Outside the kitchen, she hugs me. It would never do for her young people to see this obvious display of deep friendship between the Master Sergeant and the interloper.

"It is good to see you again, Mister McCaa. Your boy is a hard worker and seems to have this strange attraction power over the young ladies. I wonder where he got that."

"Dorothea, it's nice to see you again. Eben looks well. What are you feeding him?"

"Nothin' special. Just good food and lots of love. Something that's been missin' from your diet, I'll bet."

"That, dear woman, is my business. Anyway, Merry Christmas and I love you."

"I love you, too, Mister McCaa. But not as much as Jesus does."

"I hope he does, Dorothea."

Another hug and I'm back into the unreal world of revelers. Eben and Dorothea are human treasures. The Kileys are lucky to have found them and gracious to share them with heathen such as Jimmy B.

Turning my attention to the extraordinary groaning board, I am confronted by a server.

Bam!

Good, God almighty. She is a gasper. One look at her and I gasp for breath and my life. My eyes glaze over and my tongue feels a foot thick. My hair springs out of place. Heart begins to race and I feel flush. Sweat appears on my upper lip and armpits. My mouth is as dry as the Sahara.

"Hey, Mister McCaa, remember me? Alyssia Dermond. Would you like a canapé?"

Staring into and searing my soul. Green eyes, offset by a brown-based green overlay combination eye shadow. Jet black hair pulled back into a pony tail shows off tiny, delicate, succulent ears. A single diamond stud in each lobe. One-half carat. A gift from her folks. Not that pricey. Translucent complexion. Teeny freckles on her nose and forehead. Big eyelashes. Pencil thin, wasp lips. Lipstick to match a color in the tartan. The neck of a swan. She wears *White Shoulders,* the scent of a woman in my past. Not just the collar buttons, but two blouse buttons are intentionally undone.

She has really violated the rules. She smiles perfect teeth. These, alone, are worth three grand.

Her delicate hands offer a tray of goodies, mushroom caps stuffed with crabmeat, bacon-wrapped water chestnuts, curried chicken and almond balls rolled in parsley and basil, puffed cheese pastry, and prosciutto and melon. The portable feast only momentarily seduces my gawk from the incredible, edible beauty before me. I follow the hands and arms to shoulders, swimmer's shoulders, wide and strong. Down past the firm small breasts to a very small waist. I don't think she is wearing a bra. The body of the swimmer has been an aphrodisiac for me since my youth. In heels she is exactly my height. She smiles at my inspection. Something she wanted. Hell, I hardly took notice of her. (Yeah, sure. I just wrote my name across her chest.)

"Yes, I remember you, Alyssia. And I'll take whatever you're selling. Seriously, I'll help myself to a chicken and almond ball. You look very grown up."

I wonder if my stammering was audible. That may be the dumbest and most insulting fucking thing I could have said. Of course she looks grown up—she is grown UP.

"Sorry, about the 'looking grown up'. It's that you startled me." This was not a lie.

"How are things going at Saint Sebastian? Congratulations on the third place in the 200-free at states. I hope this will help with colleges. What are you going to do over the winter?"

As long as she talks I can't make too much of an audible ass of myself. But, I can't take my eyes off her. Her eyes, her hair, her face, her body. Do not stare. Do not slobber. Do not touch. Look away. Do something. Anything. Cough. Wave to some unknown person in a far corner of the universe. Consciously distract yourself or you'll start to drool. Bodily functions slowly return to B-A (Before Alyssia) levels.

"I swim for a club until the spring season. Helped me cut two seconds off last year's time. I see where Two gets it. The looks. For a parent, you're cute."

I think she is really saying, '*I can say anything I want as long as I don't move my lips or speak too loudly and you can't react.*' She knows she has me by the short hairs. Men don't stand a damn chance. Not a fucking chance. Maybe boys can weather the tornado of youthful estrogen. But not men. Particularly, not me.

"Nice to see you. Hope to see you again before the party's over. There is Mister Carson. I need to talk to him. Excuse me."

Actually, I needed to talk to anyone but this siren in a Speedo. Just get away. I just couldn't afford another *little head* mistake in my life. One is too many. It causes the loss of friends, family, and work, while it makes opposing divorce lawyers very righteous and rich with my money.

A leper with full-blown AIDS is more welcome than an adult male who falls in heat with a too young female. Only society determines what is too young. A millennium ago there was no taboo. Three hundred years ago, the age barrier was thirteen. Today, excluding certain mountain areas in the country, eighteen is the cut-off. That is, below that age society cuts you and your member off.

As I walk through the mosh pit of social impotence, I become acutely aware of two very distinct and equally obnoxious forms of communicating. In the first, every sentence sounds as if it were a question. The tone of the speaker's voice goes up the musical scale a few notes in conjunction with a slide in the syllabic connection of the last word or words. There are no simple declarative sentences, just fawning, bleating questions. The simple itemizing of the canapés on the serving plate becomes a cloying request for response. It is almost as if the listener is being asked to validate the speaker's existence. Sort of a subservient-master situation. Reminds me of characters from *Lord of the Rings.*

This mode is found primarily amongst the younger partygoers. Extremely infantile. Babies and immature children constantly ask their parents or peers to confirm that they are of value, simply as a function of their activity. Children fear the lack of intrinsic worth, so they ask for confirmation in conversation. Their worth is in the ear of the other. This curse seems to have permeated all levels and layers of youth from six to twenty-six. I hear it tonight and I am repulsed. Bitch. Bitch. Bitch. God, am I a *kvetch* or what?

The second sound that grates on my psyche is a dialog or trialog. Herein individuals share insignificant intimacies and regale each other with the importance of the unimportant. The conversations are always animated, visually and audibly. The members of this great discussion panel are of small minds. And, while menial employment is not a prerequisite for panel membership, it helps. The nature of #2 pencils takes on a huge significance. Laughter, oohs, and ahhs are attendant to any discussion of this item. Halyard lines, gasoline octane and business forms fall into the category of *who cares?* Small minds care. The conversations are real *us versus them*. And, we, who don't know, don't care, or don't care to know, are the *them*. The greater subject's minutia, the more inbred the conversation, the more important the us feel. As you walk down any office corridor, through any party, or sit in any public antechamber, listen to the small, *tres* exclusive conversations around you.

I'm I paranoid or just a snob? Both. Fear keeps the animal alive. It has helped me survive through some very dicey times. I am an *ohrenmensch*. I listen. I hear. I have been accused of sleeping with my ears open. And I can recall TV shows that I have slept through. Grotesque conversations come in fragments, "Every time he tries to . . . ," "The car wouldn't have swerved . . . ," "She always complains to me." "Why can't he get it right.?"

Weaving past clumps of people, I head for the family room. The family room has been cleared of any remnant of family except the wall art and photos. The photos record history from before the union to last year's party. Children's pictures. Grandparents' photos. Shots of KBY. The horses. Athletic teams. Famous people. The wall of fame if you're there and wall of shame on you if you are not. There are even pix of people most people don't know. I recognize a few. Gino for one. The silver-haired fox. Man of a thousand sexual lances.

Now transformed into a dance hall of sorts, the family room is half-full or half-empty. Regardless of your point-of-view, there is enough room to dance and people are dancing. Husbands and wives. Dear friends. Dads and daughters. Mothers and sons. Swirling and taking in the sights. Gliding and talking. Animated and intimate. Partners switch. The servers sneak in for a dance then leave before they are missed by Dorothea. The eight piece ensemble is packing the ears with lively, very danceable sound. One arm is taken by the Mayor's wife, Barbara, the other arm by Gwen Gill, wife of the president of the local utility. This is an incredible power struggle. Or am I just a vehicle for entrance.

"Now, Gwen, I saw Jimmy first. He's mine. Find another eligible bachelor of your own."

"Barbara, you are so grabby. And crabby."

"That's better than itchy and . . ."

"Now, ladies, please. Do not fight over this dog's bone. Who would think you are sisters?"

The drinks have taken over and good taste and reason abandoned. This is grab while the grabbing is good at its social best. Barbara and I trip the light fantastic. Gwen spots a young server, who foolishly stumbled into the den of cougers. She sets her sights and scoops him up and on to the floor. Pulling him very close at every single body point, she begins the slow mating ritual of vertical fornication. His life as a virginal high school student is over. He will be initiated into the young stud's life later tonight. It has been this way for the last eight years. One sister or the other. Husbands get too drunk to know or care.

The three-song set ends to polite applause. I'm never sure if this is appreciation of effort or relief from cessation.

"Jimmy, why is it that I never see you at the oh-so boring political functions? Everyone asks about you. You could do me a favor and relieve the boredom. The museum is holding a gala next week. Please try to come. If you want, I'll leave a ticket for you at the door."

"Barbara, you are most kind. I'll try, but boredom bores me."

As quickly as she attached, she detached. Gwen and her young sire were discussing something and discussing it deeply. Maybe the economic impact of an increasing trade deficit, reengineering the production and cost accounting centers of General Motors, or where they will meet after the party. I feel a tug on my arm and turn expecting to see Barbara. Wrong!

"Hey, Mister McCaa. Will you dance with me?"

The music had restarted, she was standing in my face, and I could not move without dancing. So, we dance. Alyssia beams. Her touch is delicate yet firm. The waltz. Three years in Mister Thom's Dance Class. I was and am damned good. One-two-three. Long-quick-quick. Turn to the major points of the compass. Forward and backward. Then go wild, or as wild as a white-gloved, dark-blue suited, mustachioed dance master would let eight-year olds go around the room. Images in my mind's eye of Vienna and strains of Strauss. Candles have been replaced by flickering electric sconces. The light ricochets off the glass coverings on the pictures. I am driven by the memory of showing off. Alyssia is my mate. We are joined at the hands, shoulders, hearts, and souls. Spin, twirl, whirl, and revolve around the center of the dance floor.

She moves closer. We move closer. Her grasp grows deeper. Leans her head back as we create great diamonds and arcs over the room. She stirs new images. Bodies touching, but not in a licentious way. A century-old dancing way. The more the music takes control, the stronger our dance passion becomes. The small orchestra keeps perfect time, but I feel their beat becoming more emphatic. The dancing partners' movements are in complete synch. Toes never touch. The respondent foot moves as the precipitator foot approaches. We are Fred and Ginger. Just no white tie and tails nor long multi-pleated dress. I lead. She leads. We dance. It is magical and marvelous. How many times around the room? All eyes are on us. Smiles and side comments abound. We are the only ones dancing. We are the show. In street language, "we are in the house." Her eyes stare into mine. Her smile is my smile. Her glow becomes my pride. Music ends. Applause is tumultuous. There are whistles and cheers. Alyssia curtsies. I bow. Take her hand and kiss it. Nip the flesh. She kisses my cheek. Rubs her breasts against my arm.

Bam!

Red Forty-five Weak Stunt

*R*ed . . . forty-five . . . weak stunt. Red . . . forty-five . . . weak stunt. Man-to-man full coverage. Sideline to ball. Bump hard. Drop straight back quickly. Outside the receiver wherever. Close off outside. Force inside into linebacker or safety. Do not hand off. Watch for speed and cut block. Keep one eye on motion man, then shift glance to QB. Four down linemen. Balanced with O-line. Linebacker stunts with end on weak side, backer in, end back. Strong side backer drops to fill flat. Here they come again. Balanced line. Power my side. Wideout big split. Motion to me. God, I need whole bunches of help. QB takes snap and spins. Fake dive holds interior backers. Drop back, passer looks in my direction. The wideout bumps me hard. He is pissed about the first play. This takes him off his route. Sometimes you've got to sacrifice. Can't get into a shoving match with him. Stay with him like shit on a shoe. He is ten and in. Behind the backer and in front of me. The backer's paw bats down the bullet.

Mister Alan Carson, *Deals on Wheels*. The peripatetic entrepreneur. He can be found at fine deals everywhere. No arrangement too big or small from which he can't make a profit. Basically, he introduces people, and has been doing this since the early sixties. Somebody wants to buy, he finds a seller, and vice versa. All he wants is between one-half a point to two points of the gross depending on the size and complexity of the deal. He can facilitate the navigation of the legal forms and processes. He can very often get a better deal than either the buyer or seller, depending on who is his client, 'er, friend. He knows everyone and everyone knows him. No one has ever been burnt, although a few feathers were severely singed about five years ago.

It seems the farmer didn't really own the land he was trying to sell to the mall mavens. Who knew? The old man's family had been farming the acreage for generations. Actually, it belonged to the Catholic Church. They wanted more than the farmer wanted. A lot more. No land. No mall. No growth. No money for AC. This was no good. So the old man was out and the nuns were in. This is really tough for an atheist like Alan. He could promise the farmer an inheritance big enough to take care of the kids and grandchildren. Rich is good, particularly when it is cheap for the buyers. It's all a matter of perspective. The nuns wanted richer—a hospital wing. The mall men were willing to spend enough for bandages and ointment. AC kept the two parties apart to preserve his action. With the closing date looming large, it appeared as if *kerplunk* would be the sound heard throughout the county. No budge. No deal. Nuns are great negotiators. They can wait forever. It's what they're trained to do. Suddenly the mavens found the money, and the Sisters of Perpetual Shame decided to name the wing after the head mall man. Great PR for the spoilers of the good earth. Now they were solid citizens. Alan received less than a point, but it was a large gross for the time. The developers were pissed about being jerked around. They blamed AC for the high price. So, they paid him over one year and squealed with each check. They made no bones about his soul going straight to hell. No love lost there.

Alan had been at the party for a few hours. The ocular barometer told me so. The more he drinks, the more he squints. His eyes had begun to stretch from the bridge of his nose to the top of his ears. Herringbone gray tweed jacket. Blue shirt with white collar. Orange and blue rep striped tie. The perfect shade of deep charcoal slacks and dark brown loafers. Casual, proper prep. All of this on a six-foot, two-hundred-and-ten pound body. Not destroyed by regular exercise. Black hair with matching white shocks over the ears. He was holding court.

Harry and Joan Mellis, Bill and Anne Defry, Judge Wellington Narlow and Adriane Simon. Hanging on Alan's every word. Or, just not caring one wit and too anesthetized to move. Their expressions are the same. The Mellis are a great couple. Harry is a lawyer, corporate Mergers and Acquisitions. Senior partner with the largest firm in the state. He is kind and gracious. Has a very wry sense of humor. Can always be counted on to lend a hand or give some solid, off-the-record advice. He is tall, lean, with thick bifocals beneath blonde-gone-to-gray hair. Sharp facial features and a slight stoop have earned him the nickname of *Ichabod*. Or, just "Bod." He laughs at the comparison. Loves the ribbing. Honest people do. Joan is almost as tall, about six feet in tennis shoes. Brown hair and eyes. Attractive with a comely disposition. She has on the traditional "Greenie." A few years ago she spent a king's ransom on a green gown for formal parties. Being a founding member of the "Thrifty Rich Club," she is determined to maximize her investment to approximately ten dollars per wearing. This requires that she wear "Greenie" very often for a number of years. She has worn it so often and for so long the dress has acquired a legend of its own. Her friends named the gown and they promise to replace it with one of Joan's choice, if and only if, Joan will let them burn the frock at a ritualistic Bar-B-Q. Ah, the joy of friends. Joan sells real estate. The company, the biggest in the four-county area, bears the name of her family. Her father is the tax collector for the city. Some day this area may even grow up.

Harry and Joan raised a son and two daughters, all of whom went to college on athletic scholarships. Must be nice. Now the folks fish and play tennis a lot more than five years ago and not nearly as much as five years from now. They are both attentive to Alan as he spins his tale of development, mortgages, and wealth for all. And to all a good night. Harry is interested in the fact that a major tenant will be a new corporate entity formed by a marriage as yet to be an engagement. Everything is at least two years away. Alan is a long-range dreamer. He can make reality from dreams that don't exist, or vice versa.

The Defrys have two children here tonight. A real coup. He is a humble subcontractor, except you can't put up a big building without him. Windows require a specialist in Florida's heat and sun. He has made a ton as the area grew from a swamp with cattle and orange groves. Bill is six feet. Scholarly in appearance. Thin. A ready smile and quick mind. He has a devilish side. Loves practical jokes. Once epoxyed the big wooden door of a client's ostentatious office. Bill hates obvious displays of wealth and bad taste. The guy inside had to call the fire department to remove the door. New door cost twenty-five hundred and the publicity was humiliating. He was Bill's college roommate and knew the beast. Got even by having three tons of bovine waste dumped on the Defry's front lawn very early one Sunday morning. Games like this are the fuel that makes long-term relationships never ending.

Anne is tolerant of Bill's pranks, because he is a kid at heart, loves her, and spoils her at every occasion. Flowers for no reason. Surprise vacations. Sleep-in Saturdays with breakfast in bed. She is lovely. Blonde with a well-tended figure. She could place very high in the Mai Britt look-alike contest, when Mai was younger, before the Candy Man. Impeccably dressed and clipped. A smile that starts in her heart. Both adults are very active in the preeminent Episcopal Church. Actually, most of the attendees are. Even the rector.

Their two kids inherited the best features of both parents. The boy, Warren, is tall. Has a great tee shot and can get really close with the mid-irons. Finished eighth the regional junior tourney. Twelve over after three rounds. Will play in the Nationals in the spring. Jenny is a dancer. Ballet. Hopes to pursue this in college. I never knew how much work was involved in this activity. She practices three to five hours every day. Jenny has eyes that could melt titanium. They are a chocolate black color, the color of the very expensive Mercedes, Beemers, and Porches. The ability to combine two almost excluding colors and produce a unique color, a very coveted color, belongs to German engineers and learned from *Gott*. Her eyes are a combination of savagery, sadness, mystery, and mayhem. Eyes encased in a cherubic countenance, a beacon for the boys. Two says she is an 'itch with a 'tude. Somebody told her she was beautiful and she believed every syllable. She is the replica of her mother. No wonder Bill plays only home games.

Bill is questioning Alan about the size of the new structure, trying to get a hint to its location and glass needs. Alan could sidestep a bullet fired from three feet. He gives out just enough information to keep the interested interested. Not enough to slake intense curiosity. The stuff of dreams.

"And, it will be just the beginning. My clients are looking to make this the face (faces the incoming traffic) building in the office park. Eight stories. As much automation as money can buy. Ultimate goal is two million square feet of office space plus a very upscale mall, four movie theaters, a couple of eateries, and saloons. Busy eighteen hours a day. State-of-the-art security and pedestrian traffic." AC is rolling and roiling. His audience appears rapt on the rap.

"Jimmy B, how you be?"

Always the same question, big hug, and loud greeting from Alan. Maybe that's why I like him so much. There is pleasure in consistency.

"You know all my friends don't you?"

I've been attending this party for a decade, but he feels compelled to introduce me. Solid handshakes from Harry and Bill. Warm little hugs from Joan and Anne. I extend my hand to the judge. He is somewhat apprehensive, because he is hearing my motion for a modification of child custody. Can't mix business with pleasure. Don't want to give the slightest hint of impropriety.

"Your honor, good evening. Let's make a deal. Oops, bad choice of words. I'll call you Wellington, or whatever informality you wish, and you call me Jimmy. We won't talk shop, your shop, on this glorious occasion. Besides, every time I think of the issue I get *agida*. How are you doing this fine evening, Wellington?"

He is a man of almost unfathomable patience and calm. Through all the hysterical ranting of our hearings he is calm, polite, and dead level fair. I know he is not on drugs and he is awake. Whatever he is paid, he earns it on our case alone. Her lawyer is very vindictive; he hisses like a frightened viper. Like client, like lawyer. I am doing everything *pro se*. The law library is a treasure chest of useful information, as it should be. The people who man (Or is it who *people?*) the desks seem to enjoy helping the *pro se*. I am a quick learner. Besides, the law is constructed for the lowest common denominator but obfuscated by and for lawyers. After reading a few sections of a particular book a few times, the intent and exclusions emerge. I know what the court expects and, hopefully, how to provide the right information to engender a favorable opinion. The fencing would be fun were the stakes not so high. Here, I am at a disadvantage. I care. The opposition lawyer does not.

"Just fine, now, Jimmy."

"And you Adriane? I hope things are well. You look lovely."

"Good evening, James. Yes, things are well, indeed. Thank you."

Adriane Simon. Woman of mystery. Woman of tragedy. Woman of wealth. I love the last of these. Sounds like the promo for a soap opera. Actually, her past—far and recent—is very thought provoking. Her parents, Tecer and Hapapise, were very successful farmers and growers in the middle of the state. Oranges, tomatoes, etc. The huge spread included horses and a beautiful riding course. They built at the beach, Dunes, and summered there to avoid the oppressive heat. Mother, Adriane and Aminno, the son, would live at the shore from the end of May to Labor Day. Tecer would take long weekends from the farm. As the children grew up and took on more chores and responsibilities at the farm, the entire family spent less time near the water. The fifteen weeks became August, then long weekends only. Still the beach house was a monument to Tecer's success. The three-hour drive a testament to his dedication.

Then the tragedy of Aminno's death. A farming accident. Something collapsed and a piece of machinery functioned improperly. The seventeen-year-old boy was sliced, diced, and pureed. It was ugly. The sluice was almost unrecognizable. He could have been buried in a number ten can. He had been a treasure to the family. Handsome, happy, hard working, and helpful. Not the brightest light on the tree, but he knew the farm and its business. After the ghastly event and very proper funeral, the Simons went into seclusion for about two years. No parties. No shopping excursions. No summer house. No contact with the outside world. All public business was transacted by the foreman and the lawyer. Suddenly, the Simons gradually emerged from under their self-imposed rock.

During the exile, there had been born a third child, a daughter. Aminnette. Named for her brother and sixteen years younger than her sister. Born late in life to Tecer and Hapapise, a real surprise. Not unlike Avaram and Sarah, the Simons were convinced procreation was not possible. I suspect they were not particularly careful because of their ages. Adriane was considered to be the last baby, because the Simons had held off having children until the farm was established. This process lasted until Hapapise was forty-four. So, you can image their surprise at the arrival of the third child.

The gene, which had deprived Aminno of the same high level of intelligence as Adriane, came from somewhere in the family pool and assumed an extremely dominant and distorted power in Aminnette. She wasn't just slow, she was retarded, is retarded. Hazel eyes and honey-to-tawny hair. Freckled complexion. Medium build and straight stature. These are attractive physical traits, but they don't give a clue as to the internal ones and the ones of the mind and psyche. Aggressive, progressive, recessive. It's all a conundrum.

Although the family began to creep back into everyday, out-of-shell life, Aminnette stayed at home, cared and provided for. She was capable of only the most basic human functions, eating, bathing and dressing. That's where it stopped. She was also given to fits of violence, temper tantrums in polite society. Screaming incoherently, almost speaking in tongues, throwing things, and occasionally self-mutilating. The Simons had to protect society and Aminnette from Aminnette.

After the folks died, perhaps of fatigue brought on by age and the stress at home, Aminnette was placed in an excellent care facility. There certainly is and will be enough money for the sisters. The farm continues to generate a cash flow sufficient to support expansion, as well as the life style of the rich and enigmatic. The house was torn down and the grounds were converted to additional growing. Only the elaborate barn remains. The company offices are there. Now the three residences are: New Horizons Care for Aminnette, *Dunes*, and a three-story house in downtown for Adriane, just walking distance from her office.

Eight years ago she married Robby Windor, a widower. Robby's first wife died of cancer and he was given the wonderful opportunity to raise their two infant boys. He had the help of *au pair*, a young girl from one of Colombia's best families. Robby met Adriane a year or so after he became a widower. They were married six months later and set-up house in Lansdale and Mills-On-Gulf (MOG). They had more than enough money for the homes, car, and expenses of raising the boys with the au pair, a cook, and two gardeners. When they went to MOG, they needed two vans or light trucks for all the people and stuff. They seemed to be happy. Then there was the horrendous crash of ninety-one. Not the stock market, but the gasoline tanker and the van carrying Robby, the au pair, and both boys. There was too much alcohol, point-one-five, in Robby's blood, it was rainy, foggy, and one in the morning. The winding detour off the interstate was not lighted. Only the rare blinking, yellow warning lights on the barricades. Robby had a propensity to drive well beyond the speed limit. The Windor car and occupants were incinerated. The tanker and all its contents disappeared in the inferno, but the driver was unscathed. Miraculous. No fines, no prosecutions. Just another huge formal funeral. Once again, Adriane was alone with the baggage.

"Excuse me, Alan, may I steal a member of your audience? Adriane, join me for a drink if you will?"

"Thank you, James."

"Why don't you call me Jimmy or Jimmy Bee? Everyone else does."

"Precisely. I am not everyone else. As you are not just Jimmy or Jimmy B."

The Iowa farm-girl look radiates in the dimmed electric and candlelight glow of the room. There was a strong sense of purpose in her demeanor and her speech. Her dress was fashionably short. The jacket accentuated her proportions, particularly her narrow waist. The belt and shoes were from Italy. Not an Italian designer with a store in New York. The rings, bracelet, and pearl and diamond necklace were not a set, but perfectly coordinated and worth a Testarosa. She had an aroma aura I had never experienced. Rich, deep, exotic spices. No cheap heavy musk. The warmth of this base reverberated through subtle and clean, woodsy mid-notes, and these two symphonies were accented by a hint of dry floral. It was intoxicating, the desired effect. Not since Alexandra de Necheyv Rosdorova had I experienced a parfum with this clout. The memory of Alexandra, my first woman of mystery. A real White Russian.

Make-up in all its subtly had created exciting contour and color accentuation from her neck to forehead. Her skin was baby-butt smooth, wrinkle free. She did not smile. She did not frown. Hell, how could she get wrinkles? Her eyes did not sparkle. They pierced and sought truth. They rent asunder any soul whose owner foolishly thought of telling a lie or being smarmy. She was a fabulous listener and discerner. She took no shit or prisoners. She could be ruthless.

Truly without the compassion of Ruth, yet she was graceful, gracious, bodacious, and beautiful.

"Why is that I see you only at the Kileys and that is only once a year?" I was *tres* cool.

"Because you never call."

She just peed on the iceberg.

Swallowing what was left of my machismo, "What would you like to drink, Adriane?"

"Whatever you are having is fine with me."

"Two Balvenies, one ice cube, tall glasses. Do you like single malt Scotch Whiskey, Adriane?" The bartender obeyed.

"I don't know. Do I? Will I?"

The voice sounds in my brain. *Danger, danger, warning, warning,* like Robby the Robot. Fuck it. How can this be bad? In order of priority: great booze, a fantastic party, and a beautiful woman. What could go wrong, go wrong, go wrong?

"Madam, shall we stroll and be seen?"

"You arrogant male beast. You wish to flaunt me as some helpless game killed in the wild. Your trophy. That will not do. I wish to be the hunter and you shall be the buck over my mantle. Better still, I will parade and you shall truckle behind me, whimpering and fawning. How does that make you feel?"

"Is the expression, *bag 'o crap,* clear? Sorry. I overstepped my bounds."

She leans toward my ear. Maybe to repeat the Mike Tyson maneuvers. She whispers "Gotcha."

She takes my arm and we proceed to be seen. Into the big room with the two walk-in fireplaces. A Christmas tree with a marvelous collection of antique decorations from all over the globe. The tree is thirty feet tall and approximately ninety feet in circumference at the base. The trunk will make many wonderful Yule logs for next year, as did the tree from last year. It takes the family, Eben, and Dorothea a full week to decorate the tree once the construction crew gets it upright, which, in turn, takes an entire day, excluding the two days to clear the space. Net, it is a big production from start to finish. And, here is the best part, despite the space consumed by the tree, there is room for about seventy-five people. This is the hall of the mountain king.

No blinking lights. Thank God. Among the hundreds of teeny, tiny lights, none blink. Blinking lights always remind me of Rudolph sung by some cowboy. This electric extravaganza requires a new and separate line brought in from the road by our friends at the local utility. The cost is donated, because the four top dogs of the electric company are here and have been here for ten years. The attention to detail in each and every ball, bauble, and character is staggering. European pieces from the sixteenth century, African dolls with an obvious British influence, and even Asian Christian communities provided their interpretations of the Madonna and Child. What a plethora of wonder for the throng. Each year the Kileys added a few more, more esoteric and arcane than the ones from last year. Just the right amount of tinsel, which for a tree this size is about fifty boxes. And it's lead, not plastic. Just like back in the day.

The three sets of French doors are open to the patio so the room has an outdoor coolness. People appear to be milling around like skaters in Rock Center. Circling, they form small clusters, break apart, and reform as if they were amoebae. Rarely more than eight to a group, never fewer than three. People can spin off with a sought-after group into a smaller room where conversations can be discreet, liaisons can be established, and business promises made. But we are here to be seen and to see what we already know will be visible.

"Look, there are the Bears, Paul and Mary. What's he up to now? The last time I heard anything, he had gotten out of the check-cashing business. Mary always looks so much younger than Paul."

"Well, Miss Simon, he is back in the business of helping the poor and keeping a healthy percentage. A new twist on *Robin Hood*. Remember when he sold his check-cashing company? He had to stay out of the business for three years. After his non-compete expired, he jumped back into the ersatz banking business with gusto. Now he is expanding his super stores, one-stop financial services for those who have been rejected by banks and are justifiably fearful of shylocks and sharks."

"*Redi-Money* offers pawning, check cashing, and cash for car titles. *Redi-Money* charges eighteen percent on pawns with monthly payments that can never end, from six percent for cashing company checks to twelve percent for cashing out-of-state personal checks, and a paltry twenty-four percent for short-term loans against your car title. *Redi-Money,* not surprisingly, has a substantial auto collection work force and is about to open a used car lot. Everything is legal, just distasteful to the arrogantly clean-of-hands. They are such nice people. What do you know about the new mayor, ma'am?"

"Same as the old mayor. We'll just be screwed again. The city council lost its backbone in the last election when Jane Tapper was defeated and they will now rubberstamp everything the mayor and his cronies want. I suspect the level of city service will remain at its nadir and more pockets will be picked than ever before. The housing authority is still run by the group of absentee directors. They got out the vote for their man. People live in a cinder-block hell. Urine, garbage, and broken windows are the norm, yet more and more money is budgeted each year. What's wrong with that picture? Sorry, but I do get angry at the abuse of authority with no responsibility."

"Adriane, standing by the fireplace behind the mayor, who is that?"

"I don't know. Let's find out."

As we mosey over to the dark stranger, we are confronted by two, count 'em two, servers, Alyssia Dermond and Brent Denners. Alyssia looks at me as if I had soiled the linens, kicked that cat, and lied to her. There was a definite hurt scowl on her exquisite countenance. Brent's eyes seemed to be a little glassy. Maybe he had been nipping and sipping. He stared at Adriane with his best lust-in-the-dust look. Adriane glared him down and soft.

"Is there anything you'd like, Mister McCaa? Another drink? Something to eat?"

"No thanks, Alyssia, I'm just fine." I swear I heard her whisper, 'Yes you are.'

"How about you, ma'am? Another drink? Mister McCaa seems to be ahead of you."

"Yes, that will be fine. A Balvenie with two ice cubes, tall glass"

She hands him her glass. As she brushes his hand, she looks deep into his eyes, passed his lungs and pulsating heart to his genitalia. He is dead on his feet. Did his knees buckle? The young ones leave. He will be back faster than you can say "score with an older woman".

"Adriane, you temptress. Mrs. Robinson of the next millennium. Watch out, you may start a fire that can't be extinguished in a proper way."

"He only got what he wanted. I gave him something to brag about. He will now do what I ask whenever I ask. But his reward will be only a dream. Our target is moving, hurry."

"Good evening, Sir, my name is Adriane Simon. And your name is . . . ?"

"Benton Dreisch. This is a wonderful party, is it not? Let me provide more detailed information. That is what you seek? Is it not? I recently moved here from New York. I met your late husband when he was in the securities business. I knew his first wife before they were married. And I knew Billy Ray before I moved here. So I have some history, albeit tangential. I have been imported to Lansdale to resolve the banking mess created by the recent proposed merger of Orange Grove Bank, Farmer's Trust, and Second City Bank. I am, in the common parlance a hired gun, a mercenary. I get paid to fix things for the boards of directors. I re-engineer, right size and outsource if necessary to ensure smooth, very profitable operations. Growth is someone else's field of expertise. I live alone on a farm about thirty miles to the North. Is that enough?"

"Well, other than very personal information, yes. Let me introduce my friend, James Buchanan McCaa."

"I already know a great deal about Jimmy B, thank you. I also know a great deal about you, Miss Simon. If you'll excuse me, I need to talk to Mister Carson."

"Well, he seems impervious to your delicate feminine charms. And, fuck him; he does not know me well enough to call me Jimmy B. Why was he insulting to you? Just who is that asshole really?"

"No need to get defensive on my account. I can take care of me. Hell, I can even take care of you. But your gut reaction is accurate, he is a prick. And I have a sneaking suspicion he is either more than he appears or nothing like his public persona."

"Here's your drink, Miss Simon." It was Brent and he seemed foggier. As he handed Adriane her double, he took her hand and gave her two napkins. She smiled seductively. He leered. He strutted away with his chest thrown out. Cock of the walk to his friend,s he hoped. Adriane handed me one of the napkins upon which was written in the best cursive Italics of the private school, *Call when you want KL5-4593. I want*. Game, set, and match, Adriane. Was this a contest with him or me? If it was with me, I better learn the rules of engagement.

"James, let's talk to Brent's father. Maybe he'll shed some light on the tall dark stranger."

Stan Denners. Home grown banker extraordinaire. A legend in his own mind. He inherited Orange Grove Bank and blossomed it into its present predicament. The bank built its fortune on land, groves, and farms. Did not give a fig about buildings, cars, or capital enhancements unless they were based upon lateral growth followed by vertical growth. Finally, Orange Grove had to move into the late twentieth century. Land became scarce. Much more expensive. Crop projections failed to materialize. Taxes and operating expenses did not go away. The good ol' boys began to ask for extensions based upon fraternity lineage, not reality.

The present bank *manage a trois* has been more heavily scrutinized than the ladies who work North Iowa Avenue. The state required the three banks to complete forms so detailed they had questions about the questions, monthly cycles of the female officers, job histories back to eighth grade, and attitude toward just about everything. The feds even got involved. The merger created extensive overlaps and redundancies. The loans and mortgages were intertwined. Banks lent to banks to cover loans from and to each other. It was a tangled web of near deceit. The computer systems were not completely compatible and some of the branches wound up competing against each other. The deal, which was to be closed by last April 15th (auspicious), was not yet finalized. Too much in-fighting, too much greed, and too much territorial prerogative were the concrete slabs that crushed the camel. Enter the gunslinger.

Stan is widow-dressed as he has been for years. The same non-descript tartan slacks. Black lace up wing-tip shoes. Not clunkers, but expensive Coaches. The buttons on his blazer form the centerpiece of his ensemble. Gold coins discovered off the Keys. Four large coins for the front of the double-breasted jacket and four smaller ones on each cuff. Total package; roughly twenty times more expensive than the five hundred dollar Brooks Brothers blazer. Stan found the coins in a dive off one of the smaller keys and loves to flaunt his good and large fortune. The gold coin buttons were crafted and stitched to stay. They are removed for each cleaning and replaced by a tailor thereafter. When the blue jacket need to be updated or replaced due to wear, the coin buttons are simply moved to a new home. Always a white shirt with a tie and matching pocket foulard in a seasonal motif. There is something very comforting and almost good about constancy of uniform.

"Stan, we just met your Mister Dreisch. It's so nice to have new blood in the pool. Do you think he'll stay after the merger? What has he to do with the merger? How is it going?"

"Adriane, it's nice to see you, too. Hello, Jimmy. What's shakin' your bacon? God, that's terrible. I learned that from Brent. Cutting to the chase are we Adriane? Mr. Dreisch will most likely stay in Lansdale after the merger, assuming certain conditions and timetables are met. Until that time he is solely focused on making the merger happen as expeditiously, legally, and cost effectively as possible. He has a crew of six who work here all week and return to where ever they live each Friday. There is a mass of data and information, which is collected each week as the basis for planning, which is done and reviewed on weekend by fax. The merger is going well. Our initial projections were just too optimistic. Mister Dreisch and his people are quite objective. They think corporation only. Damn the people. These hired guns will kill anyone for the enhancement of the bottom line. Why should I care? I'm just about out of the morose morass. I am expendable."

What a bomb. And, you heard it here first folks. Stan Denners is resigned to being resigned. He'll take his fifteen million and go quietly onto the boat. The gold of the trampled can span the ionosphere or cover only next month's rent and groceries. Stan is one of the lucky ones. Linda will enjoy the life on the yacht, *Banker.* They will probably sail around the Gulf and call MOG home.

"If you want to know more about Mister Dreisch's personal side or the lack thereof, you'd best talk to my former secretary, Carol. It seems that they have become very chummy. There are rumors she spends weekends with him at the farm. I know she sold me out for his promises and maybe his bed. She's not here, obviously. But call her after the holidays. Maybe she'll tell you what you want to know. I doubt it, though."

Another bomb. Stan's steady *schtupf* is sleeping with the enemy. He has been banging Carol since she came to the bank and onto his couch, seventeen years at least. I think Linda knew, but she would not do anything to jeopardize her life style. The yacht, the Country Club, vacations in the South of France, and three children through good, not great, schools. I have always suspected she was getting a little on the side. Just which side and from whom I was never sure. Anyway, theirs was a comfortable marriage of friends. They have known each other since they were toddlers. So, all's well that ends.

"Thanks for the info, Stan. Adriane and I must be going."

"That was like sticking my dick in a nest of wasps. Adriane, whatever possessed you to be so bold?"

"I am always straightforward. I have no guile. And, this damned whiskey has fueled my fire. So I must sound like a pushy broad. Are you hungry? How about a seafood salad? Big chunks of Grouper, crab, lobster, and shrimp, 10-12 size. Sweet and sour vinaigrette. Sourdough rolls and two bottles of '93 Chardonnay. And, if we are lucky, fresh fruit, cheese and forty-year old brandy for dessert. Let's have one more of these wonderful personality enhancers then leave for dinner."

"Sounds good to me. Just where is the restaurant that serves this scrumptious meal?"

"That's my secret for now. Oh, Brent, be a dear and get Mr. McCaa and me each another Balvenie. No doubles, please."

Faster than you can say promise hinted and promised not delivered, the drooler was back with the cups of nectar. As we move toward the fab four hosts, Billy Ray sees us homing in. His grin was unmistakable. He, too, had three or five too many.

"Youse guys have outdid yourseffs dis year. Me and dis fine feminine pulchritude have had da bestest time. Seriously, as always, your hospitality has exceeded your good looks and charm, which are legendary throughout the state. I am pleased to give you this small contribution for CitiMinistries."

Jeannie takes the envelope and holds it up to the light in an attempt to discern the amount. She announces to her small flock. "It's either one thousand dollars or ten dollars. Once again, Jimmy, you have underdone yourself and given beneath your means."

She gives me a hug and nips my ear.

Billy Ray smiles beatifically. Fatigue and Balvenie are a soporific combination. He gives me a big bear hug. KC and CK simply stand in the background and grin sheepishly. This ritualistic departure dance is performed every year. We stopped crying four years ago.

"Adriane, you're not leaving with this droll troll are you?"

Good for CK!

"We are leaving at the same time, that's all. Not together. Here is my donation for CitiMinistries. Thank you for the wonderful evening and the introduction to Oban, I think. Have a joyous Christmas. James, my wrap."

I am willing to bet my check that hers is larger and doesn't need to be held for deposit until January 15th.

The Kileys collect toys, food and clothes for the residents of CitiMinistries. These are given as gifts by the children of the invited. Not the workers, but the younger, stay at-home crowd. The adults are expected to donate money. Each year the donation grows significantly. The Kileys never tell, but I suspect the contributions are in the half million range.

Alyssia appears with Adriane's ankle length mink. Given Alyssia's previous display, I would not doubt if she poured red wine upon it somewhere noticeable to people walking behind Adriane. I thank Alyssia and try my best Adriane stare, deep into her soul and loins. She flinches and takes a short audible breath. Her blouse opens to reveal what she wanted me to see all evening. She is braless and her nipples are standing up. A sorceress in training in the safety of a public gathering.

As we exit, Adriane leans her head lovingly on my shoulder so that Alyssia can see. 'Don't try to compete is the message from the high priestess.' And by the empty stare in Alyssia's eyes, the message is received.

When we are outside and the door is closed, Adriane hands me her parking chit. "We will take only my car. Leave yours here. It can be retrieved later. I've had too much to drive, I mean to drink, I mean to drink to drive."

I tell the young man the plan. He chortles. In a few minutes he returns with a mint condition silver Mercedes three-sixty Gull Wing. God, Adriane has a really, really huge penis. Her appendage, the car, is a collector's item. The wings of flight are unfolded, she enters the passenger side. I will drive. God, I'm catching all sorts of breaks. Tip five dollars. Not refused despite the sign with the big letters.

"Now, where is this fabulous restaurant with the seafood salad?"

"My kitchen at the beach. Hurry." I am nothing if not a good responder. Fangio and Moss soar into the *noir*.

Blue Fifty-three Weak Blitz

*B*lue . . . fifty-three . . . weak blitz. Blue . . . fifty-three . . . weak blitz. Deep zone coverage if the wideout is on my side. Give him a big cushion. If no wideout, I am weak side and I blitz. Five down linemen. Weak side end drops into short zone coverage and rolls to outside five steps. Tackle takes wide rush to draw attention of blockers away from blitzer. Safeties and other cornerback form three-man umbrella. Here they come. Balanced line. Wideout on other side. I am blitzer. Motion away from me. Will have a very clear backside shot if disguised properly. Move up. Three yards behind and three yards outside the end. QB eyes are darting over secondary to the other side. Long count gives me a chance to start my push. I hit the line of scrimmage with the snap. Their fake off tackle holds line backer on the side as guard pulls to blocks near side. They are full of misdirection. I am behind guard as QB cocks arm to pass. Bingo! I dive onto the almost-passer chest high and he goes down. One down and more to come. Damn stitch in my side is causing a shortness of breath. Head butting all around.

The salad is before me. Lettuce so fresh it cracked when pulled apart, scallions, grape tomatoes, cucumber, red and yellow peppers, and bean sprouts. The dressing, a house specialty, sweet and sour creamy. I'll never know the ingredients. Big lumps and chunks of crab, lobster, Grouper, Pompano. Big shrimp. Now, that is truly an oxymoron. But, they're about the size of my index finger. The bowl is filled to the rim, and not with Brim. Sourdough rolls warmed. Real butter. The Chardonnay is quite chilled. Everything is as promised. There is truth in advertising.

The kitchen is a huge twenty-by-thirty. Around two walls are the works. Two gas stoves. A monster microwave. Double-door fridge beside a big door freezer. In the center is the piece de resistance, a six-by-nine butcher block. Not the wimpy kind, but two feet thick. The real deal. Used for prep and enjoyment of casual meals. Scrubbed with salt. Washed with a special antibacterial, anti-fungal, antiviral, Auntie Mame soap every six months. Above the block are hung pots and pans of every functionality. On the block, at either end, are the custom racks for the knives, forks, ladles and spoons, stirrers, cups, choppers, slicers, and dicers. The right mind with the right training and all the ingredients could prepare a feast for the President and an intern or an incredible seafood salad for Jimmy B. I find the chairs and we face off with the bowl, wine, and rolls between us.

"This looks fantastic. You have delivered. And, by the by, I love the car. Where did you get it?"

"It was Robby's. The only thing he brought to the marriage I wanted to keep. The rest is just an ever-dimming memory."

I serve my hostess, listening to the ever so subtle voice in my brain, "We, who are about to experience something very strange, salute you." Her smile is cloyingly coy. Remember to leave room for the roll. Let us not have to load too many dishes into the dishwasher. Now seated, I hand the roll basket to her. She takes. I take. She refuses. The dressing will be a sufficient moisturizer and flavor booster. I follow her lead.

My first bite of the repast is rewarded with a taste explosion. As is the second one. The fish and crustaceans are fresh and I mean caught-yesterday fresh. The piquancy of the dressing only partially masks the base of dark clover honey. I crack the roll and take a small piece. I glance up. She has nipped a substantial chunk from the helpless encrusted bread and is aggressively placing it in her maw. *Sie fressen nicht essen.*

"I was hungrier than I thought. Or, maybe it's just the alcohol begging to be sopped up. Anyway, ma'am, these vittles are raht gooood. And I do 'preciate your hositalty. I mean comin' into the big house for dinner and all. I don't have to eat in the bunkhouse. You're real nice to me. So kind. I guess it's the holidays."

"You are such a bull shitter, James. I didn't know the Blarney Stone was Scottish. Or is it owned by all the Celts? Do you talk this way to everyone? What do you do for a living? I'll bet you sell, just about anything."

"Do you always go right for the heart of the matter, Adriane? I'm a writer. I write advertising, company literature, and sales material for Great Eastern Life Insurance Group. Joined the company a few years ago after losing my ass in my own business. As a matter of fact, I lost everything. It seems I was not good enough for my wife of twenty-three years. Over the two decades, I changed. Street drugs no longer interested me. Booze was treated with respect. My two children became the focal point of my life. My wife became ill. *Mal du jour.* Yuppie flu, ADDS, Chronic Fatigue Syndrome. You name it she sought treatment for it. Went through more doctors, shrinks and experimental treatments than I thought possible and reasonable. As her illnesses became more severe and convoluted, our limited income was dwarfed by the massive medical expense. Insurance did not cover the new-age treatments. Always something newer and better just around the comer. Couple this with the recent economic upheaval and the life style of the soon to be rich and well known became the economic hard times of the desperate and infamous. The small business became a one-person operation. Clients literally died, filed for bankruptcy, or just disappeared into the night, never to be heard from again."

"The mother of our children became incapacitated. Bedridden from Monday through Friday, only to be revived for the weekend. Too sick to work at my side, shop, cook, clean, or take any care of our younger child, she was hale and hearty enough to party on Fridays and Saturdays. The *upper* medication prescribed by the numerous doctors seemed to function only on the weekend. Or, when she wanted to be awake all night and talk on the telephone to her friends in Chicago. I was not able to deal with a non-wife, a non-partner. The irrevocable chasm. Things changed. I changed. She changed. *Caca pasa.* To quote Carol King: *something died and I just can't lie and I just can't fake it.* She found Mister Right and brought him into our home. He ostensibly slept on the couch until he could find his own place. I blinded myself. I was stupid and neurotically hoped we could work everything out. One night when

I came home from my office, she handed me the domestic violence injunction papers and I was thrown out of the condo. But I was still expected to pay for everything, even her evenings out with Mr. Right. Ain't separation grand?"

"I countered. She had filed in the wrong county. She had to move out. I moved back. Mr. Right slithered back into his lair. The young son never had to change residences. Within seven months, the condo was gone to foreclosure. Bank had an offer in good faith for the mortgage amount, but chose to sell the residence at auction from the County Court House steps. No takers. They bought it from themselves and finally sold it at a loss of twenty-three percent. Assholes. I had no real steady income and had to find a room. Became a telemarketer of vacation scams. Good money, if you lie and slam. But not enough to afford a place for Two and me. For his sake, I agreed that she should have primary residential custody. She had an apartment. The alimony and support I was court-ordered to provide and the Social Security benefits for disabled mother and minor dependent child were sufficient. She netted about fifty a year. I lost him with that document. All the unwritten visitation promises went up in funny smelling smoke and ill-gotten scripts. Now I am back on my feet and fighting to bond with him without her interference. Judge Narlow is hearing the case. That's about it. More than most people know. I have no idea why I blurted it out tonight. But, I feel better. Thanks for listening. Now that I've shown you mine, you must show me yours."

"Whew, that was brutally frank and a lot more than I bargained for. Am I supposed to feel sorry, angry, or happy for the favorable turn of fortune?"

"None of the above. I expect no sympathy or congratulations. What about you?"

"If you have read the papers and listened to any member of Radio Free Lansdale, you know everything there is to know about me."

"No, I know what has been filtered and sanitized for public exposure. What I don't know, is what makes you tick. More salad?"

"Yes, and dear heart, open the second bottle of wine."

There is definite arrogance in her blood. I serve and pour. I do as I am told, sometimes.

"No more Dodges, Chevies, or Fords. I have told you my feelings and the facts. Now, what is your make-up, what revs your engine to the red line?"

"Not much. I have guarded my psyche for so many years. Each time I allow the sun to pierce the dark recesses of my soul, something bad or evil happens and I shut out the world. My parents. My brother's gory death, my sister's unfortunate state, the horrific death of Robby and the two boys. Now I work, take care of my sister as best I can, and spend long weekends here reading, walking, and working. The farm is a vibrant concern and takes many hours of off-site management and planning. We are always looking to expand. Mike Stewart, the foreman, and his crew do a great job week-to-week and season-to-season. I devote myself to the two and five-year opportunities. The options are endless. More farming. Special farming. Housing developments. Strip malls. Shopping centers. Golf courses. Roads. Sewage. Utilities. The details are staggering, but I love them. You know, idle hands and all that. I miss some things from my past, but not many. In fact very, very few. I am visible in public rarely. The Kileys' party and maybe three others through the year. I am not afraid; I just choose not to go. Why tonight? Why you? Why here? I don't know. Maybe 'tis the season. The Balvenie. If you know, please tell me."

I watched her face as she spoke. Her lips were hypnotic, very expressive, smiling, then pursing, with an occasionally downward turn. Her eyes worked in concert with the lips, just more so. I'd love to play poker with this woman. I could retire early. There was a visual hint of anger when she spoke of her parents, and wistfulness about her brother. Her eyes became soft and her lower lip protruded. An unreal frown of sadness when she mentioned her sister. There was a strange twist of rage, glaring coupled with persimmon lips, when she referred to Robby. Or maybe it was all a chimera. Hers or mine? As she concluded, her visage displayed a curious look of questioning sadness.

"I have no answers, princess."

Her appearance snapped to rage and then melted into a dispassionate stare. Something I said.

"Since I went out and caught the fish, lobster and crabs, grew the vegetables and harvested the berries for the vinegar and the honey, you, James, get to clean up. Besides I want to get out of this *ShowTime* outfit and start a fire in the sitting room. Do you mind?"

"The division of labor seems equitable. I have no dress to change out of or fresh clothes into which I could change. And I am so inept at starting fires, Smokey the Bear has adopted me. I am the poster child for fire prevention."

Clean up was a piece of cake, except there was no cake. It afforded me the opportunity to nibble on a shrimp and sip another glass of wine. They do it on the TV cooking shows. That's where I learned the joy of larder.

"Well, well, well. You have hidden talents. Verbal entertainment, very fast yet controlled driving, and now a spotless kitchen. It's as if we had never been here. Will wonders never cease? Fires are ablaze. The brandy is poured. You have completed your tasks. Join me, if you wish."

I respond to the voice in the doorway to the sitting room and turn. Bam! If I wish? As if I had a choice. The shorts were of socially acceptable length, but very loose over magnificently formed bronzed legs. The blouse was tied at the waist and the knot was the only thing holding it closed, and I say *closed* loosely. Not only was she braless, her breasts were almost completely visible. She had gone waaayyy beyond Alyssia's brazen peek-a-boo. She obviously felt safe in her own lair. Even with all the Balvenie and wine, the klaxon of alarm was screaming in my brain. What did I have to do, at least, to grab some shared control? My hope of complete control had already been lost in the silver three-sixty. No car plus being a stranger's house at the beach equals no control. Duh. Just ride with the tide and go with the flow.

After drying my hands and neatly hanging the towel in the rack, I walk toward the door. Often the best defense is an in-your-face offense. I take her face, cupping her cheeks and kiss her assertively, but not aggressively, on the lips for about ten seconds. I acted, but there was no reaction. Pull away. She smiles, I think. But, then, I've never seen the Mona Lisa's smile either. I walk past her to the couch behind the coffee table with the two properly filled snifters. She stands in the doorway and turns off the kitchen lights.

"Join me if you wish." The arrogance of a conqueror and a conquered are the same. The game is over, nothing more can change. The die is cast and we both know it. As I raise my snifter, I motion to the couch.

"We are brazen, are we not?" She speaks each word slowly and precisely.

"Speak for yourself I am tired of this cat and mouse game of yours. Flirtation is one thing. Cock teasing is another. I have no car. I am in your keep. I am ostensibly trapped. Save for a call to the taxi service, the Kileys, or the police, I can't get home. And I choose not to make any telephone calls. I would be embarrassed if my parents had to come and get little Jimmy. So, sit beside me and tell me of your wishes and fantasies, and how I might fulfill them. Tell me of your dreams. Tell me of your sorrows. Let me blot the tears of the years with the hair of my head. Make me laugh. Let me make you laugh. Touch me and allow yourself to be touched." Not idle chatter. These are fine requests bordering on demands.

She is frozen like a deer in the headlights of an on rushing car. She either has chosen not to move or is unable to move because of some primal magnetic force.

"Who was your father? Your brother? Robby? What do they mean to you? How do I represent them?"

Now, I am speaking very forcefully, because I am in control. We both know it.

She is cringing. The once looming threat is shrinking. The woman is becoming a child. The cobra has met the mongoose. Suddenly she springs forward. Enunciating every syllable at a volume that could be heard two houses over, if they were inhabited.

"That's none of your god-dammed business. You rotten shit. How dare you assume anything about me? Particularly things like that? You don't know a thing and will never know the truth. It's all buried. I am alone with my past. It is not to be shared. Especially with some social butterfly, I mean, barfly. You, who gave up your own flesh and blood, have no right to sit in judgment of me. You cannot imagine what I have been through or what I have had to endure."

She is upon me now. Standing directly before me. Hands on her hips. The woman is back with a vengeance. The cobra's hood is open to its fullest. Blouse heaving with the breathing. She is trying to stare into my soul, except she is unable to find it. I gave it to my children for safekeeping. Reaching down to my shoulders, she digs her claws into the flesh and yanks me off the couch. Confrontation. She swings a right. I block a fist, not an open hand. She punches with the left to my mid-section. Fuck! Where did she learn to attack?

I slap her. She ties to hit again. This time I grab her wrist and fold her arm behind her. This pulls her head back and draws us nearly nose to nose. Our eyes meet in a raging glare. My right hand is raised to strike.

"What the fuck has come over you, Adriane? Who are you now? Who am I?"

She pounces on to my face. This is not a head butt. She grinds her lips upon mine and thrusts her tongue to the roof of my mouth. I maintain my grip on her right wrist. This is my leverage of protection, but it is also her link to my body. I can't let go, so we remain connected at various points. She moves her left hand to the back of my neck to pull my lips into her mouth. She could bite, but she sucks. Her mouth is dry. Mine not. Her left hand moves sensually down my back to my right cheek. She begins to knead my butt as her tongue becomes more active, dancing, stroking, and probing. I slowly release my grip on her wrist and she cautiously, submissively, moves her hand to my face and caresses my hair and cheek. I can feel the moistness on her cheek. Tears of release and surrender. Not tears of fear. She knows I will not hurt her. I am betting she will not hurt me. Now both her hands are around my neck. Their hold is a mixture of trembling and strength. We pull apart.

"James, what have you done? You have touched my soul."

She deliberately unknots her blouse and feverishly unbuttons my shirt. We embrace chest to chest, exchanging bodily warmth. Another deep, much less frenetic, kiss. She unbuckles, unbuttons, and unzips my pants. I remain motionless, because this is something she wants to do, needs to do, alone. When my trousers are stepped out of on the floor, I hook my thumbs over the side of her shorts and ease them over her hips, down her muscular, warm thighs and drop them on the floor. The fires, hers, mine, ours, and the one in the fireplace are raging. She is the conflagrant. In the dancing orange light we stand. Shirts on, but opened. Underpants on. Bodies touching, experiencing, learning. Lips locked. Unlocked. Hands exploring. Squeezing, rubbing, tickling. She pulls away. Removes her blouse and my shirt, takes my hand, and leads me from the room and two heaps of clothes.

Her bedroom is a sanctuary. Plain. Almost austere. Definitely pristine. She pulls back the comforter and sheet and removes her thong bikinis with the other hand. In one large, fluid, magical motion she is completely nude and in bed. Hands uplifted, she beckons. I need no encouragement. I leave my single article of clothing on the floor on my side of the bower. We kiss. Tender as two rose petals, the passion having established our goals. I kiss her neck, shoulders, arms, and wrists. When I reach the right wrist, I whisper an apology. Back up the arm to her shoulder. I drag my tongue down each breast stopping at the nipple to suckle ever so gently, then more forcefully until I am sucking like an infant. Her breathing has changed from deep and rhythmic to gulping. Her body responds to my sucking. It almost bucks.

As I attempt to move down her to her stomach, she pulls me back to her breasts. My mouth and I go where we are told. She is now gasping. I nibble. A tiny whimper leaks from her. I bite. The whimper is a moan is a pronounced cry. Not loud, but very pronounced. She pushes my head to her stomach. I lick my way down to her navel and sense her legs begin to tremble. My lips touch her mons and the trembling becomes spasmodic. I have touched the spot. Tongue massaging brings all life as we know it under the sheet to a fever pitch. The sheet is kicked off, and her legs, with minds of their own, wrap around my head and try to pull my face inside her. It's as if the legs were giant mandibles. Her thighs are quite strong. Walks and runs on the sand engender strong legs.

Her *parfum* and musk are an intoxicating mixture. This is the scent of a woman. The more considerate the massage, the tighter the legs grip. Now there are hands on the back of my head. Hair is pulled and thighs apply the final pressure before *la petite mort*. The spasms continue for twenty seconds or so. My scalp is massaged. My face pulled to her face and covered with kisses, little kisses, big kisses, little licks, and big licks. Adriane begins to breathe in a more normal manner. I attempt entry. This is not easy as our bodies are rigid, one on top, one beneath, like two sticks. She spreads her legs and lifts her knees to her chest. Gradually I enter. Finally, the depth has been plumbed. Not hers, but mine for sure. Excruciatingly slowly I withdraw almost the entire way, then just as slowly push my hips against her buttocks. I repeat this waltz of wonder. Again and again. I move up on her to get a better angle on her spot. Her reaction to each thrust and withdrawal is manifested in her open mouth, facial contortions, and closed eyes. Tears begin to flow down the sides of her cheeks. Her ankles are now around her ears. What I give she takes. When I ride up, her gasping becomes deeper, somewhat masculine in timber. My release is forthcoming. As with all male beasts, I wish to bury my treasure in the deepest part of the cave. Like a farmer, I wish to plant my seed in the most fertile earth of the garden. My pulsating can't be hidden or disguised. Sweat drips from my forehead and upper lip. She licks every drop. I kiss her to retrieve my fluids. Primitive. Feral. This is the way it can be.

The spike and duration of the passion and the depth of release on top of the alcohol of the evening make slumber almost instantaneous and very deep. We don't snuggle. We clutch.

My eyes open with a silent bang. Remembering where I am is not difficult. Adriane has been surgically attached to me by a team of skilled medical professionals who work only at night. Slowly, I extricate my trunk and limbs from the convoluted female form beside, on top, and underneath me. I walk in semi-darkness to the sitting room and our clothes. The fire is still working. I spot the brandies. Both can be mine. I pour my fluid into her vessel and move toward the fire. If I stoke it or put a log on top, it will go out within ten minutes. The curse of Smokey. I move toward the windows. It is surprisingly light in the room. Outside the brilliance of a full moon in a cloudless sky is reflected off a black, almost calm sea. It is a near daylight aura, except the color of the light is at the other end of the spectrograph.

This blue light floods through the floor-to-ceiling-sliding -window-doors. Entrances to the deck, which wraps around the room. Thirty-feet deep and the length of the three outer sides of the house. I stare out at the still sea. The waves on this side of the peninsula are always weak sisters to those on the East Coast. They're almost dormant tonight. The brilliance and stillness are yearly signs. I have seen it since my childhood. On the snows of the Northeast, the lakes in the upper Midwest or the beaches of the Southeast, the brilliance and stillness are manifested differently, but they are pervasive. I know this now as never before. It can be bright and peaceful in our lives, too, if we let it. Peace will come to me, but only when my son is in my life again.

I gave up too much when I gave his mother primary residential custody. I want to explain my soul in him to him. Teach him all I know and what I don't know. Reclaim our relationship for the balance of my days. Terry has graciously returned the portion of my soul I gave him. Only after he cloned it. Our relationship is built upon his use of my soul. He is emotionally and mentally healthy enough to let my soul help him as he sees fit. He will live with it and adapt it to his world. When he is older, he will pass this transmuted soul, the amalgam of his and mine, to his children. This cycle nurtures the cycle of life. It is the current that changes still water to a stream or rushing river. It is the juice. Without this cycle, this giving and mutating, there is no life. No heritage, good or bad.

I want to tell Two of those who gave me my soul from as far back as I know. I want him to realize that he has, burning within him, the fires of my mother and father. His grandmother, the kickass-straight-ahead lady, as described at her wake by her eighty-seven year old life-long female friends. And the tremendously talented artist, the acutely sensitive, conservative socialist, the entrepreneur that was his grandfather.

I want to be with Two so that I can teach him how these parts of the amalgam, which is my soul, will help him grow. Help his psyche be strong. Help him make decisions, that are right. Endure the consequences of the wrong ones. As I have. How to change the seemingly, irrevocable. Only possible through faith. The life-and-death importance of faith. Not just in tomorrow, but in God and endless tomorrows. Understand that each soul is but an almost invisible and minuscule part of a larger soul. Universal. Pure in very, very few. Twisted to pornography by some. Jumbled by the human condition in all of us. If I can't explain nor pass along this force, this protector, this stimulator, this questioner, this goader, this calmer, this lover, this faith, I will have fallen short of the parental charge. I don't want to lose Two like I lost Terry.

I must get Two back in my daily life. This occasional evening and weekend are crap. The court efforts will take another six months. In the meantime, I have the wussy visits. As if to prison. Which one of us is the inmate? I put us each in our respective cells. How can I free him? Or is it me that must be freed? How can I get us closer? I want to see him every day. How can I get closer to him? The brandy is beginning to stimulate my feelings and sharpen my brain. If the mountain can't go to Mohammed, Mohammed must go to the mountain. I will do what he does. I will be where he is. He will experience my presence daily. This will break down the temporary walls of shyness, which are rebuilt after each all-too-rare visit now. I will become his shadow. He is my echo. Is that not what parents are anyway? At least until the child can be on his own. So, I have to go back to an earlier time and shadow him. I cannot go to school nor move in with his mother. Where will this new closeness be? Football! He plays, I will play. The brandy is working well. Now that I know what to do, I must figure out how to do it. There are three elements, Two, me, and the school. I don't need Two's approval, and I will give me my okay. That was easy. To get the school's permission, I must make it safe and rewarding for them. The situation must be in their best interest. Their need will be their weakness. I'll sign papers, submit to medical exams, and promise a big gift. Think of the great publicity. Hell, I'll even take out a very short-term life insurance policy to them. They can't lose. Ain't money grand?

I sense another entity in the room. Have I had an epiphany? Brandy induced hallucination? Is God here? Christ? Well, I'm naked to be received. I am, we are, between the fire's heat and orange flickering and the cool blue glow of the night, between what is and what can be. Between hell and heaven? I feel rapid, short, and strong shallow breaths on my neck, like a dog exploring. A kiss on the nape. I try to turn, but am eased back to my position of staring outward and upward. The primitive panting is not frantic. It seems innate. The nostrils through which the air is inhaled and exhaled travel across my shoulders and down my spine then back to my shoulders. I have forgotten about Two. Hands are placed upon my hips then slid languorously around to my member. One takes the shaft and caresses it. The other hand cradles my scrotum. All the while the panting continues. The touch is delicate. I do not feel fear. Then just as easily as they moved to the front, the hands glide back to my buttocks. The kneading starts indiscriminately. Becomes rhythmic. Is deeper. My cheeks are spread. Closed and spread again. A finger trails the crack. Nail on skin. No entry. The panting is becoming audible. Gentle sounds are heard beneath the exhaling.

The nose and tongue are now on my neck. Hands wrap around my waist and a right leg snakes around my right. I can feel pubic hair and a bone upon my butt cheek. Now the grinding begins. Slowly. As the panting becomes puffing and the sounds increase, so too the grinding grows intense. Which came first, the grinding or the puffing? I don't care. I have never been used like this before. I have had lovers, friends, and business associates who have fucked me over, but no one has ever used me as a fucking device. A human vibrator. But motionless. Some may consider this distasteful, but it is very erotic. Maybe the feelings are interdependent. Who cares? The grinding is now bordering on violent. With her leg wrapped around mine, I have to struggle to maintain our balance. A three-legged stool. This is my role in the coupling. Around and around. Up and down. Around and around. Up and down. God, this is like the *Peppermint Twist*. Hands are now kneading my stomach. Flab finally fulfills function. I am erect and ardently stroked. Pulled and rubbed almost viciously. The discomfort has an adverse affect upon my display. I really don't like to be hurt. Some discomfort and nipping are okay. Severe pain is not.

The pressure on my right side is intense as the grinding ascends the ladder of pleasure. The grabbing and kneading have stopped and now arms are wrapped around me as if to pull my body to the grinding point. Fingers pinch and roll my nipples. Hands, like paws, pressing hard on my chest. The arms on my side are strong. Surprisingly strong. My chest movement, my breathing, is confined. The guttural sounds of the exhaling have become noisy. Now and again I hear a whimper with the moaning. The crescendo approaches. All grinding, gripping and groaning are in synch. Her body moisture, sweat, saliva, and other fluids, role from my neck to the back of my right knee. She is rubbing them into me for some type of subcutaneous inclusion. She is bathed in them as she nearly collapses. Clutching with hands, arms, and the snaked leg. I have held us erect, as it were. My detachment has been executed with the stoicism of a Buckingham Palace Guard. As her breathing subsides, she quickly slips beneath my arm and is before me. With her back to me, she is staring out to the sea, to the future.

She leans forward, bending at the waist, and arching her back. She rubs her breasts and belly to retrieve the residue of her lust and reaches behind to grab my love wand. She gently lubricates it to useful rigidity and, at the appropriate instant stuffs it into her. As I begin the expected thrust-and-withdrawal sequence, she leans against the double pained glass. Her face and breasts are pressed flat by our forward pressure. They make a fog image on the window. An upper body phantasm. As I thrust, she slides up the window. I know the window is chilly; I touched it before her arrival in my reverie. But she seems oblivious to the obvious discomfort. Her flesh squeaks on the glass. Her panting fogs the entire upper portion of the window door. I grasp her hips and thrust. Hard. As powerful as I can. Deeper. Painful? I spread her cheeks to aid the penetration. She reaches behind and grabs my hips as I plunge. Does she want to hold me inside? She pushes me away and pulls me back. She wants to be dominated. She wants to take control by being subjugated. To be taken as if she were a mare in heat. The stallion has no option. He must perform. It is inborn. I oblige. I reach up and yank her hair back to me. She lets out a scream and a quiver. Her hips shake. Her knees weaken. A puddle of drool, her saliva and sweat, now evident on the window, is beginning to resemble a rivulet to the floor. I pull on her hair with one hand, spread her cheeks with the other, thrusting as deep and hard as I can. Her hands, now on the window, and our feet on the floor, a human builder's square. We brace for the rush to completion. Hip-to-hip motion. Slapping of flesh. I tug her hair, knead it. Massage her neck, rub her back, and clutch her hips. She is repeating the sound, *em, em, em, em, em, em, em, em,* with each yank, slap, and thrust.

Our rhythm is becoming frantic. Pushing, pulling, pulling, pushing. I lean forward and nip her shoulder. She turns and nips my lip. I bite back as simultaneous culmination is achieved. The spasmodic tremors, quivering, and shaking lead to a Vesuvian eruption. We clutch, she the window and I her, just to stay standing.

I withdraw, she turns and we embrace. No kisses, just transference of quieted emotion. The last exchange. Slowly, with arms around each other covered in our own sticky, filmy juices, we return to the bed to sleep, perchance to dream. The small clock on her bedside table says it is eleven forty-five. My folks were right. Midnight is a good curfew. Whatever is going to happen is going to happen before midnight. And nothing good can happen after midnight. Hell, nothing at all will happen after this midnight.

Straight Forty-four

Straight . . . forty-four. Straight . . . forty-four. Let them come to us. Four down and four backers. Corners off six yards. No bump. Backer on strong side has end all the way. The backers cannot blitz, just read and react. This is very difficult. They have to read the QB, the runners, the receivers, and anticipate. Truly a guessing game. Often influenced by field position and score. But this controlled scrimmage negates those two factors. Corners must also read and anticipate. We have to sharpen our skills at noticing patterns of behavior. Here they come. Wideout way out. Strong side is my side. Motion my side. This is the real deal. A big time buck white sweep . . . or the biggest fake in town. Coaches said these guys fake occasionally. They love to play smash-mouth football. But I still can't cheat and get burnt by a halfback pass. Peer over my shoulder at the safety. He has dropped five yards and thus given me the go ahead to step up. I do. God the thundering buffalo are stampeding my way. The wideout cuts back on me. He is easily chucked. The motion man hits me. We parry. The guard cracks my side. I am crushed by other bodies. I turn the flying fortress in toward the hopefully pursuing backers and safety. The stitch really stings. It is tough to breathe.

Jacob Davi Echelmann is my doctor. That's arrogant. Why do thinking adults refer to Doctors, lawyers, baby-sitters, gardeners, et. al., as *our* or *my?* This attitude is insulting. A throwback to the days of slavery. This is my possession, my object, my chair, my wife. This attitude is acceptable from small children because everything in their immediate sphere is theirs. But for adults it is crap! Dr. Echelmann is board certified in thoracic, pulmonary, and coronary surgery. He has been so for twenty-five years. One of the first in this country and few in the world for a number of years. He ain't my anything. He has performed in the best operating theaters throughout the world. His service to mankind includes saving the lives of kings, tyrants, Prime Ministers, and rebel leaders. These events normally happen during the day with lots of preparation, many minions, and all the best equipment and medicine a country can acquire. He also saves drunks who believe they can drive eighty-five miles an hour through walls. Entire upper body crushed. "Save him, save him," cry the wife and parents. Rarely accomplishable, most times failure and death. Then the explaining, the grief, and the guilt. The tirades of blame directed to the doctor's incompetence. More than once over his illustrious career, the good doctor has abruptly escorted a raging parent from the waiting room or called hospital security.

Doctor Jack also treats the derelicts and street kids who are in desperate need of emergency attention at three AM. The ERs throughout the county call Dr. Jack, because he is the best and will never say no. His gait is hesitant and sometimes awkward looking. He has two phony knees, thanks to the football necessary to acquire a college scholarship compounded by thousands of hours standing in ORs throughout the world. The fourth and fifth world countries do not have the hospital amenities enjoyed here. All of this has taken its toll on his health and his marriages, all three of them.

He has been married to Robin for twenty years. This is the last for both of them. She is loving and supportive, but not subservient. Outside of the home and two children, she deals in antiques. This is her fourth lover and the only one that pays her money. She is witness to the medical and time demands that have extracted life from her husband. Like a water torture. Imperceptible to the naked eye. (How does one clothe or unclothe an eye?) His body is weaker, sleep more fitful, yet his spirit is stronger. Perhaps because he has returned to his first avocational love, opera. He loves a challenge. A game to win. An opponent to better. He lives to win. Winning at his avocation requires many hours of voice training with a teacher who doesn't give a shit who the pupil is. God, the humility of it all.

Dr. Jack has a very small patient list. Just some dear friends he would prefer to help live longer. His other time demands and his overall attitude toward medicine are restrictive factors. He is considered quite conservative. He truly believes in the caveat, *Do no harm.* This does not mean that he will not pursue aggressive treatment of illnesses, diseases, and traumatic events. It's just that his credo does not permit him to experiment or use treatments and remedies that are not approved by appropriate governing bodies and panels. However, in those instances requiring his surgical expertise, he is incredibly fast. In and out faster than a forty-four magnum. Intrusion time, he believes, critically effects recuperation. To work at his pace requires teamwork. He demands to be surrounded only by those who share his fire. He has worked with the same group, here and abroad, for twelve years. The pay is great, but the hours are shit. For illnesses, he holds tight the truth that, in many cases, the body will heal itself with sufficient symptomatic relief, bed rest, fluids, proper diet, and the correct dosage of targeted meds. Short-term for surgery and long-term for illness. This bi-polar approach to the broad spectrum of medicine works for Jack and his patients.

When he confronted the death of his parents, he did so with great strength and compassion. He was not only their son; he was their last caregiver. He was responsible for their lives and easing them into the world of nothingness. How traumatic that must have been. They gave him life and nurtured him to maturity. Then he had to soften the final blow. Jack's mother died of cancer. It started in a breast and over the course of five years spread like a field fire. The other breast. Her lymph nodes. Lungs. She went from a vibrant, gracious woman to a trembling, withered, skeletal shell. Always seeking solace in her son's eyes and words. He did the best he could. Devoted days and nights to her, never forsaking his practice. It took its toll. Lost weight. Anger and a lot of booze.

Dad lasted eighteen months without his wife of fifty-eight years. There was really no driving force to support the fight of life. Emphysema is the most evil of the deaths. It makes every breath, normally taken for granted, feel as if there were an ever-tightening metal band around the lungs. Basic and fundamental life supporting activities are so strenuous that the sufferer concludes they're just not worth the effort. The mind and soul give up because the body cannot go on. Jack had to be a caregiver and a cheerleader. Sometimes false hope is all there is.

I know this for a fact. Jack sat with both his parents during the very last days and held them as they died. That must have been excruciatingly tough. God, what incredible strength.

I trust Jack because of his strength. I trust the way Jack thinks and acts. Besides, I only see him once a year in his office and thrice more socially. The Kileys is one of those times. My visit today is not my annual checkup, but the drill and the tests are the same. Jack's staff took blood, urine, sputum, and stool samples, as well as a chest X-ray and an EKG a week ago. Today is the day of somber admonition. I know what is coming. My loins are girded.

The walls of his office may have paper or be painted a very off-white. But you would be hard pressed to find much of it. He has the requisite certificates and diplomas on one very long wall, from table level to the molding. Then he has the rogues' gallery. All the famous people upon whom he has worked his surgical genius. The world leaders, their wives, and in some instances, their bodyguards. It's these same bodyguards who were in the operating room while their fearful leader was under. It must be exhilarating to attempt a delicate procedure knowing someone will blow your brains out if you fuck up. Certainly, no pressure there. Some of the leaders are no longer alive. Assassination is the leading cause of departure. Never old age.

Then there are the special pictures. Photos of children saved from the grip of death. Incredibly thankful parents. Smiling, awestruck attendants. These are the photos nearest to Jacks' desk. The people closest to his heart.

"Jimmy, why are you here at this time of year. Your yearly visit normally coincides with the Autumnal Equinox. Let's see what the tests tell us." He pours over the data and written report.

"Well, everything seems to be within tolerance for a man your age and life-style. You should watch your weight, maybe lose eight to ten pounds over the next six months. Your heart and lungs are strong and clear. Liver functions passable. Good blood chemistry. If you cut down on your drinking, these two would look even better.

Nothing negative in the stools or culture tests. Have you been experiencing any discomforts or abnormalities?"

"No, Jack, I feel great, and screw your weight loss request."

"So, why are you here today?"

"I want to play football and I need your permission, daddy."

Smart-ass. Straight to the core of the matter. No flinching or wavering. I didn't blink. Jack did.

"What are you saying? Football. In the park on Saturdays with a bunch of used-to-be's. Bruising your body. Macho bullshit on the lawn followed by four beers, three aspirin, and a long nap. Go for it. You don't need my permission to make an ass of yourself. But, I won't see you when you need some tape or a splint. The ER will save me the visit. So, why come today?"

"Jack, this is a lot more. I want to play football with Two at Saint Sebastian. Spring practice and the scrimmage game, the Jamboree, against Saint Peter. I need the written approval from my regular Doctor to let the Sebastian coach, administration, and board of governors off the hook."

"Well, I never thought I would live long enough to see a perfect asshole. But the one, the only one, is my office today. Let me guess your motives. Recapturing your youth and recapturing the love of your youth? Would you like my avuncular consultation or my professional vituperation? Shall I itemize the ten reasons yours is a very inappropriate, nay idiotic, dream? Or, shall I give you one reason that this death wish is fulfillable?"

"Thanks for the vote of confidence, Jack. But, let's be realistic. This is something I very much want to do, nay, must do. I am in sound medical and physical shape. I am about to embark upon a very regimented body build-up program and will go on a diet to ensure the proper nutrients for my health. I will insist upon a check-up every two weeks by your office and every two days during the training regimen by the team doctor. And, if either of you two medical wizards tells me to stop dead in my tracks, I will. Ooh, that was a bad choice of words. Lastly, if you don't provide me the letter, I'll take my medical files to a very accommodating clinic of marginally esteemed docs for their approval. So, there. Checkmate. I win. Now, will you be my curative counselor, my prophylactic professional, my medicinal mentor, and write the letter? I'll set-up the bi-weekly appointments as I leave."

"Jimmy, while I am concerned about the stress and strain this type of effort will have on your visible body, I am really worried about the banging your inner body will take. Bruises will be the least of your problems. I'm thinking hairline breaks in the bones, punctured organs, ruptured linings, and concussions. Have you thought of these?"

"Yes, that's why I will be examined by the team doctor every two days during practice."

"What does the school say?"

"I have only broached the subject to the coach. He, the Headmaster and I are meeting this afternoon. I will only go to them with a done deal. Your permission, a notarized letter absolving them of any present and future responsibilities, a promissory note to repair the football field and stands, and a term life insurance policy to guarantee they get something if my demise shortens my plan of long life."

"You want a note from your doctor. It seems you have thought of everything I could throw in your path. What's a defenseless country Doctor to do, but accede to the ravings of a lunatic friend? Besides, in the years that I've known you, I have never seen you back down. You are the most persistent animal I know. You just won't quit. So, I'll type the letter with the appropriate disclaimers and wherefores just like a fancy-schmancy lawyer. One last item. Will I be invited to see you make a fool of yourself?"

"Yes and thank you. Would it be inappropriate for me to give you a kiss? The door is closed."

"It would be very inappropriate. Besides I know every centimeter of your body and you're not my type. Seriously, I am doing this despite a voice in my brain screaming that I am contributing to the delinquency of a mental and emotional minor. Now, wait here. I'll write the letter on my computer, print a draft for our review, and the approved item on my letterhead for my signature. The fewer people who know about your insanity and my collusion the better I like it. Okay, I'm ready. Give the details."

Now I have both letters, Jack's and mine. I skip to my car and float to Saint Sebastian for my two PM meeting with Coach Lewis and Headmaster Morris. After they agree, I'll make the premium payment. All will be in place

Saint Sebastian Preparatory School. Named for the martyr about whom there are numerous paintings from the Italian Renaissance. Bernini, Botticelli, Mantegna, Perugino, and de Messina spent many hours and considerable efforts depicting various aspects of Sebastian's life, death, rebirth, and death. The fact that Sebastian died twice is no mean feat. First, he was crucified and shot to death by archers. His crime was the conversion of Roman soldiers during the reign of Diocletian. A widow retrieved the body and nursed it back to life. Sebastian, not being a shrinking violet, then went before Diocletian and announced that he was back on the conversion trail. The Emperor was apparently very pissed. He had Sebastian beaten to death and his body dumped into the sewer. Irene, later Saint Irene, had a vision of Sebastian in which he requested his remains be buried near the catacombs. She obliged. Relics of the double-death man are enshrined in the *Basilica di San Sebastiano* on the Appian Way.

A reproduction of the painting depicting the arrow-skewered and soon-to-be reborn Saint hangs in the main entrance to the school. I know it is a reproduction because it cost much more than ten thousand dollars. A copy would have cost much less. The original hangs in the Church of England. Every religion loves martyrs. It is one, if not the only, earthly thing religions share.

The fact that the school's founding fathers and mothers chose this particular Saint is not wasted on the children and the attitude of the school. Beneath the painting are three inscriptions on three separate but similar brass plaques.

Latin: *Summum bonum estfortitudo intra te. Obdura in res adversas et age vitam cum humanitate fideque.*

English Translation: *The highest good is the strength within you. Toughen yourself against adversity and lead life with faith and sound character.*

Interpretation by the class of eighty eight: *Get tough. Be tough. Stay tough.*

The colors of the school are, appropriately, pure white and blood red, a rich, deep purple and brown red. The logo is a blood red S on a field of white. They wisely eschewed any arrows or drops of blood. The teams are called the Saints. Never the Marts or Sebbies.

Extraordinarily high academic standards required by the school are matched by rigorous extra-curricular prerequisites. All these are established for each student each year and must be met for graduation. Every student from ninth through twelve grades must participate with, at least, one athletic team each year. Most play three sports. Additionally, each student is obligated to contribute to one social and one academic club each year. This means each and every student, boy and girl, coordinated and awkward, big and small. All of this extra on top of an academic load consisting of regular courses that would boggle the mind of most students in the public system and Advanced Placement courses normally given college freshmen. The students are here to learn, grow, and go beyond.

Over the life of the school, there have been three Headmasters. With each, money has been infused to conquer land and build two-story classrooms, recital and concert halls, a theater, a gymnasium for boys and one for girls, multiple baseball diamonds and soccer fields, computer labs, and a swimming complex. But, after all this time, there is just one old well-used football field and a practice field behind the bleachers.

Teachers have more masters' degrees and doctorates than in all the other schools in the county combined. They want to be here, because the pay is good, and the students are stimulating and well mannered. The teachers' efforts can make a difference. The young graduates, male and female, from Saint Sebastian populate the better schools in the Northeast, Midwest, and throughout the South—Duke, Vanderbilt, Emory, Sewanee. The Ancient Eight have yet to thoroughly fish this pond.

The young men and women at Saint Sebastian are the best of the best. Socially, intellectually, physically, and emotionally. They are from privileged loins. You would have to search long and hard to find an underachiever. And, while there is an acceptable cross-section of black, Hispanic, oriental, Indian, and Middle Eastern, the preponderance of the student body is white.

The land for the school was donated, as was the money for the buildings. Each edifice bears the name of the benefactor. These names are those of the oldest families in the area. But, the story of the land is a clear glimpse into the real personality of the school's founding fathers. A bet was made between two of the wealthiest developers in the area, both of whom had children at the school, which was then housed in an old tobacco building downtown. The bet was on the outcome of the annual football game between the two state universities. Money was not the object. That would have been boring. So the combatants bet land. Not for personal gain, but for the school. Fifty acres of then not so choice real estate. One parcel of fifty west of the city. One north. No one remembers which team won. Saint Sebastian is now located west of the city on a fifty acre tract worth over one hundred times its value when donated. The other parcel became the core of the new university, ten years later. It too is worth a small fortune today.

The fortunes of the boys' athletic teams fluctuate with each generation. Football was king fifteen years ago then wallowed in the mire of two-and-eight seasons for a decade. It has recently come back. Basketball has never been more than just respectable. Just a bunch of limited speed, no-jump-shot white boys.

Wrestling is where the boys excel. Because of its required sacrifices and extreme discipline, the wrestlers are the best athletes. District and Regional champions for the past five years. Three individual state champions per year for four years. The program started small, twenty kids, about eight years ago. Enter the young coach, who is politely described as "intense" by adults, yet thought of as Satan incarnate by his team. In college, he once threw an opponent off the mat, through the gym doors and into the hall. Never looked up. Just raised his hand in victory. Lots of parental contributions of time and energy; they are known as the Monster Mothers by the Sebastian students, as well as opposing teams and their parents. These devoted parents travel wherever the team travels. They coach their kids, the refs and other parents from the side of the mats. If Texas A&M has a twelfth man, the Saint Sebastian wrestling team has thirty Monster Mothers. Parents of graduated wrestlers never leave the support of the sport. Of course, money also fuels the fire.

Now there are forty on the JV, sixth through tenth grades. And twenty on the varsity, tenth, if you're good enough, through twelfth grades. Training is year round. Wrestling tourneys, camps and club practices from the end of the season to the beginning of the next school year. Official practice starts when school starts for all those who are not playing football. The end of the football season brings the hogs, the linebackers, and only the mean defensive backs to the pit. The pit, the notorious practice room. One door, no windows, bright lights, and the coach keeps the temperature at ninety degrees during practice. The weight room is no better. There will be no fat on no body when Districts begin. And, most important, no one has to endure the last minute weight cut that weakens the body and can cause permanent damage. This is Two's other sport. But not the one in which I am interested.

Girl's volleyball is queen and the nationally recognized sport. Ranked consistently in the top twenty of the country. All the players are part of the two clubs which play on both sides of the "season." The clubs even draw girls from the high school teams, which are destroyed by the Slammnin' and Jammin' Saints. Little girls who are not even students at Saint Sebastian, tryout for Junior squads to learn from the best coach in the area and be noticed. They hope for an invitation to come to the school, compete, become one of the best. The female athlete of the year is always a volleyball player. And, rightly so. They all get college scholarships, full rides, regardless of family income.

These two sports aside, football remains the heart and soul of the alumni spirit. Macho bullshit bragging rights start in the Youth League, take a life of their own in the county, District, and Regional high school games, and become an evil drug in college.

The male athlete of the year, regardless of the team's record, is always a football player. Obviously he plays other sports and always he is all this and all that. Nonetheless, wrestlers who run cross country and track and do very very well don't stand a chance. Swimmers who set national standards. Pitchers who never lose, enjoy an ERA of less than one. Distance runners who are invited to national AAU based on sub-four-twenty miles and nine-minute two miles. None of these superior athletes will ever receive the most coveted award the school offers in athletics. So the poor football field, with its dilapidated stadium, is my leverage point with the Coach and Headmaster. I have what they need, money to re-sod the field and re-build the stands. The money is guaranteed by my written promise and the life insurance policy. My letter clearly states that the team, Coach, Headmaster, Board of Governors, and Saint Sebastian Preparatory School are not responsible for any injury I might incur as a result of this endeavor. All very proper and squared.

Two o'clock. I am ushered into Mister Morris's office. The Coach is there. Normal inane pleasantries all around. I come right to the point. Cover all the details as if this were a business presentation. Both men are silent until my conclusion.

"Mr. McCaa, why should the school do this for you?

"Mr. Morris, the better question is why should I do this for the school? The answer is because I want to. And it is in the best interest of the school to receive contributions earmarked for specific non-recurring budget items. Say a new football field and stands. My contribution will not only take care of this major one-time expense, it will also create a showcase enticement to increase attendance and involvement by the parents. Then all the school will need is a couple of winning seasons, maybe a Regional Championship, to really stoke the fires. Money will flow because I will have primed the pump."

"But, sir, we have so much to lose and you have everything to gain. We run a huge risk and you carry the torch of fame. Plus you could set the standard for others to follow. Or attempt to follow."

"Mr. Morris, I will be brutally frank. This is a business proposition, which is win-win for the school. It will be a one-time event. No future complications. I have absolved the school and all ancillary people of any responsibility. I have pledged money for an obvious need. Saint Sebastian has absolutely nothing to lose, nada, nicht, zero, zed, zilch, and everything to gain. Think of the money, the publicity, the money, the money. I am sure both you gentlemen are very busy. So let us sign the papers and let me get on with the business at hand of getting in shape for the spring."

"I will have to discuss this matter with the Board of Governors, Mr. McCaa. I'll get back to you in a few days with their decision."

"Sir, deal today. No deal tomorrow. I'm sure Coach Lewis advised you of my position before today. And, without sounding presumptuous, I suspect you have mentioned this to a few members of the Board, got a temperature reading as it were. Like many major decisions, this is yours to make. So, no hard feelings, thumbs up or thumbs down, today?"

"Mr. McCaa, give Coach Lewis and me thirty minutes to review your documents. If you don't mind, take a walk around the campus, visit our library. When you return at three, we'll have an answer for you. Is that fair?"

"Fair enough. If you want to call someone, you may consider Billy Ray Kiley, Stan Demmers, or Harry Mellis. They'll laugh a great deal, call me a crazy ass, and tell you it's a great deal for the school. See you both at three to sign the papers."

I sit in the courtyard on *the mound,* a raised, very large lump of earth in the center of all the halls and pathways from the buildings. Students traverse the mound at least a dozen times a day. They walk, run, or race depending on the destination and tardiness. Here they check out each other. Boys check out girls and vice versa. Clothes are not at issue. Personas are. I sit, sip my bottled water, and stare at the buildings, the kids, and the occasional seemingly lost parent who has come to retrieve homework assignments and books for the child at home with a fever.

It is now showtime. As I rise to saunter back to Mr. Morris's office, Alyssia spots me. She flashes jubilance and a wave. I nod recognition.

"Mr. McCaa, I must admit that, like Coach Lewis, I have reservations about this proposition. However, the documents you provided are as you promised and the references were supportive. Therefore, we are willing to go forward. So let us make copies and sign them as originals, one each for Coach, me, the Board, and two for you. Is that satisfactory?"

"One last item. Secrecy. I want to tell my son. Coach Lewis and I will tell the other players at the appropriate time. Until then, knowledge of this is truly need-to-know, and no one needs to know. Do we agree?"

"Yes."

"Yes"

I extend my hand to Mr. Morris and then Coach. Copies are made, the signatures applied and I am on my way. Now to deal with Two.

"Dad, why? This is stupid and embarrassing. You're too old and out of shape. The hogs will kill you. Why this, why now?"

"Listen, Two. Understand that the decision process was excruciating. This is not something I am doing on whim. I have a real purpose and my purpose is sitting across from me now. I am ashamed that I abandoned you. And, while I realize your mother takes care of you now and that you love her, I feel you and I are not in each other's lives. The infrequent week-day evening and every other weekend are just not enough for me, and I hope for you. Every time we are together, we have to be reintroduced. We never have enough time to really understand what's going on in our heads. While this custody ordeal drags on, I wanted to take a bold proactive step to be with you. Plus, it will be fun."

"Bullshit! You're doing this for yourself and to embarrass me, to punish me for your fuck-up. Look at you, fifty years old and desperate to reclaim some fragment of a non-existent youth. If you want to live vicariously, you're too sick for words. Get close to me without humiliating me or making a perfect asshole of yourself! You know I love you, and I know you love me. If you want more time with me, let's work it out with Mom. Don't force yourself into a world where you don't belong."

"Terry is not around for a number of reasons. Did you ever think of that? Not the least of which is that he has no love for your mother. Her warped mind-set, while she was using, drove a huge wedge between them. I cannot extract the wedge. He must do that. But I will not let her drive the same type of emotionally needy wedge between us. Thus, my attempt to get close to my son."

His eyes are on fire. The little red flecks have either multiplied or expanded. He is pissed but lovingly curious. A grown-up interloper is one thing. His dad is another. Maybe he could deal with the situation if there were a group of *alta cacas*. That would somehow diffuse the personal involvement. His jaw is flexing with each word and his shoulders and anus are pumped. I see for the first time exactly how powerful he is. I am at once in awe and very proud. His face is forcefully entering my space as he makes his multiple points. Is he handsome or just seventeen? Youth is truly wasted on the young. The knife was driven into my heart, twisted and ripped out in one fierce, surprisingly fast motion. However, once again I have reached perfection in someone's eyes.

"Two, I have tried to speak to your mother about you and me spending more time together. Each time I broach the subject, her restrictions are so severe that increased time is impossible. She continues to use you as bait. If I want to see you more, I have to pay more. That is not only illegal, it is immoral as to the father and child relationship. So, rather than lose at continual and acrimonious negotiations over your life, I walked away from that table. Seeing you, being with you is the most important issue in my life and I will not be deterred by someone who hates me."

"Okay, slow down. You know how I feel and I know that your mind is made up. Let me sleep on this and try to absorb it. We can discuss your insanity this Saturday."

Why is it that he sounds more mature than his father? Maybe he is. He has reacted much like Dr. Jack. The role model is good.

"That's fair. Next subject. How's your weight?"

"I'm going into Districts at one pound under. This gives me a good opportunity to carbo-up the night before. I can repeat this process for Regionals and, hopefully, States. I feel stronger than ever and I am ready."

God bless my baby hog.

There is silence on the drive to his mother's. He is asleep. His calm is my strength. The serenity of sleep. The pure can and do look like angels. The mouth is open partially and breathing is audible. Is this the chaste David of yore? Nah, it's just my boy. Beauty and love are in the eyes of the beholder. His kiss and hug at departure are just a little more intense than usual. I think he is coming around.

Saturday, we do movies and burgers. I never drink when I am out with him. Am I kiddy-whipped or what?

*   *   *

"Dad, I've thought a lot about what you told me on Wednesday. I can't accurately fathom why you want to do this, and I'm not sure you even know the true reason or reasons. But it is something very important to you. And I can see the point about failed negotiations.

Therefore, my son, I give you my blessing to suffer the slings and arrows of justifiable misfortune."

Now the tough guy demeanor. A fierce glare. The threat. Leaning into me with force and without compromise. He is staking out his territory without urine but with words and body language. He knows I will enter his domain and there ain't a whole hell of a lot he can do about it.

"Two, you are an arrogant, pompous fuck. I wonder where you got that. Certainly not from my Highland gene pool. Thanks for understanding. By the way, I'm going to kick your ass every chance I get. But you'll never get to me."

"You're on ancient one."

The glove was dropped. The flags unfurled, the lances of battle are sharpened, the armor polished, and the horses groomed. Combat will be joined on a sunny, hot and humid field of play. Both will be tested and live on with new found respect.

Blue Fifty-four Double S

*B*lue . . . fifty-four . . . Double S. Blue . . . fifty-four . . . Double S. Five down, four backers. Both safeties blitz. One outside on strong side and one between center and guard on weak side. Tackle and end on weak side stunt and loop. Strong outside backer drops to centerfield, scanning receivers. Corners have deep coverage. I really, really hate this deep shit running against kids, who are much faster than I am. Hide cushion until very end of snap count. Strong side my side. Wideout is near the out-of-bounds line. Must keep him inside. Hope backer can give me under coverage. Tight end looking at backer. I yell 888 as warning to backer. If the tight end does not block, but is in the pattern, I am naked underneath. But, blitzer will have a clean shot. Long count. They smell something. No audible. QB drops straight back. Wideout takes off like a bottle rocket. My cushion surprises him. His eyes are wide open. I give him eight yards, but he closes fast. Force him inside. He wants to go post deep. He turns toward the QB. The ball is in the air to the end, who is beyond the backer running toward the other corner. Long, beyond his hands. Wideout smacks me hard in the chest and ribs. Stitch is now severe in my side and breathing is difficult.

The last twenty years will be noted for its economic explosion followed by a devastating implosion. The *e-age*, with virtual life dropped over us like a net over a sleeping lion. Fortunes were made and some even lost as fast as you could say *dot-com*. With every rampaging fire there is a fierce reaction to the fierce action. A fireball sucks back the initial blast of hot air and smoke to propel its rise to the stratosphere. It needs something to burn to give it energy. The economy in the last twenty years offered the trifecta of fuels; dot-com, housing and banking. Companies were merged or trashed to provide for rapid expansion of the feverishly healthy. Countries and world sectors mimicked companies. Asia teetered. Russia tottered. South America stumbled. Eurozone members were forced to cut their losses and embrace draconian measures to stabilize their economies. There was no hope for a quick fix to value then wealth. Ha! on them. Ha! on us. Are we next? Or can we read the signs and react in time.

We presented the false hope of an overall economic stability, low unemployment, and the technology to push the world well into the twenty-first century. But, our balance of trade fell on its ass. Cheap labor and a surplus of unused production internationally made us a dumping ground for goods. And there was grumbling and grousing under the sheets of success. The banks got caught with their balance sheets down, and the lies they told about the housing market. The companies that merged for global efficiencies had to suddenly right-size. There was no money to borrow to sustain, much less expand. This country's out-of-work force was absorbed rapidly then dumped on the unemployment lines faster than you can say no work, or was pushed into the sunset of early retirement with no pensions or retirement accounts because the stock market had fallen and stayed down like a punch-drunk fighter in the eighth. The gap between the haves and the have-nots became a chasm with no bottom. The out-of-work forces in the international markets were worse off. There was no way for them to go but further down the food chain. This lack of absorption perpetuated the global and stock market slides. Some of the companies, which had been the first to jump on the global bandwagon and were increasingly dependent on these offshore markets for fiscal growth, took it in the shorts. Sales were soft to sickening and profits were continually lower than last year. And still no relief from the capital markets. The government had to jump in. Borrow money from the public sector to prop up the private sector. Slowly the money would be repaid. Could the middle class hold on that long. How long? I will get down from this current history soap box. Then there was a third type of company, like Great Eastern Life Insurance Group, Inc.

Great Eastern was healthy and growing by leaps and bounds, until the end of the century. Then the foreign owners began to worry that the old-timers who had built the business were only a few years from retirement. Enter the young dragons. New blood aggressively seeking to inject their own DNA into the veins of the moneymaker. The reins were to be shared. (Every farmer knows a buggy can't be driven properly with shared reins). Profit goals were set, and the work begun. After three months, it was apparent that *The New Kids on the Block* were operating under the mission statement that: *Having no clear objective, we will redouble our efforts.* The bitching and moaning reached new decibel levels.

"We've never done it this way. I'll lose all my commissions. Who approved this stupid program? Why haven't you completed the . . . ? I can't make this work. Aren't you responsible for . . . ? Why are two people asking for the same project?"

This is the background to my work. I am the Director of Marketing Communications. My group develops advertising, company literature, and marketing materials. The writers work with designers. We, I, report to the Marketing Director. Before my arrival the creative process was strictly grab ass. When somebody wanted something, it was written and designed, ad hoc. There was no strategic marketing input or consistency of look. Each piece looked like it had been designed by and for separate entities. The sales forces and prospective purchasers never saw the same look twice. The three advertising agencies we used were getting fat and happy. Because we reinvented the wheel every six months, all the collateral material had to be redesigned and reprinted twice yearly. And we always printed the twenty brochures; sixteen pages of four-color in seventy-five thousand unit lots. A mere fifteen percent on top of the photographer and printer charges plus a ton of billable man-hours because no one here could make up his or her mind, created a cash infusion to the non-contributing parasites.

Great Eastern is my first brush with "business casual dress" and "jeans Friday" on a wide scale basis and I do mean W-I-D-E. Many of the employees, young and old, like me, wear clothes that compliment or disguise their various shapes. However, there is a very visible, significant minority that seems to share the herd mentality that any large shape fits into and looks good in tight, ill-fitting clothes. A senior executive was heard to whine, "Do we hire from or by the pound?"

Enter Saint James, The Pot Stirrer and Sometime Smoker. Paladin seeking a better, faster, brighter, new and improved way to create marketing communications. Hired by an old friend who wanted a trusted fellow traveler to resolve a very knotty problem. Organize the work process, produce clear marketing pieces that look like they come from one company, and save money. In fact, my base is based upon the assumption that within one year I would save ten percent. My bonus would be equal to one-tenth of one percent of all savings beyond twelve percent. They wanted a two-percent cushion. Needless to say I dove into my work. The job was a great deal more complex than anticipated. Ain't it always so. The product managers' toes were more sensitive than I could have ever imagined. Small fiefdoms were fiercely defended. The parochial protection caused much of the problem. But, I had my mandate and the promise of financial reward. I just had to make nice as I took away toys.

I like work, particularly when I can contribute, improve, and make money. Suffice it to say I did a lot of the first two items during the first two years and did okay on number three. Paid all my back taxes, delinquent student loans I cosigned for my elder son, and opened a retirement account. I hope to avail this latter in fifteen years, if I don't work myself out of a job or get politically killed by one of the petty princes in the mean time.

My workday starts at seven AM and I'm out the door by five PM. I take no work home. In the office, the particulars and the planning occupy my mind. Instead of the hodgepodge of eleven printers, we now use four, for whom we are important clients. Jobs are bid to keep a lid on prices. The hunger-satiety work cycle differs with each printer. Because of my compensation plan, I am always looking to save. But, because of the charge of producing high quality items, I will not scrimp. This is a very interesting balancing act, made dangerous by the sniping and back biting of the little people. Ain't office politics grand?

My weekends are divided between Two and Adriane. Alternate life styles, bachelor father and beach lover. I need and like them both. This weekend it's the beach. We coordinate our arrival in time for a late afternoon swim or beach walk as the sun sets. It's still winter. Adriane and I have not yet had the discussion about leaving clothes or the ultimate soul searching concerning duplicate keys. I'm not sure I want to rush to these new levels of commitment. Just really happy with the arrangement, the time with and the time without. Idle chatter about the week's events but no polemic about the future. Casual garb, some off-site jaunts, but no socializing with neighbors. There never appear to be any. Each house beside Adriane's is uninhabited. Furniture is visible through the windows. Just never any bodies in the chairs. Her, not my, house and every other weekend are havens for both of us.

It's surprisingly hot for February, mid-eighties, so we decide to swim. My work out regimen has toned my torso and leg presses and sprints bulked my pins. The bathing trunks of last year are a tad droopy, because the waist is too big. Thank God for hips. Adriane looks her magnificent self in a perfectly fitting two-piece. The pattern, colors and cut are obviously just for her. Brent, the wonder server, would pass out from a loss of blood in his head, the big one. I can avoid leering by spending time in the water and running on the beach.

"How was your week? Did the county commissioners throw any more blocks in your expansion path?"

"James, they are impossible. Either they're all idiots or they have so damned many different and interconnected agenda, they just can't come to a common point-of-view on our expansion plans. Developments with self-contained shopping centers seem to be an unfathomable concept for them. Hell, you would think we've asked them to pass judgment on brain mapping. Delays heaped upon delays. Unrelated questions and requests for information that have no bearing on our proposals. What's a capitalist entrepreneur to do?"

This was her signal that she wanted to drop this topic and move on to something less stressful.

"Race you to the water, Adriane."

Off we sprint. Over the beach to the shore, beyond the breaking waves to the valley before the sand bar one hundred and fifty yards off shore. On the sand bar, her glistening body, tawny hair, and piercing eyes confront me, the victor. Her idea of second is first last.

"Okay, mister wisenheimer let's swim out to the buoy."

Immediately she dives from the far side of the bar and starts the three-hundred-yard journey. I'm six seconds behind and the gap is widening. Her sinewy muscles, steady strokes, and internal engine are too much for my short, thrashing style of water churning. The weight work is not designed for channel swimming. She wins and is very, very smug. I arrive after she has caught her breath. About a month after she arrived at the goal.

Gasping for air and grasping the metal float, I struggle to converse. There is a tingling in my left arm and a real pain in my left side.

"You won. Happy? Why the fierce competition every time we're together? I like you and hope you like me. I fight all week with people who think I am stealing their livelihoods. You work hard, fighting with fools, bureaucrats. I don't want to fight with you on weekends. We're both too tired of bullshit. The competition affords me too little time to be with you, to get to know you."

"You want to know me. I was raised to win and I like the exhilaration of victory. On the farm, in my office, and here, with you on weekends. You are good competition, up to every challenge. I know you would never let me win. I am confident your mind would be a worthy opponent. Not sure of your soul. Maybe someday I'll know. Race you back to the sand bar."

"Not yet. Wait. Let's talk a bit more, now that I can breathe and speak. Why the alternate weekends out here with you? We have been an item since Christmas. That's eight weeks. We talk weekly, yet Two and I are excluded from your other weekends. Would you like to meet Two? I would like that. He knows where I am. Have to tell him in case of an emergency. My Ex doesn't know. He can keep a secret. What do you do when I'm not here? Do you have another playmate? Yes, I am more than just curious. How much more, I don't know. As a matter of fact, there's a lot I don't know and I want to. Remember that night I asked about your past and hopes for the future? Well, I'm waiting for answers. Are you avoiding the exposure? What do you have to fear or hide? I will not hurt you, and neither will the truth."

I'm on a roll. Driven to ask, driven to know.

"An item? What the hell is an item? Who says? Two and I will meet. In due time, James, in due time. Maybe soon. Maybe later. But definitely not here. Not now. Here's the deal for now. If you should happen to win the race back to the sand bar, a very unlikely occurrence, I'll answer three single dimensional questions. Nothing like the reporters ask politicians. Your choice. *Nichts verboten.* When I win the race, you must cease your probing, verbal only, of course, and prepare dinner. Now catch me if you can!"

She is off like Jane. I am a feeble imitation of Tarzan. The game's afoot. And the dogs of war have been unleashed. No true Scot can refuse a challenge or dare. In fact, we relish them. Dares boil our blood. Prove our manhood and independence. I'll push beyond my limit. If I throw up, big deal. I must win. I must know. Her two body length lead is fading as my weight room muscles power my crawl. The egg beater style seems to be working with the waves at my back. Swimming with the tide is easier than thrashing against it. Hope I can sustain it in the absence of oxygen to my lungs. I can see her kick. My hands almost touch it. My arms are up to her knees, hips, ribs. We are stroke for stroke. Instinctively my strokes become longer. I am reaching, digging and pulling. Breathing left every stroke. The memory of years ago in heavily chlorinated public pools throughout Pennsylvania, Maryland, New Jersey, and Virginia. Finishing third or fourth in race after race during four years of summers. Relay winner always. The tingle is returning to my left arm. The damned lifting produces muscles counterproductive to swimming. The pinched nerve is an intermittent but severe pain in the neck, arm, and side.

Have no idea how close to the sand bar we are. Her stroke is now at my waist. I am in real pain. Strenuous exercise is somewhat impeded by not being able to breathe comfortably. Can't see because the water too damned murky. Grab a peak toward the shore, no help. Pulling ahead. Pain increases. This is one dare I will not lose. Strokes now in rhythm. Not bad for an *alta caca*. Motion of waves indicates bar ahead. I see her hands beside me. She's sprinting. I must out-sprint. Nothing left but guts. Stomach churning to the kick beat. Throw up on the way. Swallow, breathe, dig. Must win. Reward is worth the embarrassment of vomit. Stand up. Winner! Pull body away from first to last Adriane and puke into the waves. She's a few strokes behind. Does not see me puke, I hope.

"Where did all that power come from? Never gave you a chance. How 'bout two outta three?"

"Your ass, bitch!"

Mock anger sounds healthy.

"You wish, bastard!"

Response is healthy.

My gasps for air are audible above the waves. Let hot muscles cool in the water. Lack of oxygen or lactose something or other makes the muscles feel very hot. Knees weak. Left side pain fights for brain domination with lungs crying for air. I am a wreck. Squint into the setting sun. She seems to be better off. Her head is up. Mine is bobbing. She is breathing through her nose. My yapper is wide open. Can't accuse her of anything. Suspicious. Why is she not in agony? No distress like me. Did she let me win? Bitch! Why?

"Let's walk back to shore. Hold me up so I don't drown."

She grins at her victory in the loss.

We weave to the shoreline, gratefully accepting the push of the waves to ease our struggles. She holds my hand. A gift to the victor? Genuine affection? Assistance for the physically ass-whipped? Who cares? I'll take attention for any reason. My suit has fallen to crotch level. Butt crack visible. With a free hand, I tug to correct the social gaff. She giggles. We plop on the blankets and towels. I am devastated. She is exhilarated—just like with sex. Why are women so damned peppy after sex? They want to talk. Hell, they'll even get out of bed to fix a sandwich. Men want to collapse and sleep, because we do all the pushing and pulling. Did she get laid on the swim to the bar and not tell me?

The pains are diminishing with each deep relaxing breath. Soon, I'll just be old and not old, tired, and achy.

"Adriane, I want my questions now. Before I die."

"Before you ask, remember you may get what you ask for and not what you want. And, if you don't ask for what you want, you will get what you ask for."

I have to pause and ruminate on her conundrum-like admonition. What the fuck?

"I'll take the bull by the horns and pose these triadic queries: Why three questions? Is there another man in your life? What is behind your push-me-pull-you approach to our relationship?"

"First, to learn what was on your mind. Second, no. And third, I told you I am frightened of allowing a relationship to develop. When I was very young, I fell in love lust. Was I in love with him, in love with lust, or in lust with love? The separation is super fine when you are in your early teens. He was my first. We did everything everywhere. And I do mean everything and I do mean everywhere. We would grope and sweat four times a day. On his bed. My bed. The barn. His car. The fields. My parents' bed. I began to love him more and more. One day he left me. I never saw him after that day. And, while this is not uncommon, I was deeply crushed.

Later, as a young woman, I made another commitment. Our passion was deep and fiery, but he became abusive. I spent years getting out of that sick scenario. He was perversely manipulative and threatened to kill himself if I left. I did and he did. More years of analysis and hiding inside my work. Then I met my husband with two wonderful children. All the material stuff anyone could want. Life was idyllic at home and socially. But, deception was his game. Spent money, his, mine, and ours, like there was a never-ending supply. When he was out of my sight, he was not alone. If he traveled, he always had a bunkmate. When he was home and I was not, he had the au pair, everywhere in the houses. Couches, our bed, the children's beds. Everywhere, the pigs. In the city, here and at our place in MOG. He was deep into coke and she was the source of all his pleasures. I became the adult female figure, not the love or lust interest. Our marriage was falling apart faster than a sandcastle in a hurricane. We were in the process of separation, when he died in the terrible crash. Most heinous was the loss of the innocents. They were beautiful children and I was beginning to love them as my own. Unfortunately, so was the au pair. That was not right. I guess, sometimes sacrifices have to be made. Oh, well."

Baammm! What is wrong with this picture? Did she say what I think she said? Did I hear what she said or what I think I heard? What was her involvement in the crash? Is this why there are no pictures of Robby or the children anywhere in the house? In fact, why are there no photos of any family in the house? The mantel, coffee table, even her bedside table are void of people's faces. This is very strange. Why does the name, Mike Stewart, keep bobbing in my brain? Is he more than the foreman? I must check into this.

"James, you look pale and you're shaking. Was it something I said? Did the little swim affect you that much? Why don't we go to the house where you can lie down? I'll shower and even cover your end of the bet. Shop for food, prepare the meal, and clean up. You just relax, nap until dinner is about ready. Maybe you're not the man you thought you were. You need to be babied. I would like to be the baby-er. You can thank me later. You'll think of some way to show your appreciation."

She has a way of twisting a nice gesture into a comical debt. There is something different about this human. She looks like a beautiful, soft female, but her emotions are those of a hardened male. I wrap myself in huge beach sheets and stretch out on one of the two chaise lounges on the deck.

Tender kisses awaken me. My eyes open to a vision of beautiful skin, sparkling eyes, and warm, loving smile. Maria Schell in my face. What a concept. Adriane kisses me tenderly on the lips. There is a strange taste in her mouth. Her eyes begin to well up with moisture.

"James, it's dark. You should rise and shower for dinner. But, before you cleanse your body, I want you to know how much I care for you. You have been sweet to me, maybe a little pushy, but sweet nonetheless. You look cute wrapped in your swaddling clothes. I couldn't resist kissing you as a wake-up device. I'm sorry if I push you away. It's just this damned baggage I carry. Even when I put it down, it leaps back onto my back like it was magnetized."

"Adriane, thank you for the sheets, the rest, the kisses, and the words of kindness. Now, without sounding like an ass, what is that taste in your mouth? It is reminiscent of an illegal plant smoked by the depraved hippies of my youth. A medicinal herb used by the older generation to fight nausea and glaucoma, and occasionally smoked as a party or intimacy enhancement."

"Why, James, you detective rat. How dare you even think I would indulge is any form of illicit behavior alone? Yes, I have partaken of a magical medicinal herb to relieve the stress of the week and the day.

I do so only upon the advice of my physician. He has recommended reasonable doses of this remedy on the weekends. And he firmly recommends that I share whenever I can. Would you like some? It would help your stomach distress, improve your appetite, and brighten your overall perspective. I have a dose and the appropriate fire creating device in my shirt pocket. We can take our medicine together here on the porch."

She fires up a stick. God, I haven't seen one of them in a while. Takes a deep hit and passes the torch of rejuvenation to me. One hard tug followed by a long draft. Hand back. She draws twice. Keeping the second in her mouth, she kisses me, opens my mouth and blows the smoke deep into my lungs as I inhale. Coughing is expected and good. The ember of enjoyment rests in her hand as a beacon of betterment in the dark. She passes it to me. This time I draw twice and return the favor. We hold our collective breaths. She takes the roach for one last hit before placing it on my index finger. My thumb closes down on the little stub. My last hit. I take the bug into my saliva-filled mount, extinguish it and swallow.

The world becomes dreamy. Time slows. My body feels frozen but not rigid. The lights are brighter and the dark is blacker. The air is clear and cool. I know I'm wrapped in sheets, but feel nothing. This shit is gooooooood!

"What other surprises do you have in store for the tired combatant? Music? Dancing girls? Whips and chains? Mud wrestling? Blind man's bluff in the buff?"

"None of the above. You will shower. We will eat. You will rest. I am concerned about your reaction to the exercise. Maybe you should see a doctor?"

"Okay. Okay. Okay. I am under the care of two doctors. I'm off to bathe."

Steps are measured but not staggered. Sheets like a wedding train spread across the floor behind me. She giggles at the sight of the non-bride. I spin and give her my best improve your stomach distress, your appetite and brighten your overall perspective.

"Silence, wench. Mock not the lord of the manor. Humble yourself before him with a comely mien. The vanquished foe, testimony to his valor and righteousness, is thine own self. He will wash the stain and stench of battle from his person only to return an earthbound deity."

"Go soak your head, asshole."

The shower from warn to hot to warm to cool to cold rejuvenates my heart and soul. I shave in the shower. Have done so for twenty years. I just bleed less this way. Adriane has these neat bath towels. Almost rough on one side and soft on the other. Can really get rid of the dead skin and gives a nice ruddy complexion all over my body. But, the exfoliating side also removes hair, a precious commodity on my head, but not my arms, legs or back. Feel great. Floss and scrub teeth to get rid of remains of the vomit. Deodorant, freshly starched Brooks Brothers pink chambray shirt and jeans. No shoes. My toilet activity, while stoned, is like watching the past all over again. Feel great. Starved. Ready to walk tall and step straight. Out of the boudoir down the hall into the living/play/great room. I hear sniffing. Tears? Spice induced. Enter the kitchen and see the mirror and straw. Six neat lines of powder. Fuck me. Andes candy for the terminally stupid.

"Hey, lovely lady, what's cookin'? Sorry, but I couldn't resist using that trite line. Smells great. Chicken. Yellow rice and black beans. *Especialite di maison?*"

She does not attempt to hide the mirror. I always thought it was ironic that the evil drug was consumed from a mirror. The mirror gives a perfect reflection of ruinous affects. The user becomes uglier, meaner, and dumber with each line. The user gets to look his demon straight in the eye. Maybe the drug is warning. That is part of the seduction. Don't touch me or you'll die. Touch me if you're strong enough to live on the edge. It's sure why people smoke cigarettes. With all the warnings and deaths, kids still are convinced they are immune to tobacco's poisons. When they start coughing up their lungs, the kids and their parents blame the companies for hooking the little darlings. When the junkie can see her nose bleed, sunken eyes, and sallow skin in the mirror, she blames the drug and not her stupidity. Signs, signs, everywhere signs. If only we would open our eyes, read, and take responsibility for our own actions.

"Help yourself, James. There's always more."

"No thanks, Adriane. It's too powerful for me. Or, I'm not strong enough for it. Whichever, no thanks."

"Should I set the table?"

Her activity is unsettling. I am scared. The weed of crime bears bitter fruit. Who knows what idiocy lurks in the nose of the junkie? The ex-user do. I want to run. Call in the dogs, roll-up my bag, fold my tent, piss on the fire, and high tail it to the hills. Hide out with Two far from the madness. Boy, that makes a lot of no sense. Stay. You don't have to fight or join. Just stay and see what will happen. Is this a seduction?

"What beverage goes with the workers' feast? How about beer? A few crisp Rolling Rocks? I saw some in the back of the fridge."

As I open the fridge door and reach in, I notice her head bob to the speculum of suicide. Two lines gone, each in a single powerful inhalation. Their former space is wiped clean and the residue rubbed over the upper gum. Turning back, I stare into her watery, piercing eyes. Anxiety has a firm grip on her nervous system. Tiny twitches, in her eyes, hands, arms and shoulders. She is there. Wherever she wanted to be she is, or maybe real close. Four more lines and she'll be beyond the desired place.

The meal is served, beer poured, and we devour our portions in silence. Fear runs through my veins. The urge to run ebbs and flows. It turns my gut. She looks bored except for the twitches. Her appetite is good. This leads me to believe she is not an everyday people. Rationalization and seduction. Seduction and rationalization. Is the drug is working on me? Or have I let my feelings cloud my mind?

"I feel much stronger, Adriane. I'll take care of clean up. After that, let's go for a walk."

The dishes are rinsed and placed into the washer. Pots are emptied and the remains stored. I let the pots soak while I take care of the table. The scrubbing is easy. Done. Tidy. I head for the room. There she is with the mirror and eight lines. Time to get out of Dodge while I'm still able.

"James, you look like a bird about to fly. Does coke make you that fearful? If so, I'll stop."

"Does the expression *shitting my pants* indicate my state of fear? I took a crash course in the stuff years ago. It cost me my job, all my money and then some, myself respect and some friends. It was my fault. I'm petrified about being around nose candy. I feel like someone who is sliding down the razorblade banister of life, because that person was me and could be me again. You are an adult and free to whatever you wish. I have no right to tell you what you can do and what you cannot do. And certainly, I will never say, "I would prefer blah, blah, blah" or "If you care about me blah, blah, blah". That said, I also don't have to be in a situation or environment, causes me so much discomfort. I care about you, but I can't deal with that shit."

"Jimmy, my dearest. I am sorry for causing you this much distress. I don't need this. I can do with or without. Look, I am scraping the coke back into the vial vile. I care too much about you to let this get in our way. Okay?"

"Thanks Adriane. Did you hear yourself? You called me Jimmy. I like the change. What am I to call you?"

"Dree. And, Dree needs a hug."

I can't refuse this invitation. But, I am leery. The change from snorting to not needing the shit was too quick, unreal. More like the reaction of a junkie, who wants to control the push and the pull, the Yin and the Yang, the seduction and rejection. Control freaks are very dangerous because they have numerous hidden agenda, depending on what they want to control. This timing is not good. But, I've won a temporary stalemate. A moment to think through my next move. She walks into the bedroom to put everything away. I listen intently for a telltale sniff. She has gone into the bathroom. She can hide the stuff and take a few last lines all the while playing the role of the good guy. Am I paranoid or what?

"Let's go for that walk you promised. Better take a sweater or jacket. And, I'll grab a blanket from the closet."

We're off to see the wizard, the wonderful wizard of soul search. A male and female, a beach, and the moonlight. What could be bad or go wrong? The only trouble is my very recent brush with white death. Anxiety level is very high. My pulse rate is seventy-eight versus a normal for me of fifty-eight. My mind is telling my body about the potential danger and vice versa.

"That must have been terrifying for you to see me snorting. I appreciate that you did not have a cow. You have greater control than most people. How did you kick the shit? Was your wife hooked?"

"It was my fiend and my fiend alone. I had gotten to the point in my daily existence that nothing was higher or lower on my priority scale. Everything was the same. Nothing mattered but the snow. When I was high or in the toilet all things were equal. I could go to the bathroom, drive to the store, shoot the President, or eat a sandwich. They were all the same to me. Coke is like that. It is the number and equalizer. Life and death are the same. I could kill or let live. I could do another line or read my pornography collection. I couldn't get it up but didn't care. I was at the bottom. The end. So, I had to kick the shit."

"I kicked it the only way I knew how. Went ice cold motherfuckin' turkey. I truly believed I had bottomed out. Lost every piece of moral and intellectual fiber. Lost every shred of truth and value. So, I just quit. Threw out all the paraphernalia. Stopped talking to my dealers, notice plural. Avoided contact with fellow travelers. Began to work out, run, and lift. Took a shit pot full of vitamins and food supplements. Ate better and more. Went from 128 to 158 in nine months. Prayed a ton and was under a doctor's watchful care. Took no tranqs or levelers, no meds whatsoever. Was frightened of getting hooked the other way. That happens, ya know. No sense in stopping one insanity and starting another. The first days and weeks were sheer hell. Mind and body went into free fall. Flashes, bad dreams, the shakes, not twitches. Each and every pore of my body cried out in pain. And I suffered great fits of rage. I paced. Took cold showers and hot baths. Drank half the OJ gallons produced in the county. Thought I was turning a delicate orange color."

"All this time I had to be father to my boys. Terry was a teen and Two was a baby. The big kid knew, and he withdrew each day, I thought. He had school and the teen experience, his misery, which diverted his attention from my misery. I was there for him at every sporting event. I think that was all he wanted. In some strange way I think my failure and redemption was an almost healthy process for him to observe. Maybe he took strength from this reverse role model. He learned that failure, like success, is temporary. Failure does not kill. Not trying kills. His mother failed to try and Terry knew it. That is why he has rejected her all these years. One clean and sober parent was not enough to make a family for Terry. Or, maybe he feared his fall into the pit. Tainted by her failure. Two never let on.

I suspect his very developed perception felt there was something amiss. But, I was able to 'be sick' for weeks."

"*My* job drifted away. Who is going to keep a junkie on the payroll? As I got healthier, I realized we were in debt beyond my ability to ever it pay back. Bills had been run up while money was spent for My *Personal Idaho.* To keep what we could, we filed for bankruptcy protection, number seven. That is a maturing process. At first I saw it as an act of desperation requiring an incredible amount of paper work. There is a huge run and lift."

"There was a stigma attached to bankruptcy, or there was then. Gradually, I realized this thing I was doing was not illegal, but a right damn near guaranteed by the constitution. A fresh and clean start. In essence, I was mimicking the action of the founding fathers. They owed the King and all the other Royalty mega-bucks and said, *fuck you, we are taking a do-over that does not include you.* The King fought to protect his interests and he lost. Big companies have insurance to protect their bottom lines so no one loses. Besides it's only money. My counsel, Livingston Elliot, was terrific. A real street fighter. Once the papers were completed and filed, he told me to answer all calls and give the creditors the case number. Then hang up. I sent all notices for collection to him. I doubt if he answered any of them. The case was heard. I was one of twenty cases in the courtroom. The judge gave a canned speech, part understanding, part warning, and part very patronizing. *And that, said John, was that.*"

"Body intact and shelter protected, I sought employment. A true lesson in humility. My dad used to say that twentieth century man was driven by debt. I think fear is the engine. Fear of failure. Fear of success. Fear of not being loved by a spouse, your parents, your children, or friends. Fear of losing the love of the God that loves you unconditionally. Fear of losing everything. Fear of not being able to provide. Fear of not working. Fear. Fear. Fear. So, to cover the fear, modem man lies, invents and reconstructs. I would tell people I had been sick. This was more of a truth than they could have possibly imagined. I was looking to get back into life. I made the mistake of offering my services for less than their value. Desperation made me stupid and therefore, undesirable. I was a pariah. A leper at a licking contest. Even my friends, people I had trained, had nothing. In fact many of them did not even return my calls or see me. On weekends they avoided contact."

"This is when I discovered the five phases of job, and therefore life reclamation. Phase One: Relief of Stress—*I hated that job and I'm glad I'm out.* Phase Two: Blind Optimism—*I'll get a much better position with more potential. I'll show them what a mistake they made.* Phase Three: Honest Introspection—*What did I do wrong? How can I avoid repeating my mistakes? What are my best talents to promote?* Phase Four: Abject Terror—*I'll never get another job no matter how many interviews I have.* Phase Five: Employment—*I made it with the grace of God.* These phases are universal and eternal. If you have not yet been unemployed, you don't know. But, take these phases into your heart. You can't circumvent the process. You can't skip a phase. You must go through each one. The only mystery is duration. Only God knows how long each phase and the entire process will last. And, she'll never tell. It is a character-building process."

"Faith held me together. As I lifted ego from crushed to full-size, but not bloated, as my posture went from slumped to erect, and as my point-of-view improved from *I need* to *If the deal is right, I will consider it,* opportunities opened. The interviewing process became hectic. I had two or more interviews for a single position. Finally, I actually turned down a job offer. This was the culmination of the process and my return to male responsibility. Within a week the second offer was on the table. I took it and danced in the streets."

"With the job and commensurate income, I rebuilt. I never want to go through that shit again. I never want to be face-to-face with that demon again. This is a battle that I could not win. It would kill me. I choose not to die yet. Ergo, my reaction. Sorry for the loquacity, but I knew you wanted to know."

By now we are seated on the blanket facing each other. She has taken my hands. Our knees are touching. My monologue is at a whisper level. As I finish, she leans forward and kisses me tenderly on the cheeks, chin, and forehead, then brushes my lips. I see in her eyes a torment usually covered by the steel of control. The streams of tears reflect the off-white glow of the moonlight. She is not trembling or sobbing, just projecting with the hurt. She feels her hurt. Unfortunately, my hurt is so far behind my present existence that it is no longer mine. This was not intended to be a mind-fuck or a Vulcan Mind Meld. I just wanted to puke my rational guts out. The spear of truth pierced her heart.

"But you drink regularly and smoke weed. How do you manage that?"

"I'm not sure how the psycho-chemistry works. I like well crafted single malt Scotch Whiskey, fine wine, and a good beer. I can drink or not. And, I almost know when to stop. It wasn't always like that, but it is now. As for toking, I can and will, but I don't ever seek it out. Maybe I'm just mature. I know I'm older."

"Dree needs another big hug. She is chilly and frightened."

Why fear? She has made me an offer I can't refuse. We pick up and head for home. Holding hands. She snuggles against me. Sleep is instantaneous. No love making. Emotions are spent.

Old Man

Old man. Take a blow. Your ass is draggin'. And besides, I want you to watch how to really play this position. It's time for you to go to school. Two is coming in at the other corner. Nickie is coming in for me. I limp off the field. Cannot hide my pain or exhaustion. Coach yells at all of the first D to get to the juice bar. It must be one hundred degrees on the field and the only breeze I feel is when people ran by me. Even my lungs are hot. The perspiration has soaked through everywhere. Why the hell did we wear our dark blues? My legs feel like lead. The juice bar. A table with benches all around. On the table huge jugs of specially enhanced fluid. Not the brand name, but four times the power. They call it Saint's Blood. Color and consistency. Chilled oranges. Even three oxygen masks. I need it all, plus a couch in a darkened, air-conditioned room. The sun has turned my arms and neck crimson. Now I know the purpose of the sun block. The tingle in my left arm is almost numbing. The pain in my side causes me to list to port. Plop on the ground. Suckin' 20 deep drafts of H2O. Gulp Saints' Blood. Gnaw an orange. Rest. Rest. Lean on something. Then I hear "what's the matter, old timer, wiped out?" I flash the universal number one sign. Arise and head for the bench presently occupied by a few of the other defenders, heads bowed, and the entire ninth grade contingent staring blankly. I play, therefore I suffer.

I remove my helmet and look into the stands. Without my glasses, no contacts, and sweat burning my eyes, I can make out shapes and colors but not too many details. A few fans wave. The men are jealous, the women are curious. These are the moms of my teammates. Most of the moms are at least a decade younger than I am. A few of them look fine. They are just as fine as their daughters. Players stare at some of the moms just like they stare at the daughters. The hogs call them MILFs (Mothers I'd Like to Fuck). And they would. I suspect the mothers would like it, too. This is the age of massive confusion for both genders. Girls as young women. Moms as young women. Young studs as men and men trying to be young studs. The senior girls call some of the dads FILTHs (Fathers I'd Like To Hump). And they would. I suspect the fathers would let them. Visual and mental groping, but never touching. *Das ist verboten.* At least, if the groping becomes common knowledge.

There it was, bigger than life, which, of course, it was not.

Banker kills two, self!

Stan Denners has no name, only a profession. The details were as lurid as the omissions. It seems that Stan came to the farm rented by Benton Dreisch. Carol Bardo was there, working late with her new boss. Stan, for unknown reasons, entered the house and shot both Benton and Carol. He then turned the 9mm Glock on himself. The bullets were *pre-fragged cop killers.* Teflon coated destroyers forbidden outside the military and law enforcement. They can eat up Kevlar vests, the ones cops wear. When inside the new host, the bullets spin out of control, they sprawl, cutting jagged, irregular paths through everything, bouncing hither, thither, and yon. They can enter the upper chest with a down leftward trajectory and bits and pieces will exit at the groin and upper right quadrant of the back. Because of their bizarre and plundering behavior, the kill rate is 99 44/100 percent pure. If not dead, the innards are so chewed up that surgeons are helpless to save the victim.

To ensure success, Stan fired three shots into each of his targets, two in the trunk and one in the head. The exit holes in the body were the size of softballs. Each head was missing a large portion. Carol had no jaw. Benton had no eyes and nose. Stan shot himself through the roof of his mouth and lost the entire back half of his skull. The master bedroom was the abattoir. Blood and body bits all over the floor, ceiling, and four walls. Bone fragments in the drapes. Brain goo on one wall. I learned later from the police that Carol and Benton were naked when killed. In fact, the bed was drenched with their co-mingled blood. Soaked nearly through the mattress. But they were draped over the bed as if they had fallen on to it from either side. When he died, Stan was sitting on a chair at the foot of the bed fully dressed, except for his shoes. Perhaps he had finished the orgies, surveyed the carnage, and politely got dressed in his best business suit. Then put an end to it all.

The bodies were found by Benton's housekeeper when she went to change the sheets for laundry day. Her call to 911 was unintelligible due to the screaming and broken English. Somehow the gendarmes arrived before the video bloodsuckers. This gave the constabulary enough time to cordon off the drive and wrap the house in the oh-so attractive yellow crime scene tape. All the cameras recorded were body bags and a State Police Department spokesperson, Captain Foley, recited the usual: names, addresses, unknown assailant, nothing concrete, lots of loose ends, et cetera, et cetera. No reason to follow the meat wagon. I can find out what I want from anonymous sources, the Medical Examiner and a Police Sergeant. The autopsy revealed that there had been lots of lovemaking immediately prior to the killings. The coroner found a lot of semen in Carol. Different places. Was not sure all of this could have come from one man. Did Stan participate? Was he first or second? Did he watch when he was done? Did he interrupt then join? Did he initiate? Just don't ask. The gun belonged to Stan. Bought in Pike County. The bullets, the cop killers. Where did they come from? The police were mum or just didn't know. Sometimes it's better to bury the mystery with the bodies.

This minor incident at the farm sure put a crimp in the bank merger. The joining of Orange Grove Bank, Farmer's Trust, and Second City Trust was in serious jeopardy. Many thought it should be called off. Lots of top level hush-hush meetings. Fed and State regulators. Directors of all three banks. The remaining hired guns moved to town. Mucho late nights and off-sites. As the oil burned and the brains churned, no money was earned and the financial institutions and their activities slowed to a crawl. The poor *schlubs* who had their money in any of the three black holes could withdraw it or leave it. And it was protected by insurance. But people get scared easily when their money is threatened. Advertising and promotion campaigns abounded. The three mergerettes struggled to keep afloat. Competitors tried to scuttle the three. Offers of bonuses and free services were the norm within two days. Offers and counter-offers. The three might have joined Neptune if regulators had not stepped in to reassure everyone that life was sane and happy days were just around the comer. It sounded like the Great Depression.

Stories leaked or were leaked. The three banks were ready. One institution was too weak. There was a cash trove waiting to kick start the new bank. The cash was being withheld. It was off the table until the wrinkles could be smoothed. The proposed President and Chief Operating Officer was in the morgue. The Chairman, Chief Executive Officer, and all four Executive Vice Presidents were in place. They just needed a dynamic leader, not a cold stiff. More wheeling than West Virginia. More dealing than Vegas.

A week after the two murders and suicide, the bank ran advertising that announced the new entity, Central Bank and Trust, the officers, locations, and services under the campaign of *Trust the bank Central to your life*. They introduced the new head man, Harv Garner. Fresh from Memphis with connections to Lansdale via his parents and grandparents on both sides. Hometown boy makes good and returns to apply his expertise to a very dicey situation. I hope it all works.

Linda and Brent Denners were stoic through it all. The funeral was closed coffin. The Catholic Church, for a substantial donation, allowed the requiem. Over six hundred people. Biggies and the inconsequential. Old timers and the newly initiated. Friends and foes alike. After the folderol, the two Denners settled in behind the walls of their gated reserve. Brent went to school. Linda stayed home. No socializing.

Lots of time and space to rebuild. I understand Linda did not get Stan's complete piece of the pie. She'll just have manage on three-point-three million. She was about to sue when the bank's lawyers detailed some information that she did not want flashed to the unwashed. She had very few long-term expenses other than Brent's college and normal living. At a crummy eight percent, she was assured of two hundred and fifty grand per year. The yacht and Stan's other toys, the XKE and Bugatti, *et cetera*, were put on the block immediately. Rumor had it that disposal of all the toys netted her one-point-seven million. That would be another hundred thirty-five per year. Certainly enough to struggle by. All she had was the house and two cars. Linda wanted to wipe the slate clean before too many people read between the lines or paid attention to the rumors. She had to reinvent herself. Not an unattractive woman, just not a stunner like others I would like to know, biblically. The gardener of ten years moved into the guesthouse. He was a rugged, handsome man of limited education who loved to be around growing things. He was kind and gentle. Devoted to Linda, Brent, and the estate. Maybe the inventor needed an apprentice. For sure the bear got closer to the honey pot.

Spin classes are less fun than having root canal work done on three teeth at once. At least you know the Novocain will reduce some of the pain and the pain will only last for twenty minutes. A spin class lasts one hour and the agony has a death grip on your body for about three hours. Enervated, not invigorated. On a stationary bike, you start with ten minutes of rapid, flat land pedaling. This becomes intense uphill pull work for fifteen. Cool down for five. Slow pedaling. Stand with the resisters at near lock for ten. Then full tilt in the downhill mode. Cool down for five. Stand with no resistance for ten. Flat out motherfucking race to the goal. All of this is lead by a little wisp of a thing in a strangely color non-coordinated suit and a damnable microphone. She has done this for years and could do it in her sleep. Her yelling is thought to inspire. I damn near expire. All the macho studs in their dripping wife beaters collapse off the circular racks of pain. I can't walk. The Hettie Green of the exercise world just bounces off to the next event.

I don't dare sit. Legs will lock-up. Can't walk, no strength. Even standing still causes cramps. Limping through the floor doesn't draw stares or looks of sympathy. This is good. If I wanted compassion, I'd go to the Red Cross. Without my glasses, every body is in soft focus. The hard-edge outline of biceps, pecs, and nipples are vaguely apparent. Sweat and sex, an intoxicating combo. I smile occasionally, but don't know anyone. There are not many people here my age and certainly no one of my social circle, or is that a rhombus? I think if some sweet young thing offered to take me home, bathe me, spoonfeed me and fuck me until death did us part, I would have to demurely decline her offer.

I'm sure that this is a meat rack, just not for me.

I can see and feel the results of my program. It's been nine weeks. Started twice a week. I needed a lot of time for my body to heal between sessions of torment. Week three, I was up to three times. A little running on Sunday. Week six, four times. Week nine, five times. All the time increasing my weight and reps. Of course, I started at very low levels to avoid tearing muscles irreparably. I just couldn't lift more than a paperweight. Arms, shoulders, back, neck, legs, and stomach. This latter is of paramount importance. A guy can have a shitty body, but if his stomach does not bulge or is flat, he is acceptable looking. At least that's what I was told when I was younger.

Each of the major areas is broken down to sub-groups, biceps, triceps (three different points), forearms, wrists, grips. Pulls, pushes, lifts, up, down, sideways, curls, bends, squats, ad nauseum, maximum nauseum. Fluid replacement between every set and every exercise. Learned to take a bottle to be refilled at the fountain. Then there is running. As far and as fast as I can. Started low and slow on days I was not lifting. Now I spin or stair step. Weight loss has been marginal. I was hoping for twenty pounds. So far it's ten. My goal may not be attainable, given my bulkamania. But, I'm happy. Besides I have a time constraint. What a copout.

After each evening at the gym, I spend half an hour in the sauna or steam room. Have been told this will help prevent stiffening. So far this benefit has not been realized. I still wake-up with some muscle group sore. At the very best, tender. The good news is that the rooms are co-ed. The bad news is that I am so tired and without my glasses. I can't focus in on anybody, and if I could, I wouldn't be able to do anything about it.

Who is Mike Stewart and why is his name stuck in my brain? Adriane's foreman. There I go with the possessive. How can I look into Mike without anyone knowing that I looked? John Feber. John and his family own a chain of high-end food stores throughout the state. Never many in one county, but each one is located in or very near the best neighborhood. That is part of their strategic planning. Another part is to own the shopping center that they anchor. Each center is home for numerous high-end or niche shops, clothing, housewares, pet supplies, and always the state's leading drug store. The total volume per store is on the low end for the industry, but the profit per square foot is the gold standard to which all other chains strive. John would know how to do deep, deep research on a person. This is a mandatory step in the hiring of key store personnel.

John and his wife, Heather, are beautiful people, physically, socially, and emotionally. Both of them are tall and slim. For me, at five-eight and one-hundred eighty-five pounds, this is a source of envy. Jewish guilt, Catholic shame, and Episcopalian envy. John is handsome, blond, lean and mean. Heather, black hair, aqua eyes, and fair skin is the personification of the word, slink. She doesn't walk. She glides. This is easy when she is indoors with a long dress or skirt. You could almost believe she has on roller blades. But she can glide or slink across the lawn in shorts and sneakers. I've seen it or I wouldn't believe it. It's not sexual or provocative; it's just a great event to observe. Their four children, nicely spaced thirteen months apart, have not taken the expected toll on the faces and bodies of the parents. On top of all this they are funny and nice to know.

John sits on the Board of Governors at Saint Sebastian. He was instrumental in securing a scholarship at the school for Two when I really needed it. John knew I was in the pits, no money and few prospects, and the teachers told the board about Two's contributions and academic achievement. After reviewing my financials, he pushed for Two to receive one of the two full scholarships. He reached out and helped me as no one else could. For that I am eternally grateful. Nothing has ever been spoken, but I learned all this from Billy Ray, who, I'm sure, seconded the motion. I am honored that they would go to bat for Two. Now I must ask for another favor. This one of a lesser value. My phone call gets right through. It's nice to be known.

"John, thanks for taking my call. I'll be brief. I am trying to uncover some factual history about an individual, and I need a source for the information. Do you know of someone who could help me dig?"

"Jimmy, it's nice to hear from you. I hope all is well. I won't ask the object of your inquiry. The firm we use for background checks is Southeast Information Service, Inc. When you call, ask for David Ellis, he is the man. The company's telephone number is 1-800-852-6097. Is there anything else?"

"Thanks for the name and number. By the by, how are Slinky and your children."

"Slinky, as you call her, is fine. The girls are getting to age of realization and that's scary. They both look like Heather, er, Slinky. I'm not sure they can glide yet, but they are beginning attract boys like flies to honey. John and James are just rough and tumble boys. Scrapes and bruises, tears and howls of laughter are the norms. They have ties and jackets. I know, because I paid the bill. They live and sleep in Saint Sebastian golf shirts and torn khakis. I dread the day all four are driving. Do you know where I can buy four Sherman tanks, two pink and two blue? Speaking of two; how is he? What did I hear about you and football? Have you slipped off the edge or simply jumped?"

"John, please. It's something I really must do and besides I will be providing a new football field and stadium, so your boys will have a showcase. Think of it as my contribution to your sons' athletic future. I really appreciate your guidance in the matter of background checks. Give my best to Slinky. Love ya' both."

Immediately, I dialed S.I.S.I. Mr. Ellis was there. I introduced myself as a friend of John Feber and outlined what I needed. Mike Stewart. Presently employed as foreman of the Simon Ranch in Pike County. No younger than forty. I didn't know if he was Mike or Michael or if he had a middle initial. David allowed that he could get a preliminary search with outline information within a week for one hundred and fifty dollars. Once I felt we were on the right path, he would do an in-depth report. Two weeks and two hundred and fifty dollars. Because I was a friend of Mister Feber, I could pay after each stage. I agreed and gave him my work and home numbers.

I also called Alan Carson.

"AC, how goes the brokerage business?"

"Well, Jimmy B. How you be?"

It never fucking changes.

"AC, I'm looking for some information and have come to the font of knowledge. What do you know about Adriane Simon and her real estate empire?"

You could have heard a feather drop. The silence lasted for five seconds or so. But it seemed like a minute.

"What do you mean, Jimmy?"

"Never answer a question with a question. I mean she owns all that land in Pike County. I know she has been buying up adjoining property in Hills County over the past years. I know she has been presenting to and talking with various county commissioners both here and there. I know she has been fighting with the road and sewage guys in both counties. What I am looking for is who is on the other side and how close is a deal?"

"You know what I know."

Silence.

"Bullshit. I know what is visible. You know what is invisible. And I need to know what you know. The stuff that only you could know, oh, broker that you are. And besides, you owe me. Remember last year when I spoke to Judge Dranger for you? Remember that really awkward issue with the three girls at your apartment? How old were they? Fourteen? Thirteen. Now, what do you know?"

"Okay. Okay. But it's just between us. Adriane has been in negotiations with out-of-towners, who want to buy up everything. The agents say they want all the land and all the rights. Unfortunately, I believe there are more than two parties negotiating. My company is set on building twelve communities, four gated and eight open, six ownership and six rental. Horse stables and a fox chase. Two of the gated communities will require a minimum purchase of ten acres. Lots of lakes and a big-ass nature preserve. There will be two golf courses, three strip centers, gas stations, a foreign auto repair plaza, and a huge mall with three department stores, all the chic shops and a Cineplex, even its own post office, water system and electrical co-generation. It will be fantastic. I know this sounds corny, but it will be much bigger than Sunshine City. Self-sufficient and for everyone who has big bucks. Adriane stands to become one of the wealthiest women in the entire country. We're talking hundreds of millions to her, a bug chunk of it up front. And here is the sad part: she has no one to share her wealth. Or does she?"

"Alan, how could you be so presumptuous? I hardly know the lady. I mean I've only seen her a few times."

God, I was stammering and blushing.

"Thanks for the information, my friend. Let's see. If Adriane gets, let us say, five hundred million and you pick-up one-half a point, your take will be—why Alan, you'll be rich! The more she gets, the more you get. That's a good incentive for you. The scales are in balance. My lips are sealed."

"Jimmy, you now know more than anyone and you have the ear of a principal in the negotiations, pillow talk and all that. I would be very interested in insider information and could reward you handsomely. My group needs to know if there is or are others bidding on the boodle. This would give us a real competitive edge. And, my group would be generous. Shared information leads to shared wealth. You know *quid pro quo*. There is enough to go around, you know."

"What information do I or can I have that you would want? I don't know what you're talking about. Adriane and I are just friends. I don't understand farm management and she doesn't understand marketing communications. We exist in mutually blissful ignorance. Thanks for the pleasant chat."

"Wait, I could really use what only you can learn. How difficult would it be to inquire and remember, I need people, dates, facts? How would you like a quarter of a million?"

"Hope to see you soon, AC. Maybe at the Spring Jamboree at Saint Sebastian."

"I have no interest in high school athletics."

"Well, see you soon, goodbye, my friend."

Nothing can piss off a wheeler-dealer more than an opponent who quits when he is ahead or before the wheeler-dealer can win. Happy with his gain and not interested in more. But, the big guy wants everything and refuses to accept or comprehend how and why the little guy just walks away. This is the leverage the little guy has if he uses his head, because now the big guy is driven by the twisted emotion of greed. I got AC by the shorts and I twisted. He knows it and hates it. I just don't give a fig. Sometimes the winner is the one who doesn't care to do battle.

*   *   *

David Ellis called and needed a fax number for the single-page report.

Name:	Michael R. Stewart
Occupation:	Foreman—CreteEnterprises, Ltd.
Time:	1990-present
DOB:	07/16/40
Married:	Yes
Div/Sep:	No
Spouse:	Marta Minnig
Children:	Two sons
	Robert (26) Ethan (22)

Previous Employers:	Southern Trucking Corporation 1989
	Department of Agriculture 1982-1989
	Pike County Construction 1976-1982
Education:	Pike High School, Class of 1974
Military Service:	Honorable Discharge 08/18/76
Misdemeanors:	None
Felonies:	None

Parents:	William L. Stewart	Gwen House Stewart
Siblings:	William L. Stewart, Jr.	Harriet Stewart Jameson

I called David and asked what more could be found in the in-depth report. I was interested in newspaper clippings, occupations, and histories of parents and siblings, etc. I was not really sure what I was searching for, except, perhaps a connection to Adriane Simon other than his employment. He would dig deeper. Much deeper. Much, much, much deeper.

AC calls. This must be my lucky day. Wants to talk more.

"Jimmy, what do you want?"

"What do you mean, Alan?"

"I mean what will it take for you to understand how much I need any information you can get for me?"

"Alan, I've told you before I can't in good conscience be your mole." Good conscience, that's a laugh. The last time I had a good conscience, Kennedy was president.

"But Jimmy, I could make you financially independent. Say, one-half a million with one-quarter reported and one-quarter in a bag. All I ask is that you think about how much that is and what you could do with that much money."

"OK, I'll think about it. OK, I thought about it and no thanks."

"You little shit, you're holding me back from a killing."

"Listen, AC, your take is more than you're worth. I say that as a friend. And, while I appreciate your interest in sharing your wealth with me, thanks, but no thanks."

"I've never taken no for an answer."

"That makes me feel special, your first *no*. Like popping a cherry. Should I have a cigarette? Maybe just a nap. As thrilling as this monologue is, I must bid you *adieu*. See you soon."

Click.

Doubled his price so soon. Not a ploy for the man in control. He must have a budget above and beyond his take. Money that is his to use for informational purposes. He must be desperate. Is the deal soft? Does he need a bigger edge? Does he need all that money? He'll be back. How much can I squeeze from him and still rationalize my deed of deception? To use his owns words: *If you can't fuck your friends, who can you fuck?* But, be careful not to get sucked into a trap. Don't get too greedy, or react too fast. Play a coy waiting game.

This is my weekend with Two. Do something special? The beach? A camp out on the beach? Not for him. He likes his stove-cooked meals and comfortable bed. When you're young these are not pleasures, they are essentials. Pick him up in an hour. We'll do a movie and chili tonight. The beach tomorrow, early. Well, early for a teenage boy on Saturday is about ten. I'll push for eight and promise not to stay the day, just through lunch.

More Oxygen

My legs tell me it's not time to stand, yet. More oxygen. An ice pack on my neck. It's a damned inferno even on the sideline with the fans going. All the other D team is flushed red. Someone told me I looked pale and should stay seated. Deep coverage is called. It's time for Saint Peter to start throwing. Glad I'm not the one chasing the wideouts all over the field. Try to yell in my vast five down experience. Two looks over to the bench or to me. I motion to the wideout's eyes. Watch the eyes. He looks where he is going. Two nods. He understands. Wideout takes off like the rocket for whom he is named. Two is stride for stride. No bumping. Pass is on the way. Wideout turns and comes back. Two doesn't anticipate. Takes three extra steps before he tries to come back Ball is in the hands of the wideout when Two arrives. Reaches in and pulls his arms down. Digs his pads into the receiver's back real hard. Ball pops loose. Receiver slumps to the ground. No steps, no catch. No wonder Serrano wants Two on the other side for the Panthers.

The Spring party is on the lawn of the Mayor's mansion. A true political feeding trough. Ins, outs, used-to-bes, wannabes, and those who can create, or think they can. Some from the Kiley guest list. Many more from the *nederland*. Old school, new school, and no school. Big money, small money, and contributors of time.

The women are decked out in their spring cum summer finery. What will be worn later is previewed today. Sundresses; the order of the day. Some boat neck, some scoop, some high collar. Body shapes are not readily apparent, but there is plenty of wiggle with the giggle. Big hats with ribbons. Designer shades to Raybans to *Cheap Sunglasses*. White shoes, beige slip-ons, yellow sandals, flats, half heels, full heels, but no spikes. Lots of glitter. Pearls, pearls, pearls. Except for the big diamonds on the wedding fingers. Mommy obviously dressed many of the girls at once. While the costumes have a similar look, the differentiation is quality, blends versus one hundred percent cotton versus silk. Big pearls versus department store pearls versus Mikimoto.

The male of the species can be found attired in tan, not white, slacks, a blue blazer, pink, yellow, or light blue shirt and a contrasting tie. Slip-on Guccis, Ballys, or Churchills. A few Topsiders and tennis shoes. No socks. Black-banded watches. Gold watches and wedding bands, except for the unmarried. Again the differentiation for the males matches that of their partners in the sun. It's all financial. The difference between personally tailored clothing, Ralph Lauren, and S&K Men's Store is readily apparent.

The party started at three. The bottom feeders were here at three-o-one. The shrimp and lobster trays were ravaged by four PM. Finger sandwiches are untouched, cooked canapés also. Most of the first beer kegs are gone. There are others. Wine and liquor bar not frequented by this group. They will gobble and swill their fill. This is their meal for the day. Hopefully no fights. But, hot sun plus booze plus politics equals trouble for many of the thick necks. It is a universal formula. Language is no barrier. At a scream level English, Italian, and Spanish take on a strong similarity.

I hear the beginnings of a brouhaha near the twin oaks by the driveway. Something about public housing and police profiling. Men are speaking in loud voices. The conversation has turned from de facto to ad hominem. Territorial imperatives are in full swing as voices become deafening. No touching yet. Other men of a similar build—squat—and ilk move in to ensure peace. The squall passes. It will be like this for the balance of the time that these people remain at the party. The dilettantes don't cotton to brawls or screaming arguments. They suppress their social anger only to let it boil over on the tennis court, golf course, or at the office. We sip and nibble while the heathen guzzle and gobble. They yell. We lock our jaws and whisper. They point fingers. We stare.

The music is upbeat early middle age contemporary. Not rock. The group is available for parties, weddings, and bar mitzvahs. Not suitable for the younger set. Alan and his movable financial feast are standing under the tent near the bar. Where else? He seems to be shepherding two strangers. Both are overdressed. Not unhandsome. Very stone-faced. Hanging on AC's every word as he spins his tale to the Deputy County Commissioner, Tax Collector, Property Assessor, and their wives, girl friends, or both as mixing and matching is a permissible sport. This is show-and-tell time. Alan will show his new, out-of-town friends who he knows and tell everybody of the glorious future his new friends can create. The trainer is debuting his charges.

Adriane and I are outing. Everyone can now speculate in public. The whispers will abound and become a tumultuous hiss by Monday. She is absofuckinglutely beautiful. Her sundress is not a print, but a sheer yellow crème lace over silk. Filmy cover for a body that makes me go weak every time I am with her. The outlines of her breasts and nipples are visible. Her buttocks bounce in her rhythmic gait. The thong bikini underpants are almost noticeable to my eye. Dress, panties, and shoes. That's it. Her smile and eyes are not hidden by a hat or glasses. She is the real deal. There is not a male eye not focused on her, and I mean all three eyes. Wives are not envious, just appalled at their husbands' pubescent behavior. There will be pointed conversations about the husband's gawking when the couples get home. Maybe even some good old fashioned screaming about "good enough", "love me", and "my body." Wives feel only a little bit of safety in the fact that Adriane is firmly attached to my arm. Her eyes always come back to me and mine to her.

As we enter the tent, Alan becomes nervous. Could it be that he wished Adriane were not so close to his protected procurers? Does he think they will try to cut a deal and cut him out? Ain't the politics of business grand?

"Adriane, you know Alan Carson, Joe Rantoleoni, Juan Hebert, and Bobbi Rivera? Hello, my name is James McCaa. And you are?"

"Ralph Castor. Steve Troy." Aha, Blackstar Ltd. Very big money developers. These are the players, or preyers. And Adriane has or is the coveted prize. "Let me introduce Miss Adriane Simon."

"How do you do, Miss Simon."

"It's nice to meet you, Miss Simon."

Boy, are they cool. Not a twitch or hint of recognition. Alan is beginning to sweat. Nanny, nanny, pooh, pooh. He's in trouble.

"What brings you to Lansdale, gentlemen?" Adriane is just as cool, although her smile is a wee bit phony.

"We're exploring possibilities to expand our business."

Steve, you liar.

"And we're looking for land to build out. Mr. Carson is helping us in our search."

Steve just let the cat out of the bag.

"Well, you're in good hands, gentlemen. Mr. Carson knows of every available parcel of land in the area and all the right people with whom you should talk."

"You're too kind, Adriane. I am just a small town broker."

Alan, you bullshitter.

"Excuse us, will you? I must talk to Mr. Garner about a personal matter." She is center stage and working the audience to a fever pitch. We shake hands all around and walk to Harv.

"Harv, do you have a second?"

A second! Harv has a lifetime for Adriane. I've heard that she owns as much as eighteen percent of the stock of the new-used-to-be-three-in-one bank. And the bank, in one of its previous incarnations, funded much of her ranch's expansion. Who owns whom and who owes whom are the multi-million dollar questions. And, to his credit, Harv understands that he is not in control, because no one person is in control. He just tries to keep the ship off the shoals.

"Adriane, nice to see you again. I see you are properly squired by the fabulous Jimmy B."

Thank God he is not a loud asshole.

"Is there any news on the K-4 matter? It's been two weeks since we met with them."

Adriane's voice is louder than a "personal matter" would warrant.

"Yes, they got back to me. Not what I thought was in your best interests, so I bounced back to them. They are due to respond by Wednesday. I hope to be able to come to you then." Now even Harv is speaking for audience.

Alan and his two associates were hanging on every word. I smile at AC. He grimaces.

Over to the bar for drinks. All this business bantering is stressful. Balvenie and cold water, tall glass, no ice. Two times.

"Jimmy, why is it that I get the feeling you are observing me? You're here but not with me. Is there someone else who has struck your fancy? Perhaps a teenager?"

"Dree, I am with you and you alone. I just don't understand what you are about, or who you are today. What is going on between you and AC? Who are his two business associates? What do they have to do with you? What is K-4? Why is Harv involved? Did I miss anything?"

"Why, Jimmy, you rascal. You see all and hear all. I'll tell all at the appropriate time. Now let's pay our homage to the politicians and exit stage left."

She slides over to the Mayor and the City Council members, who are huddled at a table beneath a huge oak.

"Gentlemen, don't get up. As usual, your party is marvelous. Thank you for inviting me. I look forward to seeing all of you very soon."

Again, she is posturing for AC's benefit. Is she a bitch or what?

"I, the omnipresent escort, thank you also."

We exit stage left.

"Dree, you are a piece of work. The rumors about us will be overshadowed by the very big bombs you detonated around Alan, his buddies, Harv, and the city fathers. Good screen. Good cover."

"Don't flatter yourself, Jimmy. Today you are an accouterment. That's what I want everybody to see. The business shenanigans, the less than subtle hints, and veiled threats were also planned. I am sure they worked. So be on your toes. Over the next few days you will receive calls from Alan, the two gentlemen and, perhaps members of the Council. They will want to know what you know about me. They may try to convince you to spy on me. They will probably offer to bribe you. Tell me when this happens and I'll explain what to do and why. Be a dear and do as you're told."

"Dree, you're trying this head-game shit again. You've set me up to be a foil. Or is that fool? I won't do anything without knowing why. So, if I am contacted, you'll know only if I choose to tell you. The contact, what they ask, and what I tell them form my leverage, my strength. You are not the only one who can play the info game. I ask you what I'll ask them, 'What's in it for Jimmy B." The ball is now in your court."

We head back to the beach house in silence. The pronounced and prolonged silence lasted until Sunday. Once back in my own apartment, I feel strangely safe. If I don't answer the telephone, I can control the tempo of the game. AC is up to one million without any prodding. What is the next step? How high? Who will take it? What can I extract from the Council members or the Mayor? Be careful, very careful.

The phone rings. I ignore it. I may be the only adult male who still has a land line, but there is some measure of security in the answer machine.

"Mr. McCaa, this is Mr. Rantoleoni. There are some matters I would like to discuss with you. If you have some time, call me. At home or tomorrow at my office. I'm in the book."

That is a cold bath. I need information before I return the mystery man's call.

"Jimmy, this is Alan. What the fuck was that all about? Call me, now."

Back to the message.

"Mr. McCaa, I am Executive Assistant to Mr. Troy and Mr. Castor. They would like to meet with you over dinner, Tuesday. The Blue Heron Club at six-thirty. If you can't make it, let us know. Otherwise they will expect to see you then."

Three for three. God that woman is good. When she yanks chains, grown men groan. Each of the callers will want the same thing, just different roads to the treasure. I was right.

Rantoleoni was curious about how much I knew of Miss Simon's business plans. I tell him nothing. He was obviously calling for the Mayor. If the Mayor wanted to know, he could call me. I would tell him the same thing I told Rantoleoni.

AC wanted to go fishing for a few days. Talk. Get reacquainted. I set aside time for next weekend, after my dinner with Castor and Troy.

Dinner will be a hoot. The Blue Heron is a restaurant masquerading as a private eating club. You need to make reservations. And they have an unlisted number. They only take reservations from people who know the land line number. This keeps out the riffraff. The food is good, but not to die for. The booze quality is unmatched in the area. The service is superior. The price is obscene.

The valet parks my car at six-fifteen. The boys are waiting. Smiles all around.

My Balvenie arrives without a request being issued. Their red wine has been poured. A ninety-one French Merlot. It ain't no screw top.

"Gentlemen, this toast is for a pleasant and productive evening. Now, it's your call. How can I help you?"

"Thank you for the toast. Ralph and I just felt we should get to know you better. You seem to be someone of influence in this market. Someone who might want to benefit from our efforts. We know so little about you, Mr. McCaa, and we want to remedy the information deficiency."

"Since I don't know what you know and therefore don't know, I don't know where to begin. So why don't you tell me who I am and I'll fill in the blanks? Fair?"

"Steve, I told you he was direct and not devious. Let's order. Then we can talk uninterrupted. What do you suggest, sir?"

"The fish in any form is always good. The meat is okay, but the pasta is not that good. I think I'll have the Grouper *en papier*."

"Taking your lead, Shrimp Jambalaya. Sounds tasty. Ralph, how about you?"

"Well, I'll be the rebel and have the twelve-ounce filet."

The waiter saunters away with our order and knows not to hurry back.

"Mr. McCaa, we know where you work. About your failed marriage. Your children. And, your relationship with Miss Simon. We know where you live, bank, and shop. Now tell us what we don't know about you. Tell us what makes your engine rev."

Bam! Nothing like the hot seat and the truth meter to spice up an evening.

"Let me cut to the heart of the matter. My relationship with Miss Simon is in its I don't-know-where-this-is-going nascence. I see her. The Mayor's party was the first time we ventured into public scrutiny. But you know this, I'm sure. Other than that, I won't fuck and tell. What do you want from me as it pertains to Adriane, Ralph?"

"We would like information about Miss Simon's aspirations, her business plans, and her relationship with Central Bank and Trust."

"Why ask me, Steve? I can only assume that Mr. Carson is unable to provide the desired information. I'll tell you this. He has already asked. And I turned him down. Now you are asking. So my bet is that you asked him to ask me and when he came back empty handed, you decided to take matters into your own hands. Is there a time crunch? The nearer you get to your deadline without valuable information, the weaker your position will be. Am I getting warm? Hot? Are you guys up against it?"

"Mr. McCaa. We are only curious, as any good business group would be. We may want to conduct business with Miss Simon and knowledge of her plans might prove profitable to us. We seek information and are willing to reward the person who provides it. There, that's simple, isn't it?"

"Ralph, you are asking me to spy on a lover. Frankly, I don't give a damn about what she wants other than during our time together. She is who she is and I know not anything more than that. Why don't you ask Adriane directly? Or would that be tipping your hand? I'm not very good at subterfuge, and pillow talk is the worst source of corporate secrets. Hookers have tried for centuries to learn trade and country secrets. We all know about Mata Hari and a few others. We don't know of the millions who have failed and died violent deaths."

"Mr. McCaa, we could give you a list of questions or areas of interest and you could probe them when you deem it appropriate."

"Ralph, is what am I saying unclear? No. No. No. But I do know something. I know that you are frustrated because you can't break through the corporate veil or find your way along the maze of interconnecting corporations. Has she built a real labyrinth? Ain't that a kick? A small-town girl ties the big-time players in knots. I'm sorry, I just can't help."

"Can't or won't?"

"What is the difference, Steve?"

"The former implies an inability, while the latter implies an unwillingness. And we can help the unwilling become willing."

"Is that a threat or a promise of riches beyond my wildest expectations, Ralph?"

"It is whatever you want it to be or both."

"Well, this is what I want. I want it to be a promise. Because I don't take kindly to threats and you are in my sandbox now, gentlemen. This is not New York or Atlanta. This is Lansdale. The home of Jimmy B. I may be a very small fish in your sea, but many of my friends are sharks. In fact, a few of my friends may be friends with your friends in New York. And they are as protective as I am territorial. So, I know that you meant it as a promise. A promise of something for services rendered. You meant it as a promise, because you would not be foolish enough to threaten me. So, thank you, but no thank you for the promise."

"Mr. McCaa, we do not take refusals lightly. Ralph and I can ensure that your information will be kept in the strictest of confidence. For a few points of interest, we are willing to pay a half a million dollars in cash."

"Shit, AC beat that offer all hollow and I turned him down just as cold. So unless you want to talk about the weather or fishing prospects this weekend, I bid you a pleasant evening. Thank you for dinner."

The drive home was uneventful. The message light on my phone was a harbinger of interesting conversations. First, David Ellis. Then AC. Then Steve and Edie, I mean Ralph.

Ellis wanted to meet and review the Stewart file. Suggested lunch tomorrow. Noon at Wendy's north of the city. Paged back and confirmed.

"Jimmy, what the fuck are you doing? Dinner with my guys behind my back. They told me what you said. This is not good for our friendship or business dealings."

Alan was nervous. Sweating howitzer shells.

"Alan, listen. They called the meet. If they choose not to tell you in advance, that's their business. But, I suspect, because you guys are up against a deadline, your inquiry and their blustering is a rendition of good cop, bad cop. A coordinated effort to extract the desired information as quickly as possible. So, fuck botcha, or all treeya."

"Jimmy, these guys are for real and what they're offering Adriane is sweet. But she is being evasive, coy. Disclosure is not her long suit. We know she owns the land we need, but we cannot prove it. There are so damned many companies that own companies that own companies that own land. Farmers, ranchers, and growers work land that is not theirs outright. But no one is sure who owns the land. They pay rent. The rent goes to several holding companies, which are, in turn, held by very private companies. Central Bank is involved just about every step of the way. Involved up to its axle vault. All legal. But they're blocking the path. We've got so many middlemen in this deal it's tough to see the sides. That's why I, we, came to you for help."

"I'll bet there is another offer on the horizon. Do you have the first right? Now time is running out. Your offer is X and you fear the other offer is X-plus. Adriane can sell all at once as one huge vista, like the guys did in *Whoreland*. Or she can break-up her holdings, sell them a parcel at a time. She makes more money doing the latter, but is very time consuming and contains a real element of substantial risk. Your guys make more money doing the former. Adriane wants only the biggest dick. Who has the biggest dick? You guys, or a new stud you fear? I'll bet she even leaked some parameters of the other offer just to cause penis envy. She is holding two johnsons and applying pressure. That must hurt. If the pain gets too great your guys will walk and you'll have invested a ton of time and, maybe, money for naught. Am I close or what?"

"My guys will play rough if they have to. We're not sure who the other player or players are, but we know you can find out for us. We just need a name. We also have to penetrate the bank. Harv Garner is an enigma. We can't reach him. He avoids me as if I am a leper. We know he is very leery of the regulators, feds and state. His skirts are clean. And he really controls the other officers. They won't or can't talk about anything. If you could help us there, it would mean another quarter."

"AC, let us stop being henny-penny for a moment. What you're asking me to do is physically possible, just not emotionally so. I have too much to lose if Adriane were to find out I was the source of information leaks. Threats do not work with me and you should know that. Check New York. I'm sure you and your guys found I was a stand-up guy. I was and can be trusted, by someone who never forgets a favor. So, cut the bully crap. Besides, what you're offering is chicken feed."

Bam!

"Jimmy, let me talk to my guys and get back to you."

Instantly I call Steve. If Alan stops to think about what he will relay, he is the second call they will receive.

"Steve, this is James McCaa. Call me Jimmy."

"Good evening to you, sir. Thank you for returning our call. Let me tell you why we called."

"No, let me tell you of my conversation with Mr. Carson. The conversation he is calling now to relay to you. Tell him you'll call him back. Listen to me. Then you'll know if he is telling you the truth. He spelled what you want, why you want it, and even offered a hint of violence. Lastly, he sweetened the pot for some side-bar info. I politely told him no. I will not be threatened. I am protected. I will not get you what you want because I do not like the concept of losing what should be mine. And Adriane would cut me and it off in a nanno second if she learned I was in her bed then yours. I'm not even sure I could get what you want, if I wanted to cooperate. So, gentlemen, that's that."

"Jimmy, we need as much information as we can get in a number of different areas. Mr. Carson has been very productive up to this point. He seems unable to wend his way through this complex maze. We need a trusted guide, and we need one now. We checked you out, both here and in New York, and you seem to be the man for this job. We are willing to pay Mr. Carson his finder's fee and send him away. We will have an excess cash situation, which could answer your needs nicely. You do have needs, don't you? Will you help us?"

They are up against a big, big, big wall. Time and a better offer are creating a severe obstacle to their success. There is a twinge of urgency in his voice now. Is that real or a sound show for me? They know they can't threaten me. Gino would not permit it. If something happened to me, Bill and Two could go to Ralph and Steve's funeral the day after mine. Except their event would be 'closed coffin' due to the disfiguration. AC must have called at the same time as I did. Another line. Relayed my hint for mo' money. Now they are willing to cut him out. This deal must be bigger than AC has let on. And he has to know he has jumped into bed with vipers. That's why he is leaning on me. His offer includes what they told him to offer and something from his cut. He gives up a little and gets a lot. Comes out a hero by not going over budget. Good boy, AC. Except, they are going to use much of what he thinks is due him. Poor bunny, AC.

"Gentlemen, I will say this slowly for the last time. I cannot and will not be of assistance. Thank you and good night."

*　　*　　*

David Ellis loves Wendy's salad bar. A real gourmet. If I remember accurately, my son Terry had to pee in a Wendy salad bar to pass his fraternity's initiation. Oh, well. David, as he prefers to be called, hands me a manila envelope about one-half inch thick. As he scarfs the salad, I leaf through the papers. There are notes on all the boring details of a person's life: children, church, civic clubs, house photos through the years (The most recent abode is really nice. Too nice?), and auto ownership (trade in every three years, trade up every six). A very complex formula for estimating income and net worth for the past ten years. Wow!

"David, are these numbers accurate? Income of seventy-five thousand and a net worth of two million? He has no mortgage. That's real good for a farm foreman. Too good. I notice his net grew upon a base established about seven years ago. Must have hit the lottery or something."

"Mr. McCaa, you will notice that his monetary value began to increase when he went to work for CreteEnterprises. Before that, his best year was twenty-eight thousand."

"David, am I reading this properly? His brother, Bill Junior, is the Sheriff of Pike County."

"Has been so for twenty years."

"What a treasure! I'll pour over this packet of good-and-plenty later. I'll call if I have any questions or need additional information. Thanks for your help. Here is the check. Bon appetite."

Peace after work. Pour a Balvenie. Pour contents of the envelope on the kitchen table. Begin to sort through, stack, and summarize. Both boys went to church schools in the county and private colleges. No debts. A Land Rover and the big Infinity, his and hers extravagances. One vacation each year, three weeks far away. House is thirty-six hundred square feet at the end of a cul de sac in the high rent district. Four credit cards. No balance on any of them. The man lives large. Further scrutiny confirms his trip on the gold yellow brick road began in '02. He went from Department Of Agriculture to CreteEnterprises. Nice bump in income. Bigger bump in lifestyle. Better house and cars. Each year thereafter, his income rose in the double digits, and the first one was never one.

What is special about '02, or maybe '01? Newspaper articles about little league, Kiwanis, County Fair. Mike and family were all 'round good people. Good 'ol country homies. Just rich and getting richer by the year. Very curious article about an auto crash involving a gasoline tanker. Killed passengers. Man, wife and two kids. Robby Windor. That was not his wife. Name of driver at very bottom. Mike Stewart only one to escape unscathed. Why is this important? Is there a cause and effect? Why would Mike be involved in the accident? Accident my ass! Bam! Bam! Bam!

Murder. Who? Why?

Dree. She was tired of supporting the philanderer and the philanderee and their habitual snowy spit-filled excursions of pleasure. How was it arranged? Why did no one dig to get the real answers? She and Robby were just fine on the outside, so no one would investigate the grieving widow. There had to be someone covering up the details. If Mike was the perp, was there a go-between? Doubt if he could have approached Dree out of the blue and volunteered his services. Had to be someone who knew them both. The Sheriff, Bill Junior, the brother. I wonder if his fortunes have blossomed since '92 as dramatically as Mike's. Note:

Call David Ellis for in depth probe on William Stewart, Sheriff of Pike County.

If it this true, it is frightening, but it could explain a great deal. A woman scorned, death, greed, and payoffs. It sounds like a Shakespeare play or a book from the bible. If I can learn this, who else can learn it? This could be Dree's Achilles heal into which AC, Castor, and Troy hope to shoot an arrow. I doubt if anyone in the city and county governments knows a damned thing. They live in the public eye and could not hide what the ill-gotten gains would buy. Harv must know something. What? How much? Another Balvenie and a deep sleep.

Abused Body

*L*ife is slowly returning to the elder's abused body. The little lights blinking before me are few and far between. They come back in a rush when I bend or move my head too rapidly. My steps are more fluid, less measured. The ice pack on the back of my neck is working. The 'Blood" seems to be replenishing my muscles. I still need a nap in a cool place. That would be to admit defeat. Kids are up and pacing. I begin to yell at the D. Telling Two to be careful of the sweep when they are strong and motion his way. What a strange formation. Power his way. Motion away. Wideout attacks the slides to QB takes hand-off, fakes to fullback and hands to motion man. Yell to stay home look for reverse. Far side end takes hand-off from motion man. Deep loop in the backfield. Tackle and guard have pulled. Two is outside and behind them. End tries to follow interior linemen. Two steps in. Gets bumped by the tackle. Pushed deeper. Tackle turns up field. Two steps up. Grabs the end, who is in full flight. Holds on for dear life. Near-side backer comes to assist Two. Both linemen are unaware of the development behind them. Two holds as Brandon kicks the shit out of the ball carrier. Folds him in half backwards. No flags. Brandon and Two head butt. Body of 'deceased' receives attention from his coach and trainer.

This is my weekend with Two. I pick him up from school. At seventeen, how humiliating it must be to have a parent as your ride. He never lets on. Always happy to see me. He knows his crew thinks I'm crazy and they love it. I am a breath of cold air in the humidity—laden atmosphere of their lives. I am what they wish their dads were more like. Not entirely, just a little. Maybe twenty-five percent. He is kind to my not too subtle efforts to be around him. He knows I am always nearby, always there. We decide to dine at moi maison. Pasta with basil, oregano, much pepper, and extra virgin olive oil. Extra virgin is an incredibly interesting concept. I thought virginity was a "yes or no" and that there were no gradations or degradations about it. Maybe it's all new age. Parmesan cheese, diced green, yellow, and red peppers, and sliced chicken breast (gently sautéed) added and tossed before serving. Bottled water for me, Diet Coke for him.

He really likes school. Is struggling with Honors Biology, bored with Honors Latin, and loves Expository English. Can get away with writing feelings. Not unlike his old man. No judgment except on clarity of message. Wrote a risqué short story, which he did not have to read in class. He dodged a bullet. Or maybe the teacher did. Got a note from Miss Rosi about his imagery and description of perception. Has dated numerous times. At Sebastian, dating is seen as a group event. The parents see it that way. Like schools of fish, the teens move in unison. No leader, no followers, no lovers, just opposite sex friends trying to understand growing up. Well, I'm not really sure about the "no lovers." I am willing to bet a quarter (that's the biggest bet I make other than the one dollar in the Kentucky Derby pool) there is a lot of experimentation that goes on for months. I say this because I have seen how they hug and buss each other. I have seen the longing looks. I have seen the glances. I notice the noticing. The extra tight volleyball uniforms and wrestling singlets. Boy, has the pre-mating ritual changed in thirty years! Where the hell have I been? It wasn't like this when Terry was at Sebastian. Or maybe it was and I was unable to notice. What I remember about Terry's era and Two's experience now is a lot of talking about classes . . . sports and classes. Not grades, but test scores. Hopes for colleges. It seems somewhat bizarre to me. The chase is hidden from the closed eyes of parents. It's a different source for adrenaline rush, but he is happy and the kids are the best. So his male parent is ecstatic.

He's tired and heads for bed after some inanity on the box with one eye. I stay up reading the file that David sent by messenger. Bill Stewart. By golly, his income shows no bump except for the yearly raises approved by the county government. But, there seems to be some strange financial paper trail for his wife, Margaret. She has three offshore accounts, two in corporate names and one personal. The corporate names are combinations of the names of the children, Sarah and William. The disguise is too thin. Money had been moved from both the Farmers and Orange Banks. No more accounts there now. That is interesting. Or, is it? There is a portfolio in Margaret's name, mutual funds and an annuity, which take monthly investments of three thousand dollars. She is obviously stashing every penny of her School Administrator's salary. They live on his salary and they live OK. The kids went to state schools. Both were there at roughly the same time. A cash drain but not crushing. Love to know how big the offshore accounts are. All three started in '92. The family has been hiding money since the crash. As the County Sheriff, Bill must have been familiar with the Simons and their land. How familiar?

The newspaper clipping tells me that Bill was the investigating Sheriff for the fireball special. He is the man. Adriane came to him with a dirty-deed need. Could he be trusted? Why trust him to begin with? Money is a good way to engender and reward trust. And she had money. He worked out a plan and found a driver he could trust. The contact for timing and location was made through the chain of command. She did not want to know how. Bill and Mike worked out the specifics over the weekend. She called Bill on late Sunday afternoon. He immediately radioed Mike. The tanker was loaded with fuel and driven to the spot of the accident. I would love to find where the tanker was loaded. Perhaps the farm or a supplier to the farm. Who sold Mike the one thousand gallons? Not important, but a detail that intrigues me. The tanker's skid marks were very evident. The truck was parked, not flipped or jack-knifed as one would expect. Mike exited the tanker. He was out of the truck five minutes before the vehicle arrived. Robby, doing sixty-five in a thirty-five zone, never had a chance. Darkness, rain, curves, and booze make a deadly combination. The bad guy and his snow sweetie were executed and the innocents were sacrificed. The Sheriff investigates but knows the answers to the questions before he asks them. So he does not ask any questions that might expose the very dirty truth. He even coaches the trucker. People never thought about the connection between Sheriff and driver. This sort of familial link is common in rural areas throughout the country, whether urban or rural. The Sheriff is beyond reproach unless he flaunts the benefits of his evil deeds, which he will never do.

This is what I feared. Now to determine Harv's involvement, if any. That can wait until Monday. Sleep is the order of the day. Check telephone. Blinking light. Retrieve message. It's Billy Ray. Call back on the private line in his study.

"Hey, big kid, what can I do for you."

"Jimmy, two rumors need to be clarified. First, are you really going to play in the game against Saint Peter? Second, what the fuck is going on with you, Adriane Simon, and Alan Carson?"

"Yes I am going to play, and you'd better be there to see me shine. One last shot at glory, ya' know. One last climax of the eternal urge of youth. As to the second, whatever do you mean?"

"Whatever I mean is that I have heard that Adriane is involved in a massive land deal that AC is brokering, or trying to. Probably fishing both sides of the stream, and you somehow hold cards that Alan and his associates want to see.

"Let me guess, AC called and asked you to help unblock a logjam. Did he tell you that he offered me a million for my help? Did he tell you that he and his associates are playing a good-cop-bad-cop routine with me? Did he tell you I've said no to all three of them? Did he tell you why I said no?"

"Yes. No. No. No. Why do I feel like a violin played by the maestro. Tell me what's happening and it will end there."

"Billy Ray, if I tell you everything, I'll have to kill you. Or at least expose your fondness for small barnyard animals. You may want to do us both a favor. Tell Alan that we spoke and I said, no thanks. Give my best to Jeannie and the initials. Have a pleasant night."

AC, you can't circle a turning man.

Saturday morning. Two and I go for a run. After showering and breakfast. He decides we want to go to the mall to check out the new clothes. It's interesting. He loves to look but won't buy a thing until the sales. He has learned the value of money. The highland frugality is real. The shopping time gives us an opportunity to giggle and tease each other. I can flirt with the females, shoppers and clerks alike. He feigns embarrassment. I know he is checking out the same shapes I am, and, simultaneously, my moves. Teacher and student. After two hours of nothing we head for the beach. A little sun. A little surf and then back to the bright lights of the big city for a movie. On the return drive, I decide to stop in and see Dree. Realizing this is out of the norm, I still proceed. The back entrance is easily accessed by climbing the stairs. We do so without sneaking or noise. The door is unlocked. We enter and listen. Conversation is coming from the big porch on the side that faces the Gulf. We head in that direction.

"Dree. Jimmy and Two just stopped by to say hey."

Up she leaps. Comes to the sliding door and stands in the middle of the doorway with her hands on her hips as if to shield us from the outside or vice versa.

"What are you doing here? I thought I made it abundantly clear that you were not welcomed on certain weekends. I'm sorry Two. I don't mean to be rude, but your father and I have discussed this numerous times. I am not throwing you out; it's just that you can't stay. I have company."

"Mommy, who is it? A bad person?"

Boom!

"Mommy." Who said that? Where is the child? Beyond the doorway and on the other chaise lounge. A person stands, very tentatively walks up to Dree, and hides behind her. Behind her skirt. This is not a small child. This is a woman. Somewhat younger than Dree and looking exactly like Dree.

"Mommy, who are these men? Aminnette is afraid. Don't hurt Mommy or Aminnette. Mommy, make them go away. This is my time. I want one not three."

This woman child is now clutching Dree. Holding very tight around the waist. Dree looks sad, confused, and angry. Aminnette looks frightened as if her life were interrupted by a threat. I had not meant for this to happen. I never want children to be frightened. Children are gifts to be nourished and fear is not nourishment. You can see fear in their eyes and hear it in their voices. Fear is an ugly emotion. I don't want Dree to be frightened. But the secret is out. I'm just not sure what the secret is.

"Dree, I am terribly sorry. Forgive this intrusion. Two, let us exit stage right."

He turns. I turn. We leave. Back in the car, looking straight ahead, he asks, "Dad, what the hell was that all about?"

"I'm not actually sure. I think a deep, dark, family secret was just exposed to the bright light of reality. The woman in front of us was Miss Adriane Simon, Dree. I've been seeing her since Christmas. We see each other on the weekends I'm not with you. I wanted her to meet you. I thought an informal drop-in visit would be the best way. The woman behind her is Aminnette Simon. Historically assumed to be Dree's sister. But as we learned today, Aminnette is Dree's daughter."

"From here on it is speculation, so bear with me. After Aminno, Dree's brother, died, Tecer and Hapapise Simon went into seclusion and raised Aminnette. As we now know, any belief that they were raising a "late child" was incorrect. Now the question is who is the father? Three possibilities come to mind immediately, Tecer, Aminno, and Mister X. I seriously doubt if it was Tecer. Hapapise would have killed him on the spot if he had committed incest. Hold the thought of extreme violence. Who's left, Aminno or Mister X? My money is on Aminno. The family resemblance is too strong to have been diluted by some outside genes. Inbreeding also produces deformities, physical and mental. Aminnette has been in a home for all these years. She is not balanced. Fits of animal-like rage. Limited cognitive capacity beyond the basic personal functions."

"Now, if Aminnette belongs to Aminno and Adriane, she may be the reason that Aminno died. Was he put to death? Remember the violence thought. Parental righteous wrath and revenge. Which of the parents? My bet is on Hapapise. Greek women are less prone to forgiveness than Greek men, and her temper was well respected throughout the two counties. If all of this is true, or directionally so, it explains the connection between the family and a certain elected official. Or, maybe the elected official was the father and Aminno did die in a farming accident, or was killed by our Mister X. There are many loose ends to tie-up before I can be absolutely positive. I can't go into all that at this time, but I will later."

"Dad, that's more than I wanted to hear. And certainly more than I can comprehend. It seems as if you have placed your hand in a tank of piranha. Don't ask me to retrieve your shortened bony appendage. Can we drop this story of incest, murder, and high crimes and move to something more pleasant? Like dinner and a nice terrorist-world-destruction movie. I love you, but this latest episodic horror is not part of my life with you."

Dinner at a local steak joint. Two loves and needs red meat. At his age, it's a necessity. At my age, it's a luxury. In the movie, the good guys saved the world and we went to bed before eleven.

Church tomorrow. I am the verger. 'An attendant, who carries a verge (rod, staff, or cross) before the clergy.' In the sixteenth and seventeenth centuries this was the individual who made sure there were no animals, animal waste, or assassins in the path of the clergy as they approached the alter. The verger was perceived as being between the clergy and the non-cleric folk, between heaven and hell. Dealt in garbage, feral and human. The verger is rather like humankind today, between heaven and hell. Does that make the verger the first human? I open the church and make it ready for the services. Start the coffee, regular and decaf, for the parishioners before and after services. Turn on the appropriate lights and sound system. Unveil the altar. Place the bulletin boards by the doors. Place the flowers on the altars, main and chapel. Get collection plates from the sacristy to the ushers' station at back of church. Insert hymn numbers in wall panels. Ensure bulletins are available for distribution by ushers. Plus any special needs of the day determined by the clergy. All of this is accomplished before seven-thirty AM. I love it. It is a way I can give back to the people and institution that kept me afloat when I tried to sink myself. I ask for no recognition. I serve. Then I attend the service. No music, just the essence of my faith. After church, the papers, a gallon of decaf, and *noshing*. Very often a brief nap. One to four hours.

Two attacks his homework while I slumber. And, as always, the quantity and quality of the assignments are monumental. He has about four hours of solid don't-interrupt-me-now-dad work. We finish our respective tasks at the same time. Go for a run. Shower and throw in a video rented last night. A light meal and then to his mother's. The shortness and regimentation of the day do not satisfy my need for closeness.

I have learned something about Sundays. One cannot take a seven-hour nap, as from ten AM to five PM, and still go to sleep at a decent hour, say ten PM. Yes, I do love my sleep. For years, I was unable to take any naps or to go back to sleep once awakened. I had the most horrific dreams, nightmares. Many of the usual ones depicting lack of control, rejection, abandonment, for which I railed against my parents in extensive and extended psychotherapy sessions. It was not their fault. They were not, are not, evil. I am who I am because of me.

The one dream that really scared the shit out of me was the one involving the black shark that was land mobile and growled in the most sinister fashion. It seemed to follow me everywhere. The last episode was in a beach hotel with French doors that opened off the massive lobby to the porch and then the beach. The hotel was old, not seedy, just old and dimly lit. I was pursued down the stairs, passed the front desk and into the shadow encased, leather chair, couch, and thick oak table, and brass-reading lamp lobby. I tried hiding behind a gossamer white curtain on one of the doors. I was outside. It was inside. I failed to disguise my presence and the growling black menace found me.

When I turned to confront my deepest fear, it dissipated into the sudden sunlight. I awoke in sweat and slightly trembling. But my anger was gone. Certainly not forever for I am a Scot, fucked over by the English for centuries. Anger will always be with me. But, the death of the black shark placed anger in its proper perspective. It drove me no long.

★   ★   ★

The message light is on. It's Castor. He and Troy want to meet. They are nothing if not persistent. Maybe I can head this off with a call. I am tired of their circle jerk.

"Hello, Steve. Listen I'm tired of this masturbatory game you guys are playing. We've discussed this issue and I'm still resolved. I cannot and will not help you or AC by spying on Adriane. So, there is no need for us to talk further." I can always hope for more money and less visibility.

"Mr. McCaa, we do not wish to talk. But, we can help you become wealthy, if you will cooperate. Let me leave you with this thought. Your son is well schooled, athletic, and very handsome. He lives with his mother and sees you on alternate weekends. I'm sure he is the apple of your eye. Your living and loving relationship is very important to both of you. Think about how important it is. And how you would feel if something went wrong. Let's say if the relationship came to a tragic end. You should do everything in your power to protect and preserve the relationship. To protect your son. Good night, Mr. McCaa."

Those filthy rotten motherfuckers. They've just gone too far. Fuck with me, but don't ever, ever, ever touch my kids. This is now war. I'll call Gino. He'll know what to do. Who to talk to. What to say. Hope he has the same address and telephone number as six years ago. Long Island.

"Hello, Gino? This is Jimmy B in Lansdale."

"My, my, my. How long has it been? Are you well? And the family? How are they? This is a pleasant surprise. What's the occasion?"

Always the family niceties before business. We must be vague in our conversation in case anyone who should not be is listening. And, they always are.

"The last time we spoke was six years ago, I think. During the summer. We talked about baseball, your passion, my boredom. This was right after Gina was married to Tommy DeStephano. How has that union progressed? Are you and Maria grandparents yet? You and Maria were headed for a three week vacation. I am well. Indeed, I am terrific. I am divorced. Never been happier. Freedom from the shackles of a bad marriage can open the mind and soul. Terry is grown and moved on to Minnesota. He works for an healthcare marketing company. Married. Two daughters. He says he wants to retire before fifty and work with kids. Not sure the workaholic will be able to leave the race. Two is still in high school. Lives with his mother. I see him on alternate weekends."

Thus the Q and A session is completed.

"I just wanted to ask if you know Steve Castor and Ralph Troy. They have asked me some very personal and pointed questions about Two and my relationship with him. They stressed how tragic it would be if something befell Two. These guys claim that we, they and I, have mutual friends, and that you are one of the friends. I never met them before they came to Lansdale. Seems they are working on some sort of enormous land deal with a friend of mine who asked me to help them. Unfortunately, I can't be of assistance in the area they wish. But, for the sake of relationships, you and me and Two and me, I want to extend them all the courtesy they deserve. I know you would want that."

"Steve Castor and Ralph Troy. The names are familiar, but I'm not sure I can place them. Permit me to do some digging. If they are friends of friends, so to speak, we should help them in every way possible. Even go out of our way to help. It was strange that they asked about Two. It sounds like they are up against a wall and are becoming desperate. Maybe I can help enlighten them as to the importance of Two's well being and safety. I'll get back to you. Let's see, it's now seven-thirty. Can I reach you at this number? I'll call you back before midnight. Oh, yes I am a nanno twice over. I look forward to an amicable resolution of this matter with you and your child."

I wish I could sleep. But that's out of the question. Maybe booze and some insipid movie will help numb my brain. If I don't think, I'll be okay.

Have no idea how long I've been asleep. The bottle of Balvenie is empty and there is a different movie on the box, *LeMans* starring Steve McQueen. The ringing of the phone continues. I was wise to unhook the answering machine.

"Jimmy, this is Gino. I did my due diligence. It seems that Mr. Castor and Mr. Troy are friends of a business associate of mine. They handle his investments. My friend was unaware of their unusual interest in your child. He felt it was improper for them to take such an interest. He did ask that if you could help them, you should. But, if you are unable to help, for very good reasons, and he and I trust your judgment here, the two guys should not put the father and son relationship in jeopardy. My friend will express his wishes to Mr. Castor and Mr. Troy this evening. He appreciates you and me bringing this to his attention. There is no need to thank me, Jimmy. Just sleep well and tomorrow give my best to Terry and Two."

So there! Do not fuck with my children, ever! Hell hath no fury as a Scot who has endured the intentional injury of a child. Two is safe. Now the big question is should I call Steve and Ralph and verbally piss on their shoes. Nah. That's already been done and they, by now, know who squeezed the bladder.

*   *   *

The morning comes too soon. Never enough sleep after an emotional and alcohol-filled evening. The drive to work seems more pleasant despite my hangover. Hell, even dealing with the petty princes is almost enjoyable. Call the Sheriff of Pike County and ask for some time in the evening. Personal time, not business time. Seven-thirty in his office.

The Municipal Building houses the Sheriff's Office. Bill is in his private suite. There are, perhaps five other officers working in a large, open area.

"Sheriff, it's very nice of you to take the time to see me this evening."

"I've been asked by some business associates to learn as much as possible about CreteEnterprises. We've dug through all the available records. You know financial, legal, real estate. The published stuff. We've spoken to their customers and suppliers. All the obvious bases have been covered. Now we're looking for some special insight. Anything that you might know or people who we should talk to would be of benefit to my associates."

"Sir, if I may, for what purpose are you seeking this information?"

"I am not at liberty to discuss details, but CreteEnterprises is in negotiations with several companies for a huge business deal. I have been retained by one of the companies. They are looking for an edge in the negotiations. Anything. Any little thing at all."

"I don't think I can tell what you don't already know. Maybe if you tell me what you already know, I can confirm or refute it?"

He asked for it.

"Well, we notice that Mike Stewart is the foreman over at the farm. And, that a Mike Stewart was the driver of the tanker that was involved in the crash that killed Miss Simon's husband and children. We noticed that you were the Sheriff who led the investigation into the horrendous event. What we were wondering is if the two Mike Stewarts are, in fact, the same man, and if you are related to them or him?"

He did his law enforcement best to hide his emotions. But with each step of the way, he became a little bit more serious. He was reacting in reverse. I noticed his jaw was clenched. But, he didn't blink.

"Mr. McCaa, the two Mike Stewarts are one and the same. Mike and I are brothers. Is there something wrong with that?"

"No, Sheriff, there is nothing wrong. So far, so good. But we also noticed some very interesting financial facts. Mike's income and lifestyle have enjoyed very substantial increases each year since the accident. And we noticed that your wife has three offshore bank accounts, most likely fed by her income as School Administrator. Yet the two of you live as if her salary was spent here, in Pike County. While there is nothing blatantly illegal about the finances of either your brother or you, what we know causes us to ask if there are any connections between you, your brother and CreteEnterprises that go beyond the apparent. And if these connections could negatively impact any business deals presently underway."

He is cool. He must know I am hinting at murder, blackmail, and conspiracy. He just smiles faintly and stares at my forehead. Then I spot the small drop of sweat as it begins to run down his right cheek near the ear. Gotcha!

"Mister McCaa, I'm sorry but I can't be of any help. So, if you'll excuse me, this is my bowling night. League Championship tonight. The Sheriff s Department against Slaymaker Lock and Frame. I can't miss it."

"Well thanks for your time, Sheriff. Oh, and good luck. Hope you roll a three hundred game."

The bomb is ticking. He knows that I know. He has to defuse it before it explodes and destroys all he has worked to create, all that he has hidden from scrutiny for years. I have stepped in harm's way. And was wise to carry the micro-recorder. Now to dupe the tape and send copies to appropriate people, Billy Ray and Livingston Elliot, for use in case of an accidental death—mine. Giving my protector and lance carrier an advanced warning as to what I suspect and where I am going with it will be my life insurance policy.

Call at work from Alan. He wants to talk. There is real desperation in his tone. Meet at his house at seven. Somehow his place seems grander than I remember.

"Still livin' large, AC? You've expanded the porch and opened the living room. Added a huge pool and cookout area. The video surveillance system looks very pricey. And is that a Bentley short in the driveway? Nice. Very nice"

"Balvenie and water, Jimmy?"

"Thanks. Now, what is the reason I'm here?"

"Look, I'll get right to the point. I need your help and I need it now. No fucking around. Just help me. I've got a great deal of financial motivation to make this deal happen. And happen very soon. I can not let it go to any other guys. If I get nothing, I'll lose everything. Can you fathom that, me lose everything? I've got guys calling in notes. I can't cover the markers without this deal. If the markers are not covered, I could be in a lot of hurt. So I am pleading with you. I'll even make you my partner, fifty-fifty, you'll get what I get. And the faster we can wrap this up, the more I get. My guys have really deep pockets and would be grateful."

"Let me repeat this very slowly. No. I can't. I think I closed any window of opportunity I might have had. I did something very stupid. Not even sure Adriane will even talk to me again. Second, your guys just got peed on. They did something even dumber than I did. Their parade was golden showered because they threatened to fuck with my kid. I know they will not be amenable to my involvement. So their deep pockets cannot help me, or you and me. If we are to remain friends, you must never raise this issue again. Notice I am not finishing my drink. That may be a first. I am leaving. Good night and good luck."

Harv Garner left a message for me to call his private line by eleven AM tomorrow. Jesus, maybe I should get all the players in a small room with baseball bats and have them Louisville it out. I'll deal with the one who emerges. Harv wants to do lunch at the bank. He will not leave base. What a coward.

I arrive at noon. Lunch will be in his private office, which is off the one the public sees. I suspect the placed is bugged and video intensive. Maybe he has tapes of managers and hookers or small barnyard animals. Too weird. No cocktails. Iced tea. This is the South. A salad, not seafood. Fair sized piece of mystery fish. Dirty rice. Okra. Fresh rolls. Cuban coffee. Mints for dessert.

"It is nice of you to come to my office, Mr. McCaa. Or is it Jimmy?"

"That depends on how well we know each other and the topic of our conversation."

"Let's be friends. Call me Harv and I'll call you Jimmy. Jimmy, there are many rumors swirling around about your involvement with Miss Simon, Mr. Carson, and his associates. More pointedly, the rumors concern a supposed business transaction. As Miss Simon's personal banker and her friend, I just want to help her. To help her, I must have very detailed knowledge of all that is going on. Facts, not rumors. So, I am asking you to help me help our mutual friend. Tell what you are doing and what you know."

"Nothing and nothing. Adriane and I haven't spoken for over a week. I did speak to Mr. Carson last evening. And I'll bet all the cash in the tellers' drawers you know the results of that conversation. As for his associates, I haven't spoken to them for a few days, because we have nothing to discuss. Now let me tell you what I do know. This bank is up to its ears in the deal. Adriane owns a large piece of your pie. You and the bank stand to get rich if the deal goes through a particular way. However, there is a chance that the deal will not go your way and the deadline is upon you. I don't give a damn who does what to whom, except to my children and Dree, Adriane. I have a deep emotional interest to protect her. Much different than your interest. 1 don't give a damn if she is rich or not. So, if I knew anything that might pose a threat to her, I would tell her and no one else. I'm sorry you wasted your lunch on this fishing expedition. Now, I must get back to work."

"Jimmy, Jimmy, why the hurry?"

"Mr. Garner, I leave because there is no reason to stay."

*　　*　　*

Drive to the beach. I'm seeing Dree tonight. Just a break in the routine.

"Dree, at the start, let me apologize for my intrusion into your time with your daughter. Please understand that I meant no harm. I just wanted you to meet Two. And I promise that whatever I saw or learned has been forgotten. That said, I must tell you that the past few weeks have been like an inquisition. Everybody wants to know what you are going to do, with whom, and when. Alan Carson has become a driven man. He calls daily. His queries have become more pointed. He has pleaded, offered a bribe, and been the good cop to his associates' bad cop. His associates have offered, lied, and threatened. Harv has wheedled and smarmed. But all of this activity, directed at me, is really directed at you. Selling out our relationship is not something I'll do."

"Jimmy, I forgive you for arriving unannounced last Saturday. You never knew. How could you? Aminnette is very dear to me as was her father. She can't be in public so she lives at the home and I take alternate weekends as ours alone. It has not been easy for me to balance the weekends, yours and hers. But, I love her and will never share my time with her with any one. And, I think I love you, too."

Boom. Bam. Bang.

Love me. I had hoped for that and feared it at the same time. I'm not sure I can make a commitment like that now. But I can't afford to lose her. She is my retirement fund in spades. Dree is my very personal 401(k) plan. Save love for a later discussion.

"I told you you would be contacted by interested parties. I also asked that you tell me when they contacted you and what they discussed. Now, tell me everything asked of you.

I gave her a sanitized version. Just enough dirt to make it seem real. Just not the whole truth.

"That's it? That's all? There must be more. I can't believe all those powerful men only asked you to spy on me."

"They are all very nervous."

We passed the next few hours discussing the details of when and where the questioning took place. It was like a cat and mouse game. I got the feeling that she already knew of the answers. Maybe even directed some of the questioning. For sure of that from Harv. I told her more about our meeting than discussions with the other interested parties. Why was she testing me? Was she just being a big time bitch? Or just using me as I hope to use her? Power and an inflated ego go together, and we had both. She used me as a fuck stick. Now she was just using me as a real stick. Beating on the bad guys or just the guys. We are means to our own ends. Ain't relationships grand?

Real Pain

---

*N*ow the pain was constant and intense. Cannot stand upright. Muscles all cramped on left side. Must stretch. Bend and pull. Bend and pull. Reach front and back. Reach front and back. Do I look stupid to the fans in the stands? Lie on back. Lift legs. Get other player to push legs back. Full stretch. Now upright. More Blood and oxygen. Two looks like he is ready to blitz or just roaming around lost. They call a forty-four cornerback special. Both corners blitz. Safety tracks wideout. If two wideouts, other is taken by linebacker that side. Tough to disguise this switch. Middle two linebackers must concentrate on runners and keeping the QB looking forward. One wideout. Two still meandering. Inches forward. At snap, sprints toward a spot. Head up to spot blocks, runners and target. QB fakes handoff and happy-feets it to pocket. Can only be three receivers, Wideout, tight end, and swingback. Swingback gets behind Two. Linemen pull. A screen. Can Two get to QB first? Linebacker on Two's side is Ben. Hog of hogs. Spots screen and charges through linemen to swingback as ball leaves QBs hand. Two is too late. He leaps. QB throws high and soft. Ball and Ben arrive at swingback at same time. Ben does not get the ball, but he gets the man. Swingman loses helmet. Ball bounces on ground.

"You are going to get your ass handed to you. You are going to hurt so much you'll wish Doctor Mengele was your dentist. Not just the muscle aches. Deep-joint-excruciating-can't-move-your-shoulders-and-hips pain. Bruises will be nothing. Your lungs will burn. Feet will weigh fifty pounds each. Vomit will become second nature to you. And, when the day is done, you will find it difficult to pee because there will be no fluid in your system. Your vicarious life will equate to extreme agony."

"Okay, Two, now tell me how you really feel about my upcoming experience. No sugar coating. Let me have it straight."

"Dad, Alex, Ben, Brandon and I will give no quarter. We will hit, stomp, twist, smack, punch, gouge. Run into, over, and through you. You are about to embark upon athletic hell. This is when we figure out who will want to come to the big dance, the Seven-Day Invasion, in August. We weed out the wimps and wannabes. Only the serious survive. They will stay for next season. Welcome to my world."

"Since I don't get any quarter, what do I get. Dollars?"

"If you survive, you will earn our respect. That will be your pay. All who stay and play share in this pot of emotional money."

"Let me tell you. All your posturing is fun, almost funny. I've reworked my body, endured the tortures of a workout schedule from hell. I am ready. I can take whatever you guys can dish out. I'll run beyond you. Out think you. Do my damnedest to stop you. Remember, as my mother used to say *Old age and treachery will beat youth and skill every time. I* am older than all of you kids and very treacherous. So you watch your ass, young fella."

"Okay, Dad, now that we have growled and postured, pounded our chests and thrown bones in the air, let's eat. I am famished."

Meat, pasta, salad. A meal fit for warriors.

Monday was easy. Playbooks. General discussions of major dos and don'ts. Uniforms. Weigh in. Time trials, twenty yards, forty and one hundred. I was slower than the deer, faster than the hogs. Strength tests. Stronger than the deer and a wimp next to the hogs. Bench, press, and leg lifts. Better than Two. The time and weight levels would be checked next week. Progress is the key.

Tuesday began with passion. On the field by three-thirty. Full pads. Very uncomfortable. Bulky. Blocking and tackling drills. The right way is the only way. The other way and they get away. Start on the dummies. Then everything is for real. The first hit is most bizarre. Everybody laughs and encourages. The wimps begin to show their color, ashen then yellow. The hogs are real hogs. Dirt, sweat, profanity, digging, and grunting. Physical exertion over pain. All of us in between must make a decision and effort to move one way or the other. Chicken or killer. What a choice for teen boys. Everybody blocks and everybody tackles. Sometimes I win. Sometimes I lose. All the times I feel it.

Then we move to the lineup. Defensive dummies are set up. Players stand behind them. The offense walks through plays. Offense is the more difficult. The slowest to learn. Defense is faster. Less complex. Or, so I'm told. Since, many of these guys go both ways, this is a double dose of learning. The system does not change from year-to-year. A few wrinkles each year, depending on the talents. More passing one year, because the QB can throw. More end runs and off—tackle traps the next year, because there are two speed burners. And so it goes.

Practice ends and I must run two miles. I hate laps. Extra time in the weight room. Wednesday we begin to hit for real. Lots of grunting. Groaning. Some screaming. A few go down. Usually these are underclassmen. If they get up and return to the battle they will have earned self-respect and the respect of their peers. We are divided into offense and defense. For now. First teams and second teams. Coaches admonish that nothing is set in concrete. We can move up or down based on performance and team needs. I have reached an agreement with Coach Lewis. I will play only defense.

Number one offense will run plays against us. We have chest pads. This is a walk through that slowly turns aggressive. Violent. Bumping becomes smacking. Pushing becomes blocking. D captain asks if we can get-it-on with the O pussies. Coach pretends not to hear. The rules of combat are very, very vague. Certainly not written. Maybe there are no rules. Chest pads are tossed aside. D hogs line up and dig in. Yelling begins. Line, linebackers have monosyllabic dialogues with the O. First combat is joined. The O's poor execution is matched by the D's poor reaction. Head butting all around. Chest thumping, too.

Ten running plays later and the spirit has been torqued to anger and nastiness. These are two ingredients in a winning team. Day over. More damned laps. Weight room and the whirlpool tub are my exclusive domains after the laps. The whirlpool helps minimize the aches and pains. Then home to bed. I still have to be at work tomorrow at six. I wish it were PM.

The Marketing Director understands. Maybe a little jealous. He knows why I leave every day at two-thirty. I promised him that nothing will suffer or be delayed for my battle with fantasy. He allowed that he could endure this for two weeks if I could. Thursday. The stiffness and soreness encompass my entire body. I think my teeth hurt. I've had hangovers like this, but they went away with a few hits. This pain will not go away with a few hits. It will become worse. The warm-up and stretching are absolute necessities. I hope I'm not the only one to hurt, but I fear that I am the only one who hurts this much. Full pads. The moisture from the previous skirmishes remains. Occasionally, drops of blood on thighs and shoulders. The badges of courage. Grass and dirt are required. Blood is extra special. D gets chest pads. O will learn passing plays. Now I get to run my ass off chasing the deer and antelope of next year's senior class. A couple of kids, who can fly all day. I love Alex but hate him on the field. We learn to give cushions, when to smack, and when to seek help from the safeties.

Hitting is minimal. The gods are kind. After the drills, Coach Lewis tells us we will have a kick-ass scrimmage on Friday. We will be taped and graded. Monday will be a review of our efforts. The kids are elated. They love the game, themselves, and each other. Run more laps. Extra, extra time in the whirlpool. Friday. There are even a few students in the stands. Stretching takes on a ritualistic aura. No kick-off, but there will be punting. The O has been practicing this for fifteen minutes at the end of each day. We line up at the forty. This is a reward for our first four days. Thirty offensive plays. Liberal substitution on both sides after the first eight plays. Coaches trying to find the right combinations. They pass too often. I am beaten twice. One was a completion for a touch. No one on D beat up on me. They were encouraging. *Shake it* off. *Get him next time. Smack him hard, he'll stop going deep.*

I did and he did. Covered the comers well. No successful sweeps. Fell on my face in a feeble blitz. The O guffawed. Dumped a pulling guard on his ass, I guffawed. My sub looked faster but not as strong. The wideout did not beat him. Two ran over him. All in all a good day, I thought. Coach Lewis chastised us. Much work to be done to be ready for Saint Peter, or it will be a long, dreadful day in the sun. Run my laps. No weights. Lots of whirlpool time. Hot shower. I'm the last one out of the locker room by about thirty minutes. Even the coaches have gone. God, to have that kind of energy and purpose. Well, it's Friday night. Maybe date night. For me, two drinks and deep sleep. Tomorrow I drive to the beach and let Dree baby me. Soothe my aches. Love me back to life.

The parking lot is abandoned. Few lights. Maintenance crew working in the classrooms. Trusty steed is parked in its usual stall. To the right of the second large oak, in the back lot. Away from the excited exitors.

I just had the car painted. There is a big SUV parked very close. I hope not parking me in. No dings or scratches. Approaching the vehicles, I see the SUV's driver door is open. Not on my side. Thank God.

"Can you help me?"

"Hey, Alyssia, what's wrong?"

"The damned thing was kicking and bucking the whole way over here. Now I can't get it started. Can you help?"

"I can take a look and see if anything is awry. Beyond that, you'll need a tow truck to take you to a garage or dealer. Let's see."

She pops the hood and I give it my best scan. She tries to turn over the engine. Battery good. Fuel getting to the right place. I can smell it. I assume no spark to the chambers. There could be a number of causes. I search for the obvious. Lightly tugging on wires, I discover the main one to the distributor is loose. Not off, just loose. I pull it off and reintroduce it.

"Try it again."

The vrrrooommm of success. As I back away from the hood to close it, I bump against Alyssia.

"Oops, sorry. Let me show you the problem. The feed wire into the distributor had worked its way out. There was no juice getting to the system. A simple thing. Better have the dealer examine it. There may be a hairline break in the cap or port. This could explain why the line popped out. Maybe all-new wiring is needed. I don't know, but the mechanic will find out. Watch yourself, the hood is coming down."

Extracted myself from the motor compartment. Released the hood support. Reached for the hood to lower it. Alyssia brushed against me. Accidentally? Hood slams shut. Motor purring. Proud of my skill of observing the obvious. Turn. Alyssia is right in my face.

"How can I ever thank you? You are a godsend."

She reaches up to my face, cups my cheeks, and kisses me ever so gently. Lips together. Hands at my side rise instinctively and wrap around her. Whoa! Gently part the engaged couple.

"Alyssia, wait a minute or more. This is not kosher. What the hell is going on?"

"Jimmy, do you want me?"

Say there chocoholic, would you like to swim in a cool vat of Hershey's best?

"What I want and what is appropriate are most often very diverse. This is not appropriate. You know it. I know it."

She has not moved from her two-inch distance, faces, chests, hips, thighs, and feet. The chasm of safety is closed. Her nipples feel like two pencil erasers. Her breath is warm, skin taut and cool, and her mouth, now opened, sweet. The senior athletes, male and female, at Saint Sebastian have a very interesting dress code. After practice, after the shower, they dress only in T-shirts, shorts and sandals. Nothing underneath and no socks. The boys do it and they know the girls do it. The girls do it and they know the boys do it. It is a rite of passage appropriate for seniors only. Anyone else caught indulging in this sexcapade is severely reprimanded. They have no right to the rite. Fantasy land. So, there I stand in shorts and a Tee, being aroused by a nymphet in shorts and a Tee. But, we both have sneakers on.

She kisses me. I kiss her back. She gropes. I grope. I breathe deeply. She sighs deeply. We rub. Our tongues explore. Her butt is small and firm. Her crotch is moist. I am erect and ready.

"Wait. Just stop. Now. This is a dangerous beginning to a no-win end. Alyssia, we both know where this will lead. Are you sure this is what you want?"

"I've wanted this since Christmas, when you left the Kileys to fuck that old crone. Why did you abandon me? I thought my signals were clear. I was ready then and I'm more ready now."

"Where?"

"My house. My parents are away for the weekend. Mi casa, su casa.

"I'll follow you there. Drive slowly. I'm old and my night vision is failing."

"I'll give you something to think about as you follow me. The promise of things to come."

She slides her right hand inside my pants and delicately strokes me. Then she lifts both our Tees and rubs her breasts against my chest. She giggles.

It is a long and winding road that leads to her door. I have abandoned all memory of my near fatal dalliance. The sweet nectar of youth is more than I can reject. She buzzes us both in at the gate. There is room in the garage for both cars. No sense in flagging my presence to nosy neighbors. The house is huge. My aches and pains have gone away.

"Would you like a drink? Balvenie and water, no ice, tall glass, I believe. There is the bar. Help yourself. One for me, too. Use the large plastic cups. I have to deactivate the alarm and reactivate it for safety. I'll turn on the hot tub. Meet you there."

Find the cups. Prepare the drinks. Take a huge tug on my jug and refill before I head toward the lanai. Three steps down to the pool and hot tub. Alyssia is already in. The steam is rising. Pull off Tee and shorts and gingerly step into the roiling pond.

"Here's to an eventful evening."

"Alyssia, it's already more than I could have hoped for."

She slides to my side and we toast. She takes my cup and places it beside hers on the outer rim. Then she closes in for the kill. I am up to the challenge. Her kisses are incredibly long and active. She grips my body as if to possess it. Keep it from anyone else. My response is imminent. The male beast takes over. I pull her onto me. We roll in the froth. It's not yet too hot to swim in. I hold my breath and pull her down. Kissing and rubbing, we toss and flip like a shark and her kill. Grab another breath. Dive to the four-foot bottom. She responds in kind. A contest. Who can hold his or her breath longer? A little pain with the pleasure. She pushes me to the surface and on the bench. She dives and dives. The kissing, licking and sucking are tender. No hurry. Just nice. She surfaces. I place her on the bench and dive. She must lean back for the same enjoyment that she administered. I surface. She hands me my drink.

Her breasts are wave high. They are one manifestation of the word *perky.* The other is a puppy. She is partially reclining. Inviting. I accept. Licking, sucking and lip tugging. Her head is back. Mouth open. Breathing is deep and audible. She lifts my face. Her smile is a fusion of animal lust and child-like rapture. She stands up and out of the tub.

"Catch me and you can have me. But you've got to find me first. And you have only ten minutes. If you can't find me in ten minutes, you must leave without a prize."

She sprints. By the time I figure out what the fuck's going on, she is gone. The only noise is the bubbling of the tub. Silence can be an ally. I'll announce my presence and purpose in each room and listen for breathing, giggling or motion. I used to catch my boys this way when we played hide and seek. It never fails.

"Okay, I'm in the kitchen and I'm looking for Alyssia. Is she in the pantry? No. How about the dining room? Under that table? The front closet? The living room? Behind the couch? Her bed room? Her closet? Underneath her bed? When I find her I'm going to fuck her. I'll make her cum so often her ears will burn. Is she in the master bedroom? Under this big bed, where we could fuck and suck for hours? Is she in the bathroom? How about her bathroom? She surely hides well. I guess she doesn't want to be fucked. Is she in the big double walk-in closet off the master bath? Let's check this last place. Not here. Just a lot of very expensive clothes. What's behind the clothes? Is that a row of boxes? Do the boxes hide Alyssia? Let's see."

She screams with delight as she attempts to bound past me to another place. I tackle her on the deep carpet of the master bedroom. She wiggles for freedom. I clamp down. Body on body. The chase is over. To the victor belong the spoils. I pin her arms over her head and force my mouth on hers. She bites. Not nips. Bites. I bite back. Use my other hand to force open her thighs. Once touched, they open wide, almost spring open. She kisses wantonly. Rips a hand free and grabs me. Tries to force me inside. She is ready. I am not. The wriggling has become rolling and rubbing. She kisses again. Nibbles my neck. I am now ready. She glides me to my appointed spot. Knees are bent and slightly raised.

Coupled, we roll on the floor. She likes being on top. The male dominant position excites her. Riding the love post makes her feel in control. I don't give a damn who is on top. Or if we are side by side. She pulls away and runs back into the closet. I crawl to catch up. She has pulled her mother's full-length Tanuki raccoon coat onto the floor and lies there waiting for me. Passion is aided and abetted by the feeling of the coat. Animalistic. Natural. Her panting is amplified by subtle moans. The meter quickens. We are in synch. Quickly she turns and is on top. Now I feel the full tactile pleasure of the coat. She is thrashing, bobbing and weaving like a prize fighter. Damp hair flapping. Hands and nails gripping my shoulders for stability. I thrust my hips upward. Tough to keep with the beat. I give it a 9, couldn't dance to it, but I really love it.

The crescendo of noises and motions is reached. She presses down with the same gusto that I push up. I am deep within her. Mind, body, and soul. Five, eight, twelve. Collapse. Breathing slowly returns to whatever normal is supposed to be.

A few minutes later she removes herself from me. I lie limp. She rests beside me. Snuggling. She kisses my arm and chest. She suckles my nipples. Licks my neck. Delicately presses her lips to mine. Increases the pressure and inserts her tongue. Her left hand is snaking its way to a target becoming aroused. I roll her on her back and let my fingers and mouth do the walking. Her aggression of a few minutes ago is now passive seduction. She moves her body to accept my advances, each and every stop of the way. Licks, sucking, nips. Mouthfuls of flesh. The taste of chlorine from the hot tub mingles with her essence. It is intoxicating. The mixture, warmed by our bodies, is bringing out the fur coat's natural odor. This olfactory aphrodisiac is overpowering. Slowly she turns on her side then onto her stomach. I rub her shoulders. Kiss and lick her back. Nip both cheeks. All the time rubbing, kneading, messaging. She folds her knees on the coat and raises her buttocks to my face. Another challenge I can lick. I move to mount her. I take her. She is face down on the coat. I grip her shoulders as she digs into the pelt. Slap. Slap. Slap. My strength returns. Pushes are met with equal force. Our timing is imperfect. I reach the destination before she does. I make sure she arrives.

My continued efforts have sustained arousal. She squeezes tight and attempts to drain every last drop from me. I push. She pushes back. I slowly withdraw. She quivers. I push. She spreads to accept me even deeper. I withdraw gradually. Almost completely out. Her hand stops total retreat. She trembles as she guides me in. Cannot conceal her feelings. Nor I mine. A third time I gently extract. But, stop at the lips. Her hand is there. It grasps my shaft and guides it back. Very slowly I penetrate. She likes this protracted attention. Once home, I rock back and forth a few times, extending my in-and-out by centimeters. Her guttural sounds are louder than I thought. She is growling and crying at the same time. The noises have increased in volume. The position, the person, the place, the performance. Holy shit! Her mouth is open and she is licking the fir coat.

"Push harder, old man. Make me cum. Don't you know how to fuck me? Push. Push. Push. Can't you do any better than that? Are you afraid, or just a pussy? Fuck me. Fuck me."

These are the commands of a drill instructor. Grab her hips and impale her. She trembles. I shake. She moans. I groan. I push. She pushes back. I come. She squeezes. Milks me dry and soft.

In between her gasps she demands, "You owe me big time, old man. And I want it now. You got yours and now I want mine. On your back."

As I lie down with my head on the coat, she straddles my face and begins to grind. My jaw, mouth, and tongue are mere instruments for her pleasurable release. An event enjoyed in less than two minutes. Now we can rest. I need it.

Our brief respite in the closet is broken when Alyssia sits up. Takes my hand and drags me to the hot tub. We sit and I melt. Balvenie, the reviver, is there.

"That was fun. Let's do it again."

"The thought is intriguing. The mind is willing, but the flesh is weak. You could say flaccid. I will say this about that. It was as good as it gets. And I mean that. I thoroughly enjoyed you and us. You are terrific."

"You were all I had hoped for and twice more. You're very, very good. Better than all the boys except one. And, you know who that is. Let's make a deal. No talking, just fun. No emotions more than pleasure. Is that fair?"

"Fair. But who is better?"

"I'll never tell and you'll never know. Why are men so competitive when it comes to sex? Just drop the subject."

"May I guess? And if I am right, you'll tell me."

"No. Now drop the damned subject or leave."

Another female tease.

We kiss to seal the deal. She turns off the system. The water calms. We step out of the tub and begin to dry off. I begin to towel her back. She turns and I drop to my knees as if I were ordered to do so. The textures and tastes restart my engine. I am ready. We stroll to her bed. She takes my towel from my waist and lowers herself. Her mouth is cool on the heated flesh, but as she sucks and swallows her saliva, the orifice and intruder are heated. I lie on the bed. She moves from kneeling before me, to kneeling over me. Oral pleasure for two. She cums a long time before I do, because I damned near can't. As I am about to come, she switches position and stuffs me inside. She sits upright, spreads her thighs and hips and takes my spasmodic discharge deep within her. Now I must sleep. I can perform no longer. She pulls the covers over us and snuggles against me. Fills the space around me. I hope my snoring does not keep her awake.

When I awaken, the sun is still asleep. I must steal my way home and then to the beach. I slide from the bed and search for my clothes. They are neatly folded on the chair. Not my doing.

A note is on the top.

Coffee in the perk. Just turn on. Hope you like it. Wake me before you leave. I want to talk.

Start the coffee. Jump in the shower. I'll shave at home. Pour a big mug. Cream. No sugar. Go to her bedroom. Sit on the edge of the bed and kiss her face. She stirs. Smiles.

"Thanks for waking me. I owe you something."

"You owe me nothing, Alyssia."

"I want to tell you that I'll be ready for you whenever you want. Day or night. Weekday. Weekend. Whatever you want. We will do everything together. Things I don't know yet. Things I can only imagine. This will be our secret. No one is to know. Ever. Now let's seal our arrangement with a special kiss."

I hesitate. She reaches up to my neck and pulls me down to her face. There are two kisses. One very gentle. The second, mouth open, full squeeze and tongues dancing. I can taste last night. She holds my neck with one hand and slides her face to my loins.

"This is what I really owe you."

The kiss *of bliss* early in the morning.

Double Stunt, Strong Blitz

---

*C*oach calls a double stunt, strong blitz. Both sets of down linemen loop. Tackles swing behind ends and come in from the outside. Ends drive to the inside. Sharp angle to give ends clear path for stunt. Linebacker on strong side blitzes off guard as end makes slant move. This will really confuse the offensive linemen. If they are running anything but a simple dive, this will catch them. Everyone else is normal. Corners cover mid. Safeties are roaming. One deep and one on the run. Motion is toward Two. Wideout is on Two's side. QB takes snap. Rolls out toward Two. Wideout is going deep. Motion man with safety coverage is shallow and out. QB looks. Turns. Dumps off to three-back on a screen to far side. Our pants are around our ankles. We were chasing the bait. Outside linebacker is the first to arrive. Run over by their tackle. Other corner and safety cause gridlock after fifteen yards. Enough time for pursuit. Final yardage, twenty.

Message light blinking. Metallic voice tells me: You *have six messages.*

Friday, 5:42 PM. "Jimmy, this Dree. I miss you already. Call me."

Friday, 7:18 PM. "It's just me. I'm not checking up on you. Well, yes I am. I'm home and lonely."

Friday, 9:03 PM. "Jimmy, please call me tonight."

Friday, 11:26 PM. "Something dreadful has happened and it is imperative that you call me whenever you get home. And I mean whenever."

Saturday, 1:30 AM "Where are you? I need you, now."

Saturday, 2:14 AM. "Goddammit, Jimmy, you little shit. You better have a real good reason for not calling me. I need you here now!"

The frequency and increasing level of emotion in the calls. From inquisitive to inquisition. Pleasantry to panic. Call to command. I don't like the sound of the last messages. I call.

"Dree, it's me. What's wrong?"

"Where the fuck have you been? Have you been avoiding me? Why? Were you out fucking some high school twit? Or a cokehead from your past? Is it really your past? Answer me goddammit."

"Slow down and I will. What's wrong? You sound emotionally beaten up. What happened?"

"I need you. I'll explain when you arrive. You better be here in forty-five minutes."

Click.

Her tone and attitude were a very bad mixture of employer and parent. Both pissed. I shave while I drive. Thank you, Braun. There in thirty-five minutes. Bounce up the stairs. Through the kitchen door. Spot her on the porch. She has a glass, bucket of ice, and a bottle of vodka on the table. The bottle is one-quarter full, or three-quarters empty.

"Okay, Dree. I'm here. Now tell me what's wrong."

"Aminnette is dead. She self-destructed in a fit of rage. Tore apart her room. Attacked nurses. Shattered everything in sight. Slipped and fell on glass. Sliced a wrist. Then ran through the facility hitting people, breaking anything in her path. Got outside. Ran free. Bleeding all the time. Chased by staff, she smashed orderlies with a shovel. Finally, locked herself in a farm building. Set fire to the shed. Burned or bled to death."

"Dree, I'm so sorry for you and your loss."

"Where were you last night? I needed to talk to my love. Share my pain. I needed your body, soul, and mind. You could have babied me as I have babied you. Where were you?"

"Where I was is not important. I was not there for you and that makes me feel like a shit. I'm here now. Tell me of your plans."

"There will be a very small and private service. She will be buried in the family plot next to her grandparents and her father."

Bam!

She was drunk, and baring her soul to the sun and me. She was saying things that were deep. Her father? Aminno was the father. Incest is a game the whole family can play.

"I loved her father. He was funny, kind, and tender. He taught me everything he knew about the farm, earth, growing cycles, weather, tractor repair, and love. Despite what people thought and said, he was intelligent. Just not good with books and writing."

"And he loved me. I was his princess. He was my prince. We loved each other. He never forced himself on me. I asked him to show me. I mean, there we were on a farm. Sex is a male-female thing not a generational or familial thing. I wanted to learn, experience, and enjoy. He was a good lover. Hesitant and gentle at first. We experimented. Worked up to aggressive, very physical. We fucked everywhere, at all times. I learned. I read all about it. This went on for almost two years, but I got pregnant. We thought cycle control was protection enough."

She was slurring her words. Stress, late night, booze and now the emotional release of decades.

"Mommy and daddy had to be told. Daddy very upset. Mommy was furious. She flew into a rage and threw things. It was agreed I would drop out of school. The story was I was very sick. The silence of doctors could be bought. One night, a truck of men came to the house. I didn't know any of them. Mommy talked to them in very hushed tones. Gave them an envelope. They went upstairs and took Aminno out to the barn. Never knew what happened. *Em*, that's what I called him, was found all chopped up beneath a harrow. The accident was reported to Sheriff Bill Stewart. He said he would take care of everything."

'Em, em, em, em, em, em.' I remember the first night.

"Sheriff Bill seemed to stop by every other Friday for about six months. Always met with Mommy in the barn. Then I didn't see him again for a long time. Aminnette was born. She was beautiful. I was not deeply involved in her life for the first few years. There was never mother and child bonding. I took care of her like a sister, and said she was Mommy's child. When she was four, we noticed strange things about her. Mommy had to hide Aminnette from the outside world. But, my baby had to go to a home. Kept away from society's niceties and knives. Mommy told me this was my sin."

"When Mommy and Daddy died and I took over the farm and the estate, I learned more about Sheriff Bill. Somehow he owned five percent of everything. So, we were linked. Joined at the wallet. I guessed how he got the one point. He was involved with Em's death. I don't know if he was there that night or just hired the thugs. That didn't matter. He was in my life and his presence constantly reminded me of evil. I showed him the books every year. Every year his wealth grew. He was happy."

"If there was a problem or I needed him for a special task, he was a there for the farm and for me. He is a simple man with limited tastes and easily sated. I needed his help a while ago. I had to extricate myself from a very bad situation. Called the Sheriff. He wanted four more points. The complexity and severity of the deed. Inflation, too. He thought five was a nice round number. Deal done. Problem solved. I also needed to hire a new foreman. Someone I could control. I had outgrown the job of day-to-day. The Sheriff helped me here, too. Mike Stewart has worked for me since the *second accident.*

Boom! Bang!

She had Robby killed. Bill and Mike Stewart are the doers of this evil. This has to be taped for posterity and my posterior. Not sure how to prove all this if I have to.

"There, now you know every black crevasse of my soul. Bill Stewart stands to make a bunch when I sell, if I sell to the right people. Mike will lose his job. But he has been living well and will get a substantial severance package if the deal is done properly. Both of these men have protected me, as well as their financial future, aggressively over the past eight years."

"Now, tell me, where the hell were you when I needed you?"

No time to get tough. Be conciliatory, *mea culpa* and all that shit.

"Dree, I got drunk with Billy Ray. Passed out on the library couch. Feel like a shit, physically and emotionally for not being here when you needed me. But, I'm here now. Do you want to go for a walk?"

"I can hardly stand. What I need is sleep. And for you to be here when I awaken. Then we'll talk about walks and food. Help me to my bed."

Her sleep is instantaneous. Her snores are as loud as I've ever heard from any one. While she sleeps, I retrieve the microrecorder and two tapes. Sitting on the porch, I tell Livingston and Billy Ray all that I know, think, and fear. Take two envelopes from Dree's desk and mail the tapes from the local post office. It's best to secure life insurance as quickly as possible.

Dree awakens about four hours later. The sun is high. The sea beautiful. We go for a long walk. The service will be next Saturday afternoon at four. I am expected. The game with Saint Peter's will be over by noon. I'm safe. Two will join me. She needs to clean up. Make a ton of telephone calls and all the arrangements. I am not wanted. I have been properly chastised and now dismissed. No problem. I have work and need my rest after Fantastic Friday.

$$\star \quad \star \quad \star$$

Three Murdered at Beach

Dree, Alan Carson, and Harv Garner are found shot to death at her beach house on Sunday. Kids selling raffle tickets for Saint Catherine's Church came to the open door. Found the butcher shop of horrors. They called their parents, who called the police, the Beach Patrol. There appears to have been hell of a struggle, or just good old fashioned unmitigated violence. Furniture overturned. Tons of stuff broken. Glass, chairs, bric-a-brac. A robbery gone very bad? All the valuables are missing from the bodies and house. Why the three of them? Why there? Why on Sunday? What really happened? The bodies were blown apart by a gun with nasty bullets, like pre-fragged cop killers. Torsos rent asunder. Body parts missing.

Dree had no face. Her body unwillingly accepted six slugs. They wiggled and waggled their way through her only to exit via large ugly apertures in her back and sides. Each shot bounced her body:

off the wall and along the floor. She must have bounced like a toy being bumped and dragged by a puppy. The driving force finally deposited her at the door to the porch. Blood and shards all over. Pretzel-shaped was her final resting pose. Not an *Avedon* look.

AC lost an arm in the kitchen and the lower portion of his left leg in the doorway to the bathroom. He, too, took extra rounds. Many more than necessary. The remaining portion of his body was folded like a ventriloquist's dummy behind an overturned easy chair, stuffed into the fireplace as if it were a steamer trunk. The ashes, remains of burned wood, blood, flesh, and bones made a strange stew under the andirons. Entry wounds in both eyes hinted that he would have no brain.

Harv was found all over. Foot and hand in the dining area. Swiss cheese chest in various parts of the living room. He was shot in both sides of the head. The result was a very thin two-dimensional orb. Pinched together. His eyes had popped from their sockets. The stuff that is normally inside three bodies was outside, littering the floor of each room. Impossible to tell which liver and heart belonged to which victim. The windows were blown open. Hunks of bloody bones were imbedded in the walls. The shooters must have learned their trade from some third-world dictator or some deer hunting-school for the certifiably insane.

One robber? Two? More? A great many rounds. The killer or killers reloaded. Had to be at least two of them. No one heard the explosions of thirty plus shots. There are never neighbors when you need them. Silencers? No. Too much velocity. Pros? No. Too much violence. Pro wannabees. Really bad amateurs. How did they get there and leave without notice? Surely someone had to see something. The police had taped off the house. It looked like a Christmas Gift wrapped by a group of very young, confused children who love the color yellow.

The grand inquisitor's query interrupted my review of the photos they were so kind to share with me. Schlock shock from the jocks.

"What do you know about the murders, Mr. McCaa?"

"Nothing more than I read in newspapers, saw on TV, read in this report, or saw in these photos, Detective. Hell, the TV stations know less than I do now, and I know nothing."

"Okay, let us both be very open."

This is the cue for I'll *tell you nothing and you'll tell me everything.* The NYPD has taken this method of questioning to an art form.

"Mr. McCaa, we know that you were seeing Miss Simon. We know you were out at the beach house on Saturday. You arrived in the morning and left in the early afternoon. We know you have been seeing her at her beach house every other weekend since Christmas. You went to the Mayor's spring party together. We can assume that you have been her confidant for the past several months. We assume you know of the large business deal involving thousands of acres. Now, what can you tell us?"

"Jesus, Detective Silva, I am the grieving lover. You have a violent robbery on your hands and you're asking me to fill in the blanks of our sex life and her business dealings! If you know I was there on Saturday and left, then you must know who arrived on Sunday. You were obviously watching the house. Or were you just keeping tabs on me? This latter I doubt. On the former I am willing to bet your pay. So, if you don't know who arrived on Sunday, your guys were asleep or they let someone in. In either case heads should roll."

"I believe there is some strong link between the murders and your force. You think I'm omniscient or you know a hell of a lot more than you are telling me. Yes, we dated. We're adults, you know. I was aware of some sort of business doings. Alan Carson was attempting to broker some sort of a deal, but that was his second nature. Like breathing out and breathing in. I know nothing of Miss Simon's relationship with AC beyond this deal. Mr. Garner was a banker. He ran the new Central Bank. I have no idea of any relationship he might have had with Miss Simon other than as the President of her bank. Were you watching the three of them separately? I suspect so. If that is true, you must have been watching the house. Then you know who came to the fire-fight fiesta. I think the real problem is that your men are involved in this crime most heinous and you are now desperately seeking a fall guy. Well, bunky, it ain't me. Look somewhere else."

"Why were the three of them there at that time? Who left prints? Whose MO is this? Junkies? Very nasty bullets, and lots of them. Who has the patience and hatred to reload? Not junkies. Who carries a gun that fires cop-killers? Not junkies. The three were obviously killed by the slug of choice of the extremely evil. Who wanted them dead? Was anybody there, other than the perps? Who got away? These are the questions you should be asking yourself And the men who were or were not watching the house. Stop wasting my time and yours by pestering me."

"Well, we were observing the house for most of the day but not all of it. The killer or killers must have entered when we were not there."

"How very convenient for your force and the killers, Detective. Why were your men not there? Do you smell the stench of collusion? Have you checked all your own men?"

"Mr. McCaa, we are doing that now. We'll have answers very soon. You know a lot more than you are telling me now. We know it. You know we know it. We know you know we know it. So come clean and you can leave."

"Okay, here is all I know. I know that unless you charge me with something, I am free to leave at any time. So, in the absence of Livingston Elliot and any charges from you, I will say no more."

"We'll be watching you, Mr. McCaa."

"That fills me with great joy. I'll be watching you, too. And, by the by, good-bye."

I love threats from officials who have their nuts in a vise. Their screaming is music to my ears. I head for home. All of this on a Sunday. Too much for my delicate psyche. A drink and sleep. Five messages. Gino called to make sure Mr. Castor and Mr. Troy were behaving. Two called to tell me I played pretty well for an old fart. Then the three hang-ups. Each about a half-hour apart. Caller ID recognizes a Pike County area code. Probably pay phones so no one can trace the calls. Who would do that?

While I'm in the kitchen, the phone rings again. This time I see the Pike County Area Code and answer after the second ring.

"Mr. McCaa, we need to talk. Meet me at P-C Diner in one hour. I'll recognize you.

Fuck me. This is not nice. I bet five whole dollars the murders and the calls are related. How? By whom? I will find out in about an hour.

★   ★   ★

The drive to the P-C Diner is fun only if you like the thrill of negotiating the extensive construction on I-17. Four lanes become two. They weave, twist, and bump over and through the eight-mile detour, sort of like a roller coaster. The drive to the diner, which now takes sixty to ninety minutes, will take about forty-five minutes when all this is completed. Until then, the interstate will remain a shitty, unsafe-at-any-speed road.

The diner is nearly full. The regulars are exercising their squatters' rites. I take a small booth in the back and order three scrambled eggs, biscuits, hash browns, and sausage. I have lived in the South for twenty years but will not eat grits. I am famished, but will not eat grits. I have not eaten since I don't know when, but will not eat grits. There has been a lot happening in my life and I am trying to sort it all out. *Learn, know, be proactive.* That's the ideal. The real is: *Have it thrust upon you and react as fast as possible to avoid being crushed by the second wave.*

My evening breakfast tastes terrific. No one makes eye contact, stares at me, or comes by my booth. I finish my second cup of coffee and the newspaper. *Nada. I* leave. As I put the key in the car door, I hear the whisper.

"Don't turn around. Just listen. After these instructions, count to one hundred very slowly and out loud. Get in your car and follow CR 561 to the CreteEnterprises Ranch. I'll meet you at the gate. Got that? If you understand, nod your head. Do not turn around or try to follow me. Someone else is watching you, and they can get very angry. Do you understand that?"

I nod in response to both questions. I know that voice from somewhere, but I can't place it now. A car door closes and my counting reaches ten. I will not cheat on the count . . .

98-99-100. Here I come ready or not."

No one laughs.

The county road is well paved, wide and clean: obvious homage to the importance of the ranch. There is no car at the gate. I stop. Get out and look around. The whisperer is in the bushes.

"Mr. McCaa. We have a situation here. Miss Simon is dead. Mr. Carson is dead. Mr. Garner is dead. You're alive. We don't know who will be the next one to die, now do we? You know those crazy junkies. When they're high they'll kill just about anybody for chump change. Robbery gone bad. That's what I think. How about you?"

"Well, well, well. Sheriff Bill. Why are you so all fired interested in the motive behind the deed? Why not show yourself and we can talk face to face? Also, ask your brother to join us, will you?"

The rustling of the bushes is their processional. They are now confrontational. Hands on hips. No guns drawn. I can't run. This is a defining moment for the three of us.

"Now, let me tell you what I know. Someone, who was very upset, killed Miss Simon and the two gentlemen. Almost like a jilted lover or a business associate who got fucked but not kissed. I think the three were killed by rank amateur idiot crazies. Who and why are the real questions. I also think you guys, particularly you, Bill, may have gotten fucked out of a small fortune. Is your situation enough for murder? Is this why you are so very interested in finding answers? Greed grabs gonads."

"Mike, you'll be okay. Bill, you lost not only a nice quiet revenue stream, but also the pot of gold at the end of the rainbow. The more that is lost, the greater the interest. So, let us go into the ranch and review what we know?"

"No one goes in there now, Mr. McCaa. As the Sheriff, I must protect the property of the deceased. Mike can't even go in there."

"What are you saying, Bill? I can go wherever whenever I please. If I want to go on the ranch property, I will. I am the foreman."

"Were the foreman as of Saturday. As of now, you are a suspect, little brother."

Nothing like a little sibling rivalry to divert attention from the real issues.

"Gentlemen, settle down. We're all here to get answers, not to squabble about who can go where."

"Why should we discuss anything with you? How can that help us?"

"Wait just a motherfucking second! You called me, remember? You dragged me out to this sphincter of land. You obviously felt I had knowledge and you did not. You hoped to extract the information from me, perhaps before I shared my knowledge with the authorities. I feel the same about you. So can we tear and compare. Cut the shit and get some answers. Where can we talk?"

"Let's go to my office. No place safer than the Sheriff's Office."

In fifteen minutes we are walking through the double doors. Up the stairs and into his private space. No doubt bugged. Maybe even watched via video. Be careful. Very careful. I must remember that Bill has been instrumental in two murders and Mike in at least one, maybe two. It's the recent carnage about which I'm not sure, yet. Hell, if they killed twice, have they killed more? Maybe again? Me? Now the sweat begins to flow. What the fuck have I gotten myself into now?

"Have a seat, Mr. McCaa. Call me Bill. I'll call you Jimmy. Okay?"

"That'll be fine."

What's wrong with this picture? A one-legged, blind chicken in the fox's den with two ravenous predators.

"Now, tell what you know about the three deceased."

"I believe they were all involved in *the* deal of the century. Really intertwined. As tight a giant ball of thread. More than could be known to the outside world. I believe Miss Simon was working two potential buyers against each other. Trying to extract the best deal for herself. As were Mr. Carson and Mr. Garner. I believe each would have sold out the others to keep a point more on the deal. There was not one iota of integrity or loyalty in the group. Truly a den of thieves to make Ali Baba jealous. I believe the men were upset with the second deal because it was her deal and hers alone. They would get little or nothing from her deal. They had a great deal to lose. The two men had great disagreement with Miss Simon, because they saw their futures and fortunes fading like the fog at noon. But, she was the queen of hearts. Her way was the only way.

I believe they were interrupted by someone or ones connected to the first deal. Alan's deal and Harv's deal. Not a messenger from one of the deal guys. The big three were interrupted by someone who was concerned that this new deal would result in the intruder losing a great deal of money. This was not a robbery. No fucking way. The ersatz robbery is a feeble cover-up. The kind of thing wise-guy wannabes would do. A horrendous argument ensued among all the parties in the house. Five people but only two passionate points of view. Hers and theirs. And then the black dogs of death spoke. Once the first bullet was fired, the carnage could not be stopped. Too emotional. A metallic feeding frenzy continued until the house looked like the stockyards in Chicago. I don't think this was a pro job. Too violent. Too much blood. Too many rounds fired. Guns were reloaded. I just not positive of the connection between the shooters and the three dead. Once we learn the connection, we can prove who the shooters were. Or, once we know the shooters, we can prove the connection. It's that simple. Okay, Bill and Mike, I showed you mine. Show me yours. Tell me what you know."

"Jimmy, we follow what you are saying. My professional training leads me to believe the robbery idea is for the public. Mike and I think, like you do, that some sort of business deal was up for discussion. Maybe Miss Simon was dumping her partners, all her partners. The dumpees were more than concerned, they were furious. Something had to be done. Meet and discuss the options. Change her mind. We surmise that her mind was locked because she saw this new deal as a way to be the only winner. To share nothing. To use those who had been faithful to her. Miss Simon was very shrewd and could be cruel, very cruel. She was singular in devotion to her own agenda. There ensued a heated argument, an argument that seemed to be never ending. An argument in which she was intractable and her former friends were pleading for their lives and livelihoods. Then someone or ones entered the house and discussion with extreme prejudice. How they got in the house is a mystery. Perhaps a door was left open. The noise of the argument could have been heard from the street or a neighbor's house, I'll bet. But there never are neighbors when you need them and, most likely, there was no one on the street. Who is this other party? Could it be Mr. Carson's associates, Mr. Castor and Mr. Troy? Could it be you?"

"Bill, nice try. But, to be *number one with a bullet* on the investigators' list, the shooter or shooters would have to have motive, weaponry, and opportunity. I have none of the big three. I loved Adriane and would never hurt her. Hell, she was my ticket out of doldrums town. I was going to share her wealth as we rode into the sunsets of adulthood. I never knew the details of her financial dealings. I didn't have to. They were hers. She was the provider. Plus, I don't own a gun. Although I had been at the house on Saturday, she asked me to leave while she made arrangements for Aminnette's funeral. So, I was not at the house. You can ask the Beach Patrol. They had the place under surveillance for the day. They would have seen the perps. Last, who would have been my second shooter? I don't trust any one in this town, or anywhere else for that matter, enough to have them join me in the carnage. I would have to kill them or they me after the blessed event."

"So, where were you two when all this happened? I'll bet you both have wonderful alibis. Wives or poker buddies, who will vouch for your whereabouts?"

"Wives. With us from Saturday evening until after church on Sunday. Who can vouch for your whereabouts on Sunday, Jimmy Boy."

No body knows the trouble I'm in.

"I was *home alone*. But, as I said I have no motive or access to the weapons and rounds of destruction."

"That's not entirely true. We have your signature on a bill of sale for two 9mm Glocks. Bought here in Pike County from a gun dealer. Not sure how you got the cop killers, but we will find out."

Sweat is now flowing big time. Mouth is dry. Do not twitch. The frame is being handcrafted to properly highlight my worst features or my shortest comings. Time for some good bluffing offense.

"Bill, is that the same gun dealer who sold Stan Demers his Glock? Maybe the bullets? Maybe Stan was not the killer. Maybe he was just in the wrong place at the wrong time. Now, who would have wanted Stan and Mister Dreisch out of the way? Maybe someone who wanted some measure of control over the bank via a banker of their choice in the position of power. But, then why kill the replacement banker? Maybe there was a replacement for the replacement."

"Bill, he asks too many questions."

"Shut up, you fool. He is just jaw jackin'."

"Bill and Mike, let me tell you what I know. I know you know who was involved in the accident that killed Adriane's husband, Robby, the two children and au pair. I think you know how it happened and why. I believe you have kept quiet all these years because you were paid to keep quiet. Money muzzles. I think, Bill, that you know a great deal about the death of Aminno Simon. His death may not have been an accident. You may not have been at the farm when the death occurred, but I'll bet you kept secret a great deal. You got hush money, some of which you may have even distributed to the thugs who killed Aminno. Then you got a piece of the estate. Your guaranteed retirement plan. Through some dummy corporation or two and offshore bank accounts your financial future grew. I think you got more of the estate with Robby's accident. Now you were set for life, unless CreteEnterprises sold itself to someone who bought you out before the deal. If there were a change in the corporate ownership, you would wind up with chump change. Or nothing at all."

"Mike, I know you have been overpaid ever since you became foreman at the ranch. Was this to purchase your silence? Your involvement in Robby's death is deeper than the hapless driver of a recently filled gasoline tanker. It seems strange to me that the driver of the truck that wipes out a family is hired by the grieving widow to be the foreman of her ranch. Bill, what can you add to this bank of knowledge?"

"Nothing, because you are guessing. And without proof, you are ranting like a man whose nuts are being squeezed."

"But, Bill, what about Aminno and Robby? And, you said he knew about our money."

"Mike, shut the fuck up. Now!"

"Jimmy, I think the Beach Patrol would like to learn the whereabouts of the killer guns. Maybe search your apartment tonight and find some interesting evidence. What do you think?"

"Is that why you got me out here? So far all we've done is some guessing. I will leave now. Shame on you, Sheriff, if you planted evidence. How much were you going to make on the deal? How much did you have to lose? What is it, ten million, twenty, thirty-five? I'll bet you were going to share the mother-lode with Brother Mike, weren't you? But, Miss Simon's second deal was going to ace you out. You and Mikey didn't like that."

I doubt if Mike knew of the size of his coulda-been riches. I get up to leave. Mike rises behind me. Bill motions for him to sit.

Once in my car, I remove the microrecorder from my sock. It is wet from nervous sweat. Turn it off and retrieve the tape. Stop by my office before I go home, dupe the tape. Send copies to Billy Ray and Livingston. There is no real proof, just a lot of uncorroborated suspicions and half facts. But how did Bill know there were never any neighbors and that no one was on the street outside Dree's beach house on Sunday? The only way he could know this . . . he was there, and he had been there before. He knew of each house's isolation caused by the paucity of neighbors. He knew it would be safe to watch and wait for the most propitious moment to enter and assert his force.

Three cruisers in the parking lot of the apartment complex. I pull into my assigned spot. The uniforms exit and approach me.

"Excuse me, are you Mr. McCaa, Mr. James Buchanan McCaa?"

"Yes, officer, I be he. The one and only Jimmy B. How may I help ye?"

"Sir, we need to talk. Can we go inside?"

"Yes, I know we need to talk. Since you have already searched my place, allow me to tell you what you found."

We head up the stairs, four uniforms, Detective Silva, and the suspect, me.

"You found two 9mm. Glocks and a half empty box of pre-fragged cop-killer rounds. The guns and rounds are now at your ballistic lab. You may even know that they are the guns used in the three murders. They have been fired recently, very recently. Killed Miss Simon, Mr. Carson, and Mr. Garner. You also know that my prints are not on the guns, nor on the casings found at the crime scene. The guns have been wiped clean. Now that's pretty stupid for me to wipe clean my own guns, my recently fired guns, and leave them in my apartment. A place any self-respecting cop would look."

"While the working officers stand, won't you sit and be comfortable, Detective Silva?"

"Mr. McCaa, how do we know you didn't wipe the guns clean to throw us off? You could have committed the murders and planned to dispose of the guns when the heat died down."

"Detective, I knew I was a suspect from the very beginning. It's only logical. Fuck. You even admitted to tailing me on Saturday. It was your own bozos who let the killers enter the house and do the dirty deeds. You know it and so do I. You better be on this path real hard. The scene at the Mayor's party was for everyone to see. You saw it. The warring camps were clearly delineated. Miss Simon was the provocateur. I was intimate with her. Those currying favor knew this and you knew it. I'll bet you even knew that I was being pursued by the players to help them play better. It would not surprise me if you even kept electronic and video tabs on all of us. Since I knew this, why would I commit a murder most heinous and then leave the guns just hangin' out in my apartment? Why not pitch them in the bay? Off some bridge as I drove away from the murder scene? Why stash them where I knew you would look immediately? Jesus, Detective, how dumb do you think I am?"

"You're no genius. For the moment, lets suppose what you say is accurate. The pieces were planted. Who would do that?"

"The killers or someone in their employ. The same guys your guys let into the house hired some scum to plant the pieces. Either they or he wiped the guns clean. And, who are all these people, you ask? I do not know for sure. I have a few ideas, but all I have is speculation. First of all, the evidence-planter is not smart. To wit, the wiped pieces and where they were found. I'll bet the stasher was a local. Just doing a dishonest day's work. Someone very small, who was paid off very big to do this task. Ask around. See which of your favorite low-lifes is flashing a wad. This will be the beginning of the path to truth. God, do I have to do your thinking and work for you?"

"We know how to conduct an investigation, Mr. McCaa, and we'll touch all the bases. So, stay in town and in touch. Okay?"

"Now, gentlemen, if you'll forgive me, I am exhausted and must go to sleep. If you are truly interested, I am also under investigation by the Pike County Sherriff's office. They have taken a very personal interest in the recently departed and CreteEnterprises. I'm sure I'll be talking to you within the next thirty-six hours."

Backs Together

oach Lewis yells for me. I am ready. Revived. Well, just not dead. I am to go in for Nickie. Jimmy B and Two on the corners. He is to move with the wideout. I take strong side. Two has the speed. I have the muscle, or, maybe I'm just a bit crazier. White forty-four . . . Safety Blitz . . . Corner fade. Whiteforty-four . . . Safety Blitz . . . Corner Fade. We drop as safeties move up to blitz. Basically unbalanced away from me. Tight end my side. Wideout over with Two. Motion toward me. Looks like a big sweep in the making. QB takes snap and sprints back. Weak side back dives to suck in linebacker. Strong side back turns to take hand-off. Runs parallel to offensive line. Outside backer took step up to stop fake. He is trapped in. Safety with running start is in the backfield a touch after the hand-off. Far side guard hits him full thrust. Small log jam. Runner has to go deeper than normal. Middle backer shot gap and is chasing. I have to hand fight the end. Prick outweighs me by forty pounds. Lots of confusion caused by D. Back can't turn the corner. Gets five the hard way. I am winded and in intense pain. Very little sensation in left side.

The local morning news is sort of electronic innuendo, smear and half truth. Most of what they read happened yesterday or the day before, but never the night before, rehashed with a few more gory details that are deemed fit for exposure to the unwashed and unawake. Never any national news. Never any business news. Never any insights or blinding truth. Just trash, drivel, and weather every three minutes. How much can weather change in three minutes?

"This just in. A teenage girl was hospitalized as a result of a savage beating by her father. Wealthy developer, Aubrey Dermond was charged in the brutal beating of his daughter, Alyssia, an eighteen-year old senior at the exclusive Saint Sebastian Prep School. Barbara Dermond, the teen's mother, brought the charges against her husband of twenty-two years. What could rock and shock the exclusive gated community, The Lakes? The Insider wanted to know, because you need to know.

"Insider learned that Mr. Dermond became enraged at his daughter's behavior during the weekend when the elder Dermonds were away fishing. We were told that young Alyssia entertained someone or ones at her parents' house over the weekend. This, according to our reliable sources, is strictly forbidden by the father. The police are, as expected, tightlipped as to the events. But we did learn that the telltale clue of the weekend's intrusion was a single coffee cup. Alyssia suffered multiple contusions of the face, shoulders, and chest. Even Mrs. Dermond was not immune to Mister Dermond's rage. As she attempted to stop the beating, Mrs. Dermond received a cut on her forehead requiring two stitches. Alyssia was admitted to Lansdale General Hospital for treatment. Plastic surgery may be required. She will stay a few days for observation, both medical and psychiatric. Mrs. Dermond was released after receiving emergency treatment. Mr. Dermond is spending a few days and nights as a guest of the County. No bail has been set. We will keep you updated on any breaking developments. Now a check of traffic and weather."

That rotten little shit. Someone should take him into the woods, break both his legs and tie him to a tree. Then set fire to the woods and see if he can escape. I did her in. I can't call to find out anything. Can't tip my hand. Can't get me or get Alyssia in more trouble. I can't let anyone know I was the one. I'm not sorry for what we did, or what I did, only what her father did to her. She knew what we were doing. She initiated the evening. She is a big girl. She had a good time and so did I. Did she expect this type of response from her papa? Was he angry or jealous? The closet, fur coat, and her command to me. Had she had done this before? Was daddy doing her? In the closet? I have to stay away, for a while at least. Stay away to protect me. Can't stay away from something that good for a long time, or I'll go crazy. When it comes to young women my little head is the boss. It's not my fault.

The morning newspaper, on the front page of the Business Section, coronets a huge land deal between Apollo Futures and The Simon Family Trust. *Chicago—The Simon Family Trust sold all the acreage owned by CreteEnterprises, part of the Simon Family Trust. Proceeds of the sale will benefit charities as outlined in the Trust's Charter. These charities include the Wild Life Fund, Save the Land, Save the Manatee, and numerous state and national health and research organizations. The Trust was recently created. A spokesman for Apollo Futures stated that the gross amount of the deal was in the magnitude of $800 million dollars payable over a ten-year period. There is no reliable estimate of the net proceeds. After taxes, liens, and mortgages, the net amount could be as high as $500 million dollars. This has not been confirmed or denied by The Simon Family Trust. In a related story, Miss Adriane Simon was murdered recently. She was the last family member who could have administrated the trust. Now, the proceeds of the sale will be held and administered by Northern Trust in Chicago in conjunction with the law firm of Hale, Mellis, and Smith of Lansdale. Harry Mellis, Senior Partner of Hale, Mellis, and Smith, will make a public statement shortly on behalf of the Trust and the Simon Family.*

Harry Mellis makes good. Real good. Good for Harry.

In the lead article on the first page of the Metro Section, I see that the investigation of the triple homicide at the beach continues with police asking anyone with information about the murders to call. This is standard fare for the constabulary. I know they are closer than they want anyone to know. I saw to that. Maybe catch some fish bigger than just the small local species. Telephone rings.

"This is Father Kiley, your saintly Catholic priest calling." His best Barry Fitzgerald is miserable.

"You need to confess your sins and save your immortal soul. Seriously, tell me what's going on . . . what you know about the local slaughter. I need to know what you know if I am to help you. And I know you need help. You're up to your nose in feces. I'll help you find and pull the plug in the toilet. Consider this a telephonic confessional. What you say will be held in the strictest confidence. What the fuck is going on? First you bed the Ice Queen. Visit her every other weekend to rekindle the flames of some abhorrent sexual life. Then AC, the Ice Queen, and the Money Mole get blown away. Then this land deal with all the money going to charity. I repeat, what the fuck is going on?"

"Billy Ray, nothin' no more is going on. The maelstrom is over. It's now time to sweep up the pieces. Throw out the trash. Unmask the bad guys. Learn where I stand in the whole mess. And how to extricate my body, soul, and dick from the messes. How do I keep my face out of the public's eye and my ass out of jail? You got the tapes, I hope, 'cause that's all I got. As to the Ice Queen, I was shooting, oops bad word, for a long, luxurious retirement. I had long-range plans and only she could make them happen. Her body and her money. The future was going to be *sitting on the beach earning twenty percent*. The money was to be her concern. I was going to worry nil, except how to get it up on a regular basis without the aid of drugs, prescription and otherwise. The good life with an interesting and beautiful woman. Debauching my way into oblivion. Unadulterated hedonism. All paid for in advance by services and servicing rendered. I was good and kind for a reason. No bills or payments. But Dree's sudden disappearance from life put an end to my dream. After all the shit I took for her and from her, I deserve more than zippo. I deserve what I worked for. Her death was not fair."

"Yes, I got the tapes and the paper work and this mess is in a file in my safe. I listened to the tapes of your meetings with the good 'ol boy Sheriff Bill. That fucker is up to his holster in inextricable shit. How did he know there would be no one on the street outside the beach house, if he wasn't there? The investigating state and federal police will not be overjoyed to learn that one of their own grew the hemp, wove the rope, cut the tree, built scaffold, knotted the noose, stepped on the trapdoor, inserted his head, and pulled the lever. Little brother by his side. Did you send this information to the authorities? You should have so they can clean up this mess. Help them solve the conundrum as quickly as possible. That way you are safe and don't need protection from me or anyone else."

"And, let me add that I think your self-serving blather about how much you deserve and your retirement expectations does nothing to alter your image as a rodent. How can you be so selfish? You are a grown-up, I assume. Any relationship with another grown-up should, if one is honest, be based on trust. This is a concept, which is apparently foreign to you. I realize, as a priest, I should not pass judgment. But your words are contemptible and warrant my comment."

"Thank you for the vote of no confidence. Only you and Livingston have the tapes and papers. I am using them as insurance. Life insurance. They contain only speculations and conversations that could be interpreted a number of different ways by a number of different lawyers. I think the state investigators are leaning on the locals. The Beach Patrol came by to see me. Found planted evidence. They're now on the path of righteousness. I gave them a good lead. God, I had to pull them by the nose. I do not want to trip them by going public with my less-than-corroboratable sound bytes. They have to supply a third party validation to my thoughts. I, then, become the invisible hero. Out of chaos, law and order. I get the credit from those who matter. Fuck the public."

"You are always covering your ass with your own ego. Or is that vice versa? If you weren't dirty, you wouldn't need the protection or the insurance. Bill Stewart is a bigger loser than you are, at least financially. The Simon Family Trust will distribute the money to charities and CreteEnterprises will retain about ten million. Bill's five points would get him five hundred thousand not twenty-five million. I hope he hasn't spent more than he will get. Bill and Mike have to be the shooters. Were they invited to the meeting at the beach, or did they barge in at an inopportune moment? Try to convince Adriane to sell to someone else, perhaps Castor and Troy, and reward the Stewarts properly. Adriane blunted this and they flew into a rage. Rage ruins. I think you're night about their involvement in Stan's demise. But why? Did they want to get their banker into the job? Was Stan just in the way? Poor Carol. All she wanted to do was please and be pleased. Was the real target Mr. Dreisch? Where does Harv fit in all this? Who was he?"

"Billy Ray, Harv was just a guy trying to squeeze too much from a stone. I should know. He tried to squeeze my stones. No one controlled Harv. His appointment by the various directing boards with guidance from the regulators was based upon his past cleanliness. But, what they didn't know was that Harv was a greedy son-of-a-bitch. Knew his salvation was to handle the entire deal through Central Trust. He must have learned of the new Family Trust. It would have to be filed in the Capitol. Someone would leak him the skinny. He knew the end was near unless he could convince Adriane otherwise. When that dissolved, he became desperate. Now, not only would he not make money, he would lose it."

"All of the money of CreteEnterprises and Adriane would leave the bank. All their loans would be paid off. Cash could be recycled. But there would be far less revenue with new, lower interest loans. Swapping big loans that earn nine to eleven percent for small loans that earn six to eight percent is not the way to increase the profits of a bank. Plus, I suspect he was going to skim a point or two for 'ol Harv. Certainly earn a huge bonus on the biggest deal of the decade. Maybe two or three million. He had lots of ways to make money and only one way to lose money. He lost. I doubt he was the Stewart's boy, but I think he sought allies and they were truly hired guns. They shared the knowledge they would be losers. If he was the boy for Castor and Troy, then they were deeper into this community that we should have tolerated."

"Alan is not much nicer. He was working both sides of his deal. He thought he could get some from Adriane. Get her a better deal and she would reward him. Plus, get a broker's fee from Castor and Troy. Adriane knew he was a double dealer and shoved his greed right up his ass. He couldn't talk his pals into raising the ante, so he tried to get the seller to see it his way. If she does not sell to his pals, AC gets *nada*. Nothing from Adriane and no broker's fee. He had already spent a great deal of the money. He was into somebody for a bundle. And that somebody wanted his bundle back. He was in deep shit and she knew it. Time was running out. The sharks were circling and AC's blood was in the water. She, not the boys from the Bronx, was cutting him and holding him under water as bait for the big hungry fishees."

"She used me as a foil for both Alan and his buddies. Maybe even Harv. I'm not so sure she didn't plant information with the three sides of the triangle just to watch us shimmy. I had to say no at every turn, if, for no other reason than mommy was listening. Billy Ray, what did you find out about Castor and Troy?"

"Gino told me that AC's associates were dirty. *Sehr schmutzig.* The bad boys had their hands in everyone's pockets. They plied AC with money and future connections in the state. They tried to get to Mr. Dreisch, but he was unapproachable. He kept an eye on them. I think for the feds. I think he worked for the feds as long as he was able to see. But, Mr. Dreisch got dead. There is a strong possibility that Castor and Troy set up that deed. Then they plied Harv with the promise of future considerations as they built the new Eden. They, no doubt, worked the Stewarts with hard, cold cash. They must have known about the Stewarts' nefarious involvement with the Simon family. How they would know this, I don't know. But you found out, so they could have also. But, they couldn't get to Adriane. You saw to that. But as you say, she got to them. I'll bet when all this is in the open, we'll learn that there were different shooters at each carnage. It is interesting that no one can find the out-of-state dynamic duo. They left their hotel last Friday. The limo took them to the NordAir terminal for a three PM flight to the Big Apple. Maybe they got on the plane. Maybe they got off up North. Maybe they went somewhere else. Maybe they are still in Lansdale. Or in the Lansdale Bay with special concrete shoes. They failed, you know. They pissed off their boss and left a trail of mistakes and bodily fluids from here to there. They'll turn up. I'll ask Gino. He'll know. He always does."

"So, Adriane was the puppet master. Did she really want mo' money and mo' powa'? She wanted to watch men hang themselves. I think she really didn't like connivers. Or, maybe, she didn't like men. She wanted to watch as they slobbered all over their own ties and shoes to be nice to her. To get her to do things their way. And all the while she was manipulating them to do her bidding. And then they fail flailing. The introduction of the Family Trust was her not-too-subtle way of taking the game board pieces away from the little boys. Game over! Apollo offered more. She probably had that deal for weeks, maybe months. She just wanted to have fun at everyone's expense. She thought she had won on all counts and spanked the little boys for trying to fuck her over. She took everyone down. Very few people deserve to be murdered. She did not deserve this, but it could be viewed as a logical conclusion to her ill-conceived and ill-tempered game of I-win-you-lose. I hope there is a quick public resolution to this crap and we can get on with life. She was certainly not perfect, but I needed her for my future. Without her I have *nada.*"

"Jimmy, I'm concerned that there has been no announcement of arrest of the Stewarts. Who is stalling? Why?"

"I think that the seizure is close at hand. Only the big dogs know. When the law boys stomp on one of their own, they have to be damned sure there is no wiggle room for the stompee. I'll bet they are talking to a gun planter, a gun dealer, a Sheriff, and his brother. Checking with Apollo, examining everybody's finances, getting permission to review the offshore bank accounts. This requires the help of the feds and they always want a quid pro quo for their help. So, there will be or has been some serious negotiations. Between being swift and being sure, being sure is more important. Another week and all this will be over and old. No one will escape the iron fist of the legal avenger. The public must view the *statspolizei* actions as good and necessary. You know, removal of a cancerous growth so the patient may live."

"What can we do with and to Aubrey Dermond? His action is insane beyond belief. I have the vague feeling he must have been sexually abusing his daughter and became furious when he thought she had found another dick. His reaction was more than an angry father and more like that of a jealous lover. That's why Barbara flushed him. I think I know who the mystery *schtupf* was for the weekend. The one and only Jimmy B. I couldn't help but notice how you and Alyssia were panting after each other at the Christmas Party. Hell, everyone at the party noticed. Your tripping the fantasy life was none too subtle. You couldn't keep your eyes off her chest and backside. You went out of your way to make yourself an easy target the entire time. She catered to your every reverie. You encouraged her actions by your thinly veiled, non-verbal promise of sexual bliss. Alyssia's little flash dance at the departure ceremony was not subtle on her part. I saw it. Jeannie saw. The kids saw it. Adriane's hammering the stake of lust through Alyssia's heart by putting her head on your shoulder and giving the girl an icy stare in front of everyone was the clincher. This was not cupid's arrow in Adriane's glare. Count Vlad could not have survived the assault. When did you start to bed the teen? I thought you had learned your lesson with the previous episode. Your actions made Humbert Humbert look like a celibate misogynist. God, man you've got to get a grip on your hormones before the staff of life becomes the wand of eternal woe."

Busted. I have to play a new role. Cold and aloof. Not defensive.

"I was aware of Alyssia's actions at the party. Yes, I danced with her. It was her idea. She was stalking me. Not the other way around. She stopped me in every room. Brought me food and drink. Touched my arms and hands, rubbed her nipples on me. She was putting the make on me. I tried to stay away. I never gave her any reason to be hopeful. The dance meant nothing sexual. It was just fun. I know she flashed her breasts at me. But, believe me, Billy, I learned my lesson two years ago. Alyssia's sexual appetite is her problem. She should sate it with any number of classmates. Not me. Besides, I was in love with Dree. And Dree loved me. Our future was together. She was all I could need and then some. So, dispel those evil thoughts from your sick and twisted libido."

"Sorry, Jimmy. But your track record and seasonal actions seemed to indicate otherwise. Last, are you set for Saint Peter? Will you last the entire scrimmage?"

"I'm as ready as I'll ever be. I will play only defense, so I'll last. Now, for you. Keep the tapes and papers at the ready. And if anything should happen to me. If Castor and Troy or the Stewarts make me disappear, promise me you'll carry the torch and get the information to the news media and Gino. And this is most important, you'll look after Two. Deal?"

"If you turned this info over to the proper authorities, you would not have this paranoia."

"I can't. They must seek the truth on their own, or else I become a real suspect. I don't want to be entangled at their level. Remember that I am here because I am hiding. This whole thing is giving me too much exposure."

"Okay, you got a deal. See you Saturday, 'ol timer."

"Yes, you will, large one."

Work was just as difficult as I had feared. People asking inane questions. Sympathy from strangers. Could not concentrate. The evening finds me with a full belly and heavy eyes. Early sleep is a foregone conclusion to the very long days.

Little boy in snow suit playing around a small Lilly pond next to the house. Middle class, pleasant neighborhood. Bright sun and cold air. Winter. Building something out of snow, leaves and twigs. Extends length of the pond. Boy is alone. Lost in the imagination of construction. He slips. Arms flailing. Grasps into air. Legs stumbling and bumbling. He falls into the pond. Thin layer of ice breaks. He screams. Thrashing. Crying out for mommy. Sinks as the snowsuit absorbs water. First the legs, then the back and chest. Arms and hood are soaked and pull him down. Panic is fully operable. His screams go unanswered. No one to help. Fights to pull himself up on the side of the pond. Slippery from algae on ice. He takes in water. Spits. Coughs. Reaches. Grasps at the air. Gasps for air. He goes down again. He is a bobber. His head turns downward. Now the shoulders, arms, and hood weigh more than the trunk and legs. Boy goes down again.

Mother appears through the door. Calls for her baby. Stares at the pond with apprehension. Sees the feet of her boy child. Blood chilling scream. Runs to pull him from water. Very heavy. Very cold. Very pale. Lips blue. Unzips the snowsuit. Yanks frail body from cold, wet encasement. Carries baby to house. Calls the hospital. She clutches child to her bosom. Exchange of body heat. Hysteria is in full force. Calls husband. Office behind the house. He races to help. Wraps boy in blanket. Ambulance arrives. Intern pronounces *no life signs*. Works on child with electric resuscitator in back of ambulance on way to hospital. Rush to ER. Staff detects very faint life signs. Keep resuscitator working. Child coughs and spits. Screams for mommy. She is there as she will be for the rest of her life. Pond filled with concrete.

Fast forward tape.

Speeding along a county road in a Buick. Two not-yet legal boys. Just a teenage joy-ride. Car stolen from school parking lot during a basketball game. The road and car bounce hard. Speedometer reads sixty-five. Posted speed limit is thirty. The river to the right is frozen. The bank of earth to the left is ten feet high. The crescent moon gives little light. Headlights are up and down, up and down. Here comes the big bump. Almost a ski jump. The car is propelled skyward, then glances off an earth wall. Twists from parallel to perpendicular and over to parallel. Carousel. Round and round.

Down side down, then down side up. Once. Twice. Slams to earth. Lands upside down. Slides on its top for one hundred-fifty yards. Crashes against a sycamore by the river. Car is upside down and perpendicular. Six more feet and occupants would be swimming in the ice river. Windshield is popped out. Driver and passenger step through. They are unscratched. Unbruised. Walk two miles to diver's home. Walk over snow-covered farm fields.

Driver's father is working on his Ukrainian egg decoration, Pisanki, in the basement of home. Asks and is told. *Stole and wrecked a car. Deep trouble. No one was hurt.* Dad placed the call to the State Police. Spoke to an old friend, Captain Johnny Aumend. Driver arrested by Township Police. They acted tough. State Police were always there in the background. They loved Dad. Restitution and probation. Each family owed one-thousand, one-hundred, ninety-one dollars. All my savings and my summer earnings for the next two years. Dad was firm about debt. Probation was lifted after one year. Dad always stood by his boys. Never to shield them from reality, always to help is the path of life. When we went far astray, Dad never wavered.

Fast forward tape.

Had to miss a very big client meeting. Annual review of account and plans for future. Wife had emergency surgery. Baby needed to be watched. Taken to Mom for breast-feeding. I had to stay home to be sure mother and child could bond during her recuperation. Creative Director went in my place. Promised to call me upon return. After visit to the baby's food source at hospital, baby and dad came home. Call from office manager. Plane crashed returning from client meeting. All were killed. Creative Director died in my place.

Three times saved from death: shoulda, coulda, woulda. Three times given a new lease. Why? Not my time. What's planned? Who writes the words? Who holds the book? Who turns the pages? Who reads the words? Make the pronouncements? Why is it important to learn the answers? Must I have an edge? Who is my opponent? What is the game? Are there rules? Who made them up? I already got my do-overs. The indomitable spirit requires that, despite death, I just want to kick once in a while. I want life on my terms. But, my terms are situational. What's next? Who cares?

There must be guardian angels. Like the ones at The University of the South in Sewanee, Tennessee. Known as just Sewanee, the past, present, and future of the university and students are guarded by angels. This world-renowned university sits on ten thousand acres of awe-inspiring Tennessee hilltop just west of Chattanooga. As you leave the university, custom requires you to tap the roof of the car to let the angels know you are leaving. With that knowledge, a dutifully assigned angel lands on your car and protects the vehicle and its occupants. When you exit, the angel perches your shoulder, or simply hovers above the protected. When returning to the university, you must tap on the interior roof so that the angel can leave its protecting station and return to its regular and appointed station over the school. This is true. Terry told me. So it's true. Maybe that's why Sewanee is known as "The University. The Mountain. The Domain." But why a guardian angel for me? Why can't I see this protector? Or, maybe the protector is before, during, and after me. This would make sense in the continuum, which is eternity. Do I have an angel now?

White Forty-five Strong Blitz

*W*hite . . . forty-five . . . strong blitz. White . . . forty-five . . . strong blitz. Blitz from tight end side. Wideout side, if not the same, has deep coverage. If overloaded, take mid-coverage. Safety has deep coverage behind me. Inside linebackers jump into holes in defensive line. Outside linebackers drop to watch for sweeps and short passes. Middle linebacker, safety have short middle coverage. Like a fire drill. But all choreographed. Some move to stop. Some move and wait. Line up strong and wideout on Two's side. He is blitzer. I move to cover wideout. Motion away. I follow. He begins to move and curls at the snap. Going deep. Hand him off to safety. Look back to backfield. Strong side guard has pulled. Linebacker has filled gap. Mass moving my way. Outside linebacker my side smacked by lead blocker. Two chases. I move up. Side block from end pushes me way outside. Runner has to turn in. Cuts back. Two is there. Collision. Ball bounces loose before runner goes down. End is there first. I dive. Too little, too late. Pile-up is huge. Pain in side gone. No more tingling in arm. Breathing labored. Strange taste in mouth. Metallic syrup. Can't seem to move legs.

The fans are ecstatic. Dr. Jack, Billy Ray, everybody. Even Terry made a visit. Fans of his cluster around the rock star. I think everyone came to see me. To see for themselves. That last rush of testosterone. The MILFs and FITHSs. Once more out of the trenches and into the breach. Yelling for the team, Two and Jimmy B. It's brutally hot. The sun is searing the back of my neck. Has it come to earth? Melting everything in its path. I can't see anything, but I know the sun and the players are there. Face down in the dirt. Can't move. A soldier fallen to earth. Players are calling for the coach and trainer. Huddled around me. Two is asking, pleading to know. Telling me to just move. Trainer eases me over. Copper tasting syrup oozes from my mouth. Down my chin onto the uniform. My badge. I am a hog and damned proud of it. Bright light dims. Darkness sets in, in the middle of the day. No shadows. No discernable faces. Some gray shapes. It is not as hot as I had thought. The sun is far away. Just a pinhole in the sky. Cool breezes all around. Voices are muffled. Sounds seem to be drifting away. Am I moving? Someone takes my hand. Two? Barely feel the squeeze.

I hear the voice. The voice of calm and love. The voice of all eternity. Two.

"Dad, you are one crazy mother. I love you."

His voice is the last sound. His face is the last sight. Blackness. Silence. I can't hear my teeth click. I hope Dorothea is right. I am at the door of forever.

Metro Section, Page One of the local fish wrap:

Local Dies in Football Game

James Buchanan McCaa, local businessman, died of a massive coronary hemorrhage today during the annual Spring Scrimmage between Saint Peter's Episcopal School and Saint Sebastian Preparatory School. Blah, blah, blah, blah.

Bodies Foul Fish Nets

Fishermen found two male bodies entangled in their nets. The entrapped men had had their throats slit and their tongues pulled were through the openings in their necks. This is called the Colombian necktie. All ten fingers were amputated from each man. Their jaws and teeth had been smashed. Identification is nearly impossible. Police suspect drug involvement. Twenty-first and twenty-second drug related murders in last twelve months. The area's number one import, drugs, brings its own baggage, violent death. Blah, blah, blah, blah.

Sheriff, Brother Arrested for Murder

State Department of Law Enforcement arrested William Stewart, Junior, Sheriff of Pike County, and his brother, Michael Stewart, foreman of CreteEnterprises, for the murders of Adriane Simon, Alan Carson, and Harv Garner. Although reporters questioned the two Stewarts, there are no printable answers other than no comment. Blah, blah, blah, blah.

Two weeks later, a regular monthly event with all the anticipated hormonal swings and physical discomfort does not happen for a teenager . . . Alyssia Dermond.